KRAKEN MARE

JASON CORDOVA AND CHRISTOPHER L. SMITH

SEVERED PRESS
HOBART TASMANIA

KRAKEN MARE

Copyright © 2016 Jason Cordova and Christopher L. Smith
Copyright © 2016 by Severed Press

WWW.SEVEREDPRESS.COM

ISBN: 978-1-925493-03-0

ACKNOWLEDGEMENTS

Jason: This book would not have been possible without the assistance of Charles Matheny, Mike Massa, Michael Z. Williamson, and the rest of the gang. Too numerous to be labeled here, but each and every one of you is appreciated. It is purely coincidental if your name appears in this book, just as the disclaimer states.
Honest.

Chris: I would like to thank M.B. Weston for convincing me to submit my first short story; Kacey Ezell, for making me write even when I didn't wanna; Speaker, Doc, Cathe, EP, Stephen and Brian for encouragement and moral support; Kristen and the kids for putting up with my bad moods when blocked, and Mom and Dad for unending support. I love you all.

DEDICATION

For every mother, father, son, daughter, sister, and brother of a soldier who never came home.

CHAPTER ONE

"Victorious warriors win first and then go to war, while defeated warriors go to war first and then seek to win."
–Sun Tzu

The atmosphere of the woods was peaceful and picturesque. Birds flew from tree to tree, crying out their mating calls into the midday air. Other animals moved swiftly through the dense underbrush of the thick forest, some hunting, others gathering, all with a steady purpose to complete the circle of life. This deep into the vast forest, there was little sign of humanity's colonization of the small, alien world. It was a quixotic, tranquil scene of nature and life itself.

It was almost a shame that I was about to blow it all up in a few moments.

Almost.

I exhaled slowly as the first of the rebel scouts came into view. Despite the fact that I had whittled their numbers from somewhere near one hundred down to twenty over the past seven days while I've been on the run, they had continued with their dogged pursuit with a determination that had surprised me. I was running on practically no sleep, hadn't eaten anything other than something which may or may not have been poisonous since four days earlier, and I was almost certain that the sores on my feet were becoming infected. They certainly hurt like hell at the very least.

Granted, I figured that my pursuers were in just as bad shape. Their lone ATV had tipped over and fell into one of the many ravines that I had skirted during the chase, the men inside screaming as the vehicle tumbled down the steep slope. A few of the rebels had tried to recover the vehicle, but I had put four rounds into four heads to disabuse them of that notion. Naturally, that had pissed them off, and the next three hours were a bit of a blur as I barely dodged a non-stop artillery bombardment and somehow managed to not only escape, but continue to whittle their numbers down further.

My mission debrief, assuming I survived this, would include some choice words at the intelligence officer who had given my now-dead Special Forces platoon the pre-op briefing. "Lack of obvious artillery presence" doesn't ever mean "no artillery around, you guys don't need to worry about it."

That rat bastard. I briefly wished that the guy's starched and ironed BDU's would slit his throat while he was taking a dump in a field latrine on a rainy day in the middle of a swamp. It was the kind of death that a horrible intelligence officer like that deserved.

I shook the random thought from my head as the rest of the beleaguered unit of rebels came into view. For rebels, they maintained a certain degree of professionalism during the chase, which I probably would have lauded them for, if not for the fact that they were trying to kill me. Experience also told me that professionalism would go the way of the dodo if they managed to catch me. I had heard stories about what the Socialist India Revolutionary Army did to soldiers they captured, and could only surmise what they would do to me if they caught me alive. Everyone seemed to hate Special Forces, and especially hated the snipers in those units. I can't blame them, really. I hate enemy snipers as well. They're dicks.

My heart rate slowed to a crawl as I zeroed in on the radio operator. It would be a tricky shot, taking out the radio and the man simultaneously. The wind was always unpredictable from this range, and while my .50 caliber rounds should easily destroy the comms, if the rebel was wearing reinforced armor under his camouflage, I'd have to take more shots than I wanted. I'd probably end up giving away my position either way.

Fuck it. I was tired of running, my feet hurt, and I really wanted a beer.

Their voices rose faintly in the distance as they discovered my trail, growing more excited when they saw the blood. The stray round had grazed my hip – shallow, but leaky enough to leave the equivalent of a sign that said "This way!" It burned like crazy, and the constant rubbing drove me nuts. It had continued to ooze and bleed due to the friction. However, it had also given me an idea.

Two days before, I had circled back to the ruined ATV. Ignoring the smell from the decomposing bodies, I snagged a few supplies, grenades, and a couple blocks of C-4. To my surprise, a few detonators had survived both the environment and the fall. I added them to my stash, figuring they would come in handy, as would the remote detonator. The command radio was still inside, thanks to my earlier insistence that the rebels not try to recover the ATV. It joined the rest in my pack.

It was Christmas come early. You could say that I was extremely pleased, but that would have been an understatement.

The remaining twenty rebels stepped closer to my kill box, excited by their find and completely unaware that they were supposed to find it. A few heads were up and looking around, but, at over a mile away, mostly buried in muck and dead leaves, there was little chance that they would see me until I took my shot. I clucked my tongue under my breath. It surprised me that they hadn't questioned why they were still following my blood trail so easily. It should've been their first clue that something was just not right.

Not that I was complaining. It's my policy to never interrupt the enemy when they're making a mistake.

The kill zone was set. The carefully placed explosives were ready. The electronic reticule of my high-powered scope was fully zoomed in. I held the detonator in my left hand, ready to squeeze the detonation sequence. My right hand rested on the grip of the sniper rifle, finger poised on the trigger. The gun was hidden better than I was, and the tripod I had rigged out of broken sticks and small rocks kept my aim steady. I was ready and in a second I would bring Hell down upon the bastards who were trying to kill me.

Granted, I would need more than a little luck on my side, as well as a healthy dose of religion to intercede on my behalf, but I figured that all the gods in the universe would align to help me out against a bunch of godless Communists hopped up on peyote and hash.

I mentally shook my head to clear my thoughts and get the train back on track. I was more than ready. "Never trust something that bleeds for seven days and doesn't die, you stupid fucks," I whispered and stroked the trigger.

Even though the design was almost 150 years old, the Barrett M82 .50 caliber sniper rifle was still in high demand despite the vast technological advances of the day. With its distinct recoil, an effective range of just over 2,000 yards, and a maximum range of 4,400 yards, it was the preferred rifle of a classist who knew his weapons. People might have said I was a bit snobbish when it came to rifles, but that would be a lie. I was extremely snobbish about my firearms, and the venerable .50 caliber was one of the best rifles I'd ever fired.

The newer titanium alloy and composite material weighed less than its ancestor, but was still heavier than most modern firearms. Any sane human would have discarded the rifle long before in the pursuit. A normal individual would have used speed to escape instead of retreating at a slower pace and using their wits and rifle to whittle down the enemy numbers.

I was a Marine, though, and there was nothing sane nor normal about a Marine.

I fired a second shot almost instantly after the first and began to mentally count.

One.

I wonder if they've informed my family that I'm missing in action yet, I asked myself as my heart rate slowed to a calming beat.

Two.

That would really suck. God, I could cut a bitch for some of Mom's enchiladas right now. And a cold beer.

Three.

I clicked the detonator and watched as my pursuers were swallowed by a massive wall of flame and debris. The directional anti-personnel mines were filled with steel ball bearings and jagged metal bits, perfect for causing maximum carnage against unarmored troops. The rebels were caught completely off-guard and men were flung violently into nearby trees and rocks, their bodies torn asunder by the force of the explosion. Smoke filled the little clearing and would have made visibility hard and any further shots extremely hazardous had I not been prepared for it.

I peered through my scope and began to target anything in the kill zone which moved. I was down to guessing which direction they would move before I fired at this point, which wasn't entirely a bad thing. I had already scouted out where the most likely places to hide would be and the barrel of my rifle was moving before conscious thought took hold. The rebels were painfully aware of my presence now, though they still didn't know exactly where I was. They scrambled around, though a good majority of them were lying on the ground, broken from the explosion. The radio operator, the target of my second round, was missing his head. My first round had struck true and destroyed the radio he'd been lugging around.

There would be no artillery cover for them this time.

A warm, gentle breeze began to blow through and I adjusted my angles, taking the strength of the wind into account while shooting. It wasn't too difficult to judge how strong the wind was once it really started blowing, thanks to the reed-thin pine tree which sat near the front of the clearing. The rhythmic swaying told me all that I needed to know, and years of training helped with adjusting my shots.

I began to methodically scythe through the survivors, switching easily from target to target as they tried to find cover. Most of them were still suffering from the massive explosion and were in no condition to retreat in an organized manner. This was fortunate – for me, in any case – as it made tracking them that much easier. They lay on the ground, their rifles firing in every direction but the correct one. I fired again and removed another person from the equation. Three more shots in rapid succession and I waited.

The smoke began to clear, courtesy of the steady wind. Nobody was moving. I stayed calm and waited patiently for someone to twitch. Nothing. My breathing remained slow and steady for another five minutes, just in case. Still nobody moved.

I slowly dragged himself out of the shooting blind and looked at my ammunition count. I grimaced. Only three shots left with the .50 caliber, then all that would remain would be my pistol. I usually preferred to eliminate any threats from as far away as I could. The idea of someone shooting back at me from close range made me decidedly uncomfortable. Death from afar and all that.

The mile and a half walk took me almost an hour, slowed by the steep descent and my own natural cautiousness. As I drew closer, my senses grew heightened in preparation of further conflict. Smoke assaulted my eyes and made them watery. I could smell something sweet and pungent burning, like mango, which paired well with the all-too-familiar scent of charred flesh. I carefully approached the kill zone, looking for any sign that some poor soul had managed to actually survive this deadly trap. I couldn't see anybody moving during my initial approach, and as I drew closer I began to understand why.

I had timed the detonation and my following shots perfectly. The lead element had borne the brunt of the blast, ten bodies peppered with debris and ripped apart. Any exposed skin had been shredded by the force of the explosion and heat, leaving nothing but charred remains inside their camouflage. Half of the pursuit team had died without even realizing what was going on. The other half had not been as lucky, and there were signs that a few had died in agony, their guts ripped open by the blast and debris making short work of their skin and clothing. A few lay on the ground with massive holes in them, including one individual who was missing an ungodly chunk out of his shoulder and chest. I recognized the work of my .50 caliber. I began to root around, looking for the flamboyant young man I'd identified as their leader two days before.

I found him ten minutes later. The dashingly attired leader had been blown to the side of the clearing, his body largely intact and surprisingly unbloodied. I prodded him with the barrel of my rifle before I turned him over with a boot. The man's head flopped about limply, which told me just how he had died. The concussive force of the blast had snapped the rebel patrol leader's neck clean in half. Pleased with not having to perform a *coup de grâce* on the now-deceased rebel, I began to rifle through his pockets and search for something useful.

I hoped to find something good.

A few minutes of searching turned up a few bills of local money (which seemed to proliferate despite being banned and not officially worth anything; the black market was an amazing thing), MRE's that looked suspiciously similar to the ones that the Corps issued, and the only item of real value– a map. It was in excellent condition and covered the quadrant in fine detail. It also showed fire locations and varying rally points for the rebels. I smiled. Good maps were always a nice bonus when one was on the run.

I looked over the pristine map and blessed my relative good fortune. Sure, the situation absolutely sucked, but at least I had shed my tail at long last. Granted, it took me killing every single one of them. I quickly pulled out my GPS locator and used it to determine my position in relation to the map. While the GPS was handy, the area in question wasn't covered in as fine detail within the computer as it was on my new map. Used jointly, I could figure my way out of this Godforsaken jungle in no time.

After a close inspection and comparison, I let out a heavy sigh, folded the map, and stuck it in my back pocket. I looked at the overhead sun and cursed in every language I knew, as well as a few I undoubtedly invented.

I was still eighty miles from the secondary extraction point and the heat and humidity promised to be another day in hellish paradise. The hills made me long for the days of my relatively flat hometown and single-story homes. I made a mental promise to myself that if I ever owned a home, it would be a single story in the middle of the flattest part of North America. Screw climbing. I needed easy walking conditions, not what I had found so far on Soma.

I also needed a secure radio because I was also fairly certain that there would not be anybody on the side of the angels waiting for me at the extraction point. Not after this long.

I sighed and looked back at the pulped and mashed bodies. I shuddered. The jungle air was already growing thick from the heat and humidity, and the planet's version of mosquitoes were beginning to come out in full force. I tried to talk myself out of it, but I really didn't have a choice in the matter. What if one of them had a personal comm link of some sort? It could potentially save me a lot of hassle. I took a deep breath and headed back into my kill zone. Would a personal comm even work this far out?

There was only one way to find out and it was probably going to give me nightmares for months.

CHAPTER TWO

"The biggest problem was the politicians knew nothing about fighting a war."
–R. Lee Ermey

I scooped up what could only be identified as green mush with meaty bits and inspected it. Normally, chow on a naval base was top notch, since the demand for high-quality food amongst personnel is what drove people to enlist in the Navy. Chef was an actual, honest to God specialty in the Navy, and they liked to brag about how much better their food was than the other services.

However, when on deployment to a newly colonized alien world and fighting against a murderous local warlord intent on burning everything in the name of his ideology, the culinary arts were oftentimes the first casualty of war. I told the argumentative voices in my head to shut up and shoved the loaded spoon into my mouth. I did my best to ignore the horrid screams of protest from my gut and began the chew earnestly.

The rescue op had gone rather smoothly, considering everyone had written me off over a week before after the rebels had bragged publicly about their massacring a special ops platoon deep behind their lines. The company commander had been the least surprised by my return from the dead, but that hadn't mattered. The mission debrief had been horrible as psychologists and intelligence officers took turns bombarding me with questions about my whereabouts, the enemy's location, my subsequent and seemingly impossible escape and miraculous survival, and even my final stand. It had seemed too unbelievable for most but, given the lack of evidence arguing the contrary, there had been little choice for them to accept my story.

They had not liked it, though, not one damn bit. They made certain that I knew it as well by giving me a medical discharge and sent me back to the main base, safely away from the forward operating base and the remnants of my unit. The FOB, while a crappy little hellhole tucked away next to a desolate mountain range, was still more welcoming that the sterile and cold environment of the long-established Soma Bay Naval Station.

At Soma Bay, I was nothing more than a man to be prodded and poked, second-guessed and questioned repeatedly, my integrity and honor doubted by people who had probably never seen combat before. I had patiently given my statement again, been threatened with charges stemming from my eradication of the rebel pursuers amid accusations of war profiteering, and suffered through low-level harassment until a compromise had been made. They did not have enough on me to justify a dishonorable discharge, so one day a medical discharge proposal had arrived. Truth was, my patience had been exhausted by the strange turn of events at this point and had accepted it. All the harassment, everything had stopped after that and I was left alone, waiting until the last of the paperwork had been taken care of and I could finally go home.

Two months of my life gone as shrinks tried to crack me open so they could declare that I was insane and command could wash their hands of any responsibility for me and my team's work behind enemy lines. While we had done some troubling stuff while out in the field, none of it warranted the treatment I was getting. We hadn't broken any of the Rules of Engagement we'd been given during our pre-mission brief, and they knew it. So they attacked. They pushed, doing whatever they could to ruin my dead comrades' reputations in order to cover their own butts. I ground my teeth together at the memory of their accusations and my grip tightened on the spoon in hand. While I knew I wasn't insane, I would be the first to admit that I was extremely pissed off.

I felt a pair of strange eyes upon me. It's a second nature thing one picks up after years of running around backwater hellholes, the sensation that you're being watched. I paused, looking up from my plate. A man who clearly thought highly of himself and his abilities stood across the table from me. It was obvious that he was trying not to stare, but it's hard when there was only one person at the table.

Slightly older than I was, shaved head, with a muscular build obvious in his pin-striped overcoat. The suit beneath it looked expensive and he held a small PDA in his left hand. His right remained free, which confirmed for me that he was prior service. He carried himself well, though with a hint of haughty and arrogance that reminded me of Marines who had gone into the corporate world once their hitch was up. He definitely didn't look like any of the psychologists who had been nagging at me, in any case. I glanced around the crowded cafeteria but nobody else seemed to be staring. I looked back at the stranger in front of me and cocked an eyebrow.

"Can I help you?" I asked, trying not to sound rude. I had a feeling that I was doing a poor job of it.

"Are you Sergeant John Manning? The Marine sniper?"

"Aw, shit," I muttered in a low tone. I didn't have the time or patience for any sort of investigative journalist right now. They were like leeches, sucking the blood out of unsuspecting creatures for their own benefit. Plus, no matter what you said, they'd spin it to make you sound like you had a bloodlust for killing babies or something. I gave him my best angry face. "You some kind of reporter? I have no comments to any actions that may or may not have occurred in the field."

"Huh? No, no reporter. Far from it actually." The man gave me a smile that wasn't quite patronizing. No reporter could have managed that. *Spook*, my mind whispered in warning. The man continued to talk, unawares. "Mind if I join you for a few minutes?"

I shrugged. "Sure, can't stop you. So long as you keep away from any reporter-type questions, I'll refrain from stabbing you with a spoon."

"I can do that," he laughed politely, then grew somber. "You seem awfully bitter from someone who came back from the dead. One would think that after what you went through – excuse me, allegedly went through – you would be thrilled to be eating Navy-issue green mush again."

"Them's the breaks," I said through another mouthful of horrid organic material. At least it was supposed to be loaded with protein and carbs, something I had sorely lacked while out in the field. No matter how much it tasted like rat shit. "At least I can get real beer again soon."

"Real beer? What, you leaving this fine establishment of culinary opus?"

I chuckled darkly and decided that I liked this man, despite his probably being some sort of spy. I had heard that many intelligence agencies preferred us special op boys and oftentimes recruited them directly from active duty for clandestine operations. The pay was amazing but the travel was oftentimes sheer brutality. "Pretty much. I'm getting shipped home."

"Rotation's up?"

"Medical."

"That's pretty shitty," the man grunted. "Sorry. I know how crappy that can make a man feel."

"*They* say I'm medically unfit for active duty," I couldn't keep the anger out of my voice. "*They* say I failed the psyche eval after I took an unwanted field trip through hostile territory. *They* say I've got some sort of PTSD so they handed me my walking papers." I shoveled another spoonful of food into my mouth, chewed and swallowed. "It's all bullshit but whatever. I'm processing out this week, and heading home. Wherever that is now."

"Do you?" the man asked. He waved his hand a little. The confusion must have been shown on my face. "PTSD, I mean. Do you have it?"

His tone was curious and not accusing in any way. It was the only reason that I decided to answer.

"Yes," came my reply. "But what soldier doesn't?"

"Do you think the PTSD affects your performance in the field?" the man pressed. I stopped eating and looked at him, a furrow creasing my brow. Something was definitely up.

"You mean, will I curl up into a ball and start to cry if I get stuck out in some godforsaken forest again?"

"Something like that," the man nodded.

"Hell no."

"You sound pretty sure of yourself."

"Of course I'm sure. I love my job," I took a calming breath before I explained. "Loved. No, I was right the first time. Love it. It's hard to explain."

"Give it a whirl."

I pursed my lips thoughtfully as I framed the right response in my head. How does one explain the inner workings of the irrational, anyway? I took a breath and began.

"You look at me and see just another weirdo with a gun, some kind of sociopath who gets off on killing people. That's not who I am, or what I do. I'm a professional soldier, defending my nation, following lawful orders, and when it all hits the fan, I do what I was trained to do. Whether it's from two miles or two feet, nothing changes the fact that my job means that I have to take lives at times. Why is it so fucking difficult for people to understand? An infantryman gets into a firefight and kills twenty poor schmucks during a pitched battle in door-to-door fighting and he's regarded as a hero. I kill the bastard who sent those poor schmucks into battle with a rifle from a mile away before the battle even begins and I'm a sociopath suffering from PTSD? Fuck that. I'm just more efficient at doing my job than the supposed hero."

"Interesting."

"So would you mind telling me what this is all about?" My heart rate was up and my breathing was a little ragged. Anger is not always a good thing, but sometimes you just need to get it out of your system. "You didn't pick me out at random, and you've probably guessed that I don't swing that way. I'm pretty sure you're not a reporter, since you're not preening at.

"Yes," he said, "I was looking for you. No, I don't swing that way either. And you're right, not a reporter. What I really wanted to know is... how would you like a job?"

"Huh?" I asked.

"I'd like to offer you a job."

I stared at the man, earlier suspicions confirmed. He was a spook, all right.

"Who are you?"

"My name is Piotr Mierzejewski, and I'm a recruiter from Xanadu Securities," the man said, sticking out his hand. I shook it warily. "A buddy of mine-- who may or may not work in out-processing--talked to my boss a few weeks ago. Mentioned that you were getting shafted for being a bloody hero in a politically difficult war. We're looking for young talent with combat experience, with a good head on their shoulders. Our firm specializes in contractual work for the government – more specifically, the Navy. There are some things that they can't do but need done, so they hire us. We provide our services…for a price."

"Great. Mercenaries," I said, shaking my head.

I had been wrong. Not a spook, but a soldier of fortune. I'd heard good and bad things about mercenaries, most of it bad. Piotr brought his hands up defensively.

"Completely the opposite, in fact," the recruiter said. "We're closer to security contractors. Quite frankly, we don't work for just anybody. Our security clearances and contractual obligations dictate what jobs we can take. And, since we're at the top of the heap, so to speak, we only work for one nation. In return, we get the best contracts, the juiciest ones that make everyone else green with envy. We protect diplomats who have to go into hellhole on third worlds and try to negotiate a peace." He leaned in, lowering his voice slightly. "We protect... more interesting stuff as well."

"My mistake. Not hookers. More like high-class call girls."

"I like that better than mercenaries," Piotr admitted with a wry smile. "We don't want just dumb grunts. We want specialists, operators like you who can think on their feet and react to anything and everything. Our company used to deal less with veterans, but our CEO has seen the error of his ways and is now looking to find the brightest of the Armed Forces. Quite frankly, you surviving in that hellish forest after four weeks of almost no food and in the midst of a civil war is remarkable. The fact that you completed your mission is simply amazing. You should be getting the Navy Cross for your actions at the very least, not drummed out of the Corps. Let me put it this way: our standard recruiting method is sending a message via public comms. My boss sent me to talk face to face. You made that much of an impression on him." He sat back, studying my face, before continuing, "We'd like to bring you in and interview you more fully, one of those meet and greet kind of things, and probably offer you a job."

"Huh," I grunted. He pressed onward, undeterred.

"Think about it. A six-figure job standing around, babysitting some functionary, and with company provided tools. You like the .50 cal as a round? A bit old fashioned, but doable. How'd you like a bullpup version of it with a thirty-round magazine that weighs less than what the Marines forced you to drag around while in the field? We work closely with a certain firearms manufacturer's R&D department…all I can really say is wow. Plus, it's a hell of a lot of money. Good money. Easy money."

"There's no such thing as easy money," I pointed out, though my heart wasn't really into it. Easier money was definitely possible, especially given my current situation. Plus, I had to admit that I was more than a little curious. I mulled over my future for a moment. A medical discharge killed any retirement I would get, and if I was lucky, I might qualify for some VA benefits one day – after jumping through sixteen million hoops. Plus, I'd become a bit of an adrenaline junky. Going home to do…what? Yeah, I really wanted to see my family again, but knew that I would never really fit back into that the social order of things back home. I'd seen too much, experienced more, and there were too many memories. Memories I had spent the past ten years trying to forget. If I was going to be honest with myself, I also knew that being back home would suck the life out of me, no matter how much I missed my parents.

The ghosts of our past haunt us all, and some things should remain a memory.

I thought it over for a few more seconds before I began to nod, decision made. "Oh, what the hell. Why not? I'll go in for an interview. Where's it at?"

Piotr grinned and pulled out a PDA. He tapped the screen a few times and it chimed in response. His smile grew wider. "I just bought you a first class ticket back to Earth. Chicago, actually. You leave Friday at 1700 local."

"Just like that?"

"Just like that. We don't waste time when it comes to talent."

"That's a nice change of pace." I hoped that out-processing would be done just as easily, though past experience in dealing with the military suggested otherwise. Still, one could hope.

♌

Despite what I had expected, out-processing was done in an efficient and timely manner. I found myself boarding the lift to the orbital station precisely on time, which was a rare thing indeed. From there it would be a two-week trip back to Earth for my job interview. It would be a very tedious fourteen days, but I had downloaded a few books to my PDA and planned on reading almost the entire trip. Either that, or sleeping.

Flying first class on someone else's dime meant all of my meals would be free, even the booze. While I wasn't a heavy drinker by the standards of your average marine, I did enjoy the occasional bourbon, a habit I'd picked up while serving with a guy from Kentucky. And this flight, I guessed, would have top-shelf bourbon. I'd been eager to try some of the more refined stuff since my first sip. First class business did offer some amazing perks.

As I settled into my seat and tried to get comfortable, the attendant came by to take my meal order. Since it would be four hours until they could serve anything due to the need for constant acceleration to break free of Soma's gravitational pull, I was a little confused by their promptness. The attendant glanced over at me and immediately recognized the look on my face. She explained.

"During that boost time, it's difficult for some fliers to adjust to the sudden loss of gravity and the artificial gravity coming online. You never know who suffers from severe space adaptation syndrome and they'll usually not want to eat or drink. But because they run the risk of dehydration, and we like to use IV lines as a last resort, we take their orders now and gently remind them to continue ingesting fluids while lifting until they become acclimated to the change of pressure and loss of true gravity."

"So no booze?" I asked, just to make certain.

"Oh, after the initial burn, you can order an alcoholic drink, sir," she stated. "For the time being, may I recommend a mineral-infused bottle of water?"

"Sounds good," I nodded. The attendant smiled and moved on to the seats behind me. My eyes followed her posterior for a moment before I looked away, mildly embarrassed. It had been awhile since I had received anything more than passionate disinterest from a female and, even though the attendant was merely doing her job, it was nice to have the attention.

Once I was fully situated and strapped in for liftoff, I pulled out my personal digital assistant from my jacket pocket and began searching for something to read. After a moment, I found something I hadn't read since I was a kid. I pulled it up and tapped the screen to go to the first chapter.

I'm a bookworm at heart, and love nothing more than going back into a book I had already read once or twice before and discovering more in it.

"This flight is going to be fuller than expected. Glad I bought the seat next to yours," a familiar voice interrupted from near my elbow.

"Oh, hey." I looked up from my PDA at Piotr.

"You didn't think I'd let you fly to Earth all by yourself now, did you?" the recruiter asked as he sat down. He smoothed his tie before strapping himself in. "That would have been rude of me." He jabbed a finger at my PDA. "What're you reading?"

"*Beowulf Ascending*," I replied. Seeing Piotr's confusion, I added, "It's a science fiction novel. Written a long time ago."

"Oh! I didn't know anyone published those anymore," Piotr admitted. "I just read a lot of thrash fic myself. And famous ships, you know?"

"There are a few publishers out there still, putting out this kind of stuff. Picked the habit up when I was a kid," I said after marking my place on the PDA. "It's about a boy who is the reincarnation of Beowulf, a legendary king and hero, stuck in the middle of an alien invasion. It's pretty good, actually."

"Aliens, huh," Piotr nodded thoughtfully and pulled out his own PDA. He tapped a few commands into it. "You comfortable with the idea of aliens?"

"We've found them already," I said. "Soma has creatures that are like nothing we've ever seen before and they're on an alien planet. So, aliens."

"I meant aliens that are, well, like aliens from your book," Piotr amended.

"Uh... I guess I'd be okay with them," I nodded thoughtfully. "If we ever found any who were smart."

While it was true that humanity had discovered alien life ten times over as it had begun traversing the stars, none of the beings found had been any more intelligent than a loyal family dog. We had not found any gleaming cities of diamond on rogue worlds, nor had they made contact with peaceful, enlightened races. Initially, humanity had been depressed at the idea that it was truly alone in their corner of the universe. Then it sank in that unlimited colonization meant staving off an all-consuming "final war," and the idea quickly gained in popularity. At the end of the day, it wasn't just the granola crunchers that wanted to save the earth, but guys like me, too. Just different ideas on how to do it.

However, on a few worlds such as Soma, aliens were few and far between. There was an argument amongst scientists as to why this was. Some believe that the odd atmospheric combination on Soma – which was not harmful to humans, though it took a little getting used to – inhibited the development of life on the planet somehow. The more popular belief was that Earth's sun and water combination had led to life emerging faster than the rest of the universe. This asked more questions than answered, however. The general consensus in the scientific community was that humanity was alone – for now.

It still didn't stop people from dreaming about a real First Contact and all that humanity could learn from it.

"Aliens." Piotr's face had the barest hint of a smile on it. "No qualms. Ever wanted one as a pet?"

"God no," I said, chuckling. "The base's PAO tried to keep one of those little somacats as a pet. Had it for about a week. The demonic little thing shit acid and chewed holes through his housing wall. Ended up getting the captain docked two months at half-pay and restricted to base. He got off easy, too, in my opinion. No thanks."

We shared a laugh at the idea of some unsuspecting public affairs officer having a demonic alien pet from Hell. It was karmic justice, really.

"We'll be slowly transferring from Soma's atmosphere to Earth's on our trip back home," Piotr said, "You know that Soma's oxygen content is different from Earth's, right?"

"So I learned," I remembered the initial lightheadedness when my unit had first landed on the planet, many months before. Soma's "air", with a slightly higher nitrogen percentage than Earth's, caused some breathing difficulties for noobs as their bodies adapted to the lower oxygen levels. It was almost the same as living at higher altitudes on Earth. Thus, the planet's original colonists had been selected from regions of Earth like Peru, India and Pakistan.

Unfortunately, this combination of ancient tribal feuds and religions led to the current war on the planet. Human beings were a stubborn species who harbored grudges like no other.

"Never fails," Piotr stated. "Just when I'd gotten used to Soma's air, it's right back on a flight to Earth."

"Such is the life," I quipped. Piotr flashed me a strange smile.

"I'm going to take a quick nap." He pushed his seat back to recline. "We'll talk more later, chill?"

I grunted and turned back to my book.

CHAPTER THREE

We're not so old in the Army List,
But we're not so young at our trade,
For we had the honour at Fontenoy
Of meeting the Guards' Brigade.
–Rudyard Kipling, "The Irish Guards"

"Welcome to Kraken Mare," a booming voice greeted me as I exited the shuttle. I looked around the cavernous hangar in awe as a short, burly man with an impressive beard approached. I quickly refocused and accepted the proffered handshake. "More specifically, Mayda Insula Research Station. I'm Gerry Martin, security supervisor here for Xanadu. You must be John Manning."

"That's me, yes sir." I nodded, looking behind me as I shouldered my small bag containing all of my belongings. With the exception of the flight crew, I was the only person getting off the shuttle. That was weird. I would have thought the others on board would depart as well. I turned back to Gerry. "So you're my new boss? They spoke highly of you back at corporate."

"That's one way of putting it," Gerry said, waving for me to follow. "Another is that I'm a tough but fair bastard to work for. I bet you were wondering why you landed such a posh but boring assignment, am I right?"

Truth be told, I hadn't given much thought about it. I had practically sailed through the interview on Earth, personally meeting the CEO and founder of Xanadu. I'd impressed him enough to be offered a spot on the top security team right then and there. Shocked, I agreed to the offer even before we talked numbers.

The six-figure salary had been an extremely pleasant surprise, as had the initial-signing bonus. An influx of money tended to make one forget the harsh and stark realities of military life in a hurry.

On second thought, my discharge paperwork did just as good of a job.

"I don't know," I admitted after a moment. "I was surprised to hear that the station was even operational. I thought I was going to be running some sort of location security while they were working on the place. I heard that the atmospheric pressure was slowing down construction."

"Heh. A lie with a kernel of truth inside makes it that much more believable," Gerry said, chuckling. He gave the flight control officer a wave and led me out of the large hangar towards an elevator. The doors opened and we stepped inside. "The atmospheric pressure is why there are liquid methane lakes here on the planet. The station is a self-contained structure that is able to withstand five thousand tons of pressure per square inch. We tested it by dropping it here from orbit once we had it built."

"*Damn*," I whistled, impressed. That's one way to see if your engineers were full of crap or not. "Is this place almost indestructible or something?"

"Pretty close," Gerry nodded. "Without going into the technical details of the station, you could say this place could survive…quite a bit."

"That must have cost a fortune," I guessed. "Why'd they spend so much money on a station here, anyways?"

"Why, indeed," Gerry said. "Must be something pretty damn important here for them to lie about the timing of the construction, as well as pouring almost fifteen dreadnoughts worth of money into a planet-bound science station."

He was good, but I didn't take the bait. I wanted to play it cool.

"A crewman of the shuttle that brought me in mentioned that there's a Navy task group above the planet. What're they up there for?"

"Well, Titan is technically claimed by the United States," Gerry explained. "But since Russia and China protested the US claiming planets within the home solar system, it's under UN jurisdiction for the time being. But this is a moon, and one that doesn't orbit Earth, so things are in legal limbo, for lack of a simpler description. The

US task group above is there to maintain a UN presence until a relief force can be provided."

"But we're the nation primarily funding the UN," I looked at him, surprised. "Who's going to be sending a ship – much less a small fleet – here to operate under the flag of the UN?"

"Who, indeed?" Gerry's smiled was filled with mirth. "We expect that a coalition of Chinese and Russian military vessels will arrive to relieve the US of security duty here at this station in three years. At which time, we'll pack up and leave."

"And the station?" I asked, though I had a sneaky suspicion I already knew the answer to that question.

"What station?" Gerry looked at me as innocently as a child caught with his hand in a cookie jar was able to. "It's not scheduled to be completed for another five years. We were running so far behind that the station was never completed."

"Devious. Of course, there is still a station here... I bet there's a plan in place to render it unusable and uninhabitable, like we used to do at embassies in hostile countries back in the day. Maybe even sink it to the bottom of this lake and call it an 'engineering accident'." At Gerry's silence, I pursed my lips in thought. "Okay, so perimeter security is handled by the Navy. So what, exactly, are we here for?"

He pushed a button, holding it down until it turned green. The doors slid closed. "Fingerprint scanner. Just in case."

"That was a weak dodge," I said. "Should have tried something a little more subtle, like talking about the amenities or chow."

"Yeah, good catch on that one. There's always a good reason why they send a noob here. It's easier for me to show you than to explain everything, though."

"Show me what? And who're you calling a noob?"

"What we're doing here," Gerry explained. "Why we need security when the Navy is orbiting around the moon with enough firepower to take on a small fleet."

"That's no moon..." I said in a mock-somber tone.

"What?" Gerry looked at me, confused. "This is a moon. Why would you think it wasn't? Didn't you see that big blob in space while you were en route? You know, Saturn? Of which this hunk of rock is a satellite of, which by definition makes it a moon?"

"Never mind," I sighed. Some people had no respect for the classics. "It's a geek thing."

"You're a weird guy, you know that?"

"So…the elevator shows that there are fifteen levels," I said as the elevator began to descend. "That tells me that this station is a hell of a lot bigger than it looks from the outside."

"Yeah. That's only because only the top two levels are above the lake's surface, though," Gerry explained. "The observation deck and the hangar. Not including The Well, we have…a few levels below. Most you're cleared for, a few you aren't. So according to your knowledge, at this time there are 'a few,' okay?"

"Fine. So what is The Well?"

"Ahh…caught that, did you? Smart kid. It's something else better shown than explained, sorry." My new boss shrugged apologetically. I struggled not to sigh. The elevator's descent ceased and the doors slid open. "Welcome to Central, the main level of the Mayda Insula Research Station."

I immediately began to size up the room and started nodding before we had even stepped out.

Low plasteel walls were placed throughout the large open room, creating avenues for foot traffic which led to a primary control station set in the middle of the room. The room was fairly well lit, with the transparent plasteel fulfilling its dual purpose as a steel wall and a glass window.

To the left was a guard station, manned by a solitary individual who appeared bored yet attentive. I was impressed. She quickly gave me the once-over and dismissed me just as fast. She had the look of a former special operations soldier, though I couldn't think of any off the top of my head who recruited Amazonians.

A strange object distracted me. It was a bit of a conundrum. A solitary tube of what looked like liquid methane ran through the room, which made absolutely no sense at all. I didn't understand why the designers included it. Best guess? Something to do with buoyancy. *Perhaps this Well he mentioned earlier acts like a keel or something,* I thought.

"What's that tube for?" I asked, curious. I pointed at the cylinder filled with liquid. Gerry smiled.

"You'll see in a bit."

I sighed a little more loudly and rolled my eyes so hard that I almost hurt my brain. "You like to build up the suspense a bit, don't you?"

"Like it? Nope." Gerry's grin was wide. I could already tell he was one of those guys who would kill you with suspense. "I absolutely love it."

"It's annoying."

"Oh yeah, you're going to fit in nicely here," Gerry said, laughing. We walked towards two men who were seated in the center of the large room at a large circular desk filled with electronic equipment. It reminded me of the control desk at Xanadu's headquarters in Chicago. The two guards had their heads down and were watching various monitors at their station, their faces shadowed by the lights of the screens. One glanced up and nudged his fellow guard with an elbow.

"Control desk," Gerry confirmed my earlier assumption as he nodded to the two contractors on duty. They looked almost like twins, close enough for me to comment on it. Gerry chuckled and replied, "That's Gary Poole and Kelly Lockhart or, as they like to be called, Thing One and Thing Two. Not twins, not even distantly related, though they look exactly alike. We know this because the scientists here thought that they were lying and performed a DNA sequence test when they first arrived. Strange, though. Just creepy if you ask me. Still, solid guys. You'll be working with them a lot, actually. They run Control during their shift, with five roving guards moving around the station independently. Their fifth slot is open after Regina retired, so you'll be working on the job with them. It's less about guarding our prisoners and more about making the scientists comfortable about security in the first place. Control runs the ops, Central is the backup in case something weird happens."

"Wait…prisoners?"

"For all intents and purposes, we're both a research station and a military prison," Gerry stated. We passed the control desk and into a small corridor. Inside were ten white spheres separated by walls. The corridor was brightly lit with a stark white light. It took me a moment before I realized that this was a cell block, though it was unlike any I had ever seen before. The honeycomb and white design reminded me of a wasp nest a little bit. I mentally shuddered at the thought. I hated wasps with a passion.

"Military prisoners?" I tore my thoughts away from traumatic childhood memories involving flying murderous rage insects as we neared the first prisoner's cell. "What sort of military prisoner gets transferred to a top secret research station? That doesn't make any sense at all."

"It's actually easy to explain. You see, we only get certain types of prisoners. Volunteers, actually. For instance…" Gerry stopped and pressed a small silver button next to the cell. "They accept a plea deal, they don't get executed. It's a solution to advance science while ensuring that the most dangerous convicts are removed from both a general prison population and still legally remain in military custody. Win-win."

The protective barrier changed from cloudy white to perfectly clear, revealing the sparse interior of the cell. On one side, a cot, a table, and a chair. On the other side, a low wall afforded some privacy to the privy.

A man sat reading, his dark skin contrasting sharply with the cell's sterile white interior. His bearing was that of a lifelong military man, as though he wore Dress Blues, not just dark blue scrubs and slippers. I turned away, taking a step before recognition set in.

I stopped, eyes narrowing as the man's familiarity slowly dawned on me. I glanced over at Gerry. He read my expression, nodding before I could ask the question.

"Yeah, that's him," Gerry acknowledged. "Captain Emery Holomisa, United States Army."

"I thought he was still locked up at Leavenworth," I muttered as I inspected the prisoner from outside the protective barrier. The man inside the cell was a legend, one that gave me a smidgen of respect for the Army. It was also one of the few times when I wasn't entirely sure that I was the best in the room; a strange sensation for any Marine. It was especially unsettling for my ego, since it *knew* I was the best and yet it was also convinced I was looking at the best. It was all very confusing.

"He escaped from there twice," Gerry explained. "So they stuck him in the Maelstrom on Mars. He somehow rigged a breathing apparatus out of an apple juice box and a lump of charcoal and escaped from there as well. Survived for three weeks in the Martian wilderness before they found him. He'd almost completed building a transport shuttle out of spare parts in a waste disposal pit outside Antiquity. He was shipped back to Earth and put in prison of all his own. He escaped, despite having two guards watching him at all times. He was sentenced to death for that one, since a guard died during the escape. They say he murdered the guard, but…well, they offered him a deal instead of shooting him right then and there, so something smelled a little fishy to me. But the deal? Come here and help with some science experiments, or death by lethal injection. Unsurprisingly, he chose this."

"I heard what he did at the Battle of the Pyre," I breathed as I locked eyes with the only man to win both the Congressional Medal of Honor and the Hero of the Russian Federation Medal, the two highest awards of separate rival nations. The Pyre Front had been nasty, a dirtier fight than Soma could ever have been, and the casualty ratio had cracked ninety percent at one point. The Battle of the Pyre was the culminating effort at bringing the rebellious colony world of Delphin back under UN jurisprudence. I was glad that I had managed to avoid that hellish pit of despair, though a tiny part of me was embarrassed at my relative good fortune. "He's a hero. A bonafide hero."

"CENTCOM thinks otherwise, and he was convicted of war crimes at The Hague when the EU demanded his head after embarrassing them at Delphin." Gerry shrugged, disgust evident in his tone. "Not that I believe the original charges for a moment, if you can't tell. For now though, we mostly just babysit him. He helps the scientists do their thing and is a pretty compliant prisoner. No escape attempts so far, but we try to take care of his needs without pissing off the military or annoying him. Plus, you've seen what it's like out there. We treat him with respect and don't let him forget that he is a man. He's more inclined to stay put and be a model prisoner this way. Plus, he has some hellaciously funny war stories. And some…not so funny."

I had my own opinions of the united central command of the US military (or CENTCOM), so I completely understood the implications. "So he's fairly sociable? I can talk to him sometime?"

"He talks only when he feels like there is something to talk about," Gerry said, pressing a button next to the cell. The material frosted over once more, obscuring the view of the prisoner. "As I said, we try not to bother him. We have a dozen condemned men down here who volunteered to take part in what the scientists are trying to do here. Captain Holomisa is the only one who I don't find revolting and actually is worthy of my time."

"The others?" I asked and turned away from the cell. I felt a little ashamed at the idea of imprisoning a war hero.

"Murderers and rapists," Gerry explained as we continued down the hallway. "Convicted of crimes that would have normally gotten them hung after a military tribunal. A very *short* tribunal, I'll add. Other than Captain Holomisa, the men who volunteered are truly damned men. They're just prolonging their lifespan by volunteering for this project."

"So...what are they volunteering for, exactly?"

"You'll see."

Yeah, I thought as the tour continued, *extracting information from this guy is going to be a pain in the ass. Just like I thought.*

♂

"Welcome to The Well."

I'd been introduced to some strange things. Fascinating things. Things all over the Galaxy. The Well beat them all.

Ok, definitely top five.

I have to admit, it took me off guard just how far down it ran. Intellectually, I knew that a well could be deep, hundreds of feet at times, depending on where the water was trapped beneath the surface. Still, it never hit home until I had the chance to stand at the top and see all the way *down*.

The Well extended below the station, delving into the darkest depths of the lake. I found out later it went deeper than anyone had originally anticipated, with some of the craggy valleys reaching as far as five miles down. Inside the station, it was over forty feet across, filled with the same liquid methane as the lake.

A thick layer of plasteel covered the reflective surface. People could walk across it without any danger whatsoever; a few of the civilian contractors and scientists did just that as I watched.

For the record, I am not afraid of heights. I had made orbital drops onto battlefields before, as well as jumped out of perfectly functioning aircraft from two miles up. I had never flinched when looking down from the highest peaks and trees when I was a kid. I used to hang glide for fun. Simply put, heights had never bothered me before.

Standing above The Well, however, drove home just how alien everything in the universe truly was when compared to Earth. The station's lighting, leaving faint, colorful ripples where it touched, allowed me to see for quite a ways through the clear liquid. Beyond the reach of the light, however, the liquid methane became very dark and foreboding.

I shivered.

It had felt, for a fleeting moment, that I was standing above the abyss, gazing into the very heart of Hell itself. It was a strange sensation, one which I was unused to. I fought the uneasy feeling in my gut for as long as I could before deciding that I had had enough. Sixteen seconds. That's all it took to go find somewhere else to stand. Gerry followed.

"I feel the same way sometimes," he'd said after we had stepped back into the elevator.

I shook my head as the doors closed. I enjoyed science, I truly did. But what the station was doing on Titan, and what it was researching was beyond anything I had ever hoped to understand in this lifetime. I understood the how of it, mostly, but I still wasn't entirely sure as to the why. I said as much.

Gerry's laugh caught me off guard. I looked at him and raised an eyebrow.

"Sorry," he said, still chuckling, "A year ago I didn't even know what half this stuff was. It's funny."

"I get it." I said, shrugging. "You gotta adapt to the situation."

"Some of the things that they're looking at here is chromosomal sequencing," he said. "Humans are inquisitive beings at heart. Tinkerers and all that. Explorers of the unknown. We look at something and then ask how we can make it better."

"Okay, sure." That had been yet another dodge. My irritation was growing with each passing moment. Eventually, he was either going to tell me what was going on, or I was going to be forced to slit his throat. And *that* would not look good on my resume. I had managed to get a lot of out of my new boss, but was almost at wit's end trying to pull a few final bits of information out of him. A root canal was kinder, gentler and, I was beginning to believe, one typically got more out of it.

"The last level of the tour is really cool. You have any biotechnology knowledge? Anything about Ethology?"

""Uh, marine biology used to interest me. Sea lions, seals, stuff like that. It was something I liked as a kid," I said, keeping my annoyance out of my voice as best as I could. "Grew out of it when I first joined up, fell back into it in Sniper School. Well, the science part of it. More physics and math than biology, though."

You heard that correctly. The Marine Corps weaponized math. *Oorah.*

"Well then, you'll probably find this pretty interesting," Gerry told me as they exited the elevator. "This is the primary research level here at the station. You'll be down here a lot once you're cleared for transfer duty. Escorting the prisoners. We run three guards with each prisoner transfer, two behind, and one in front. They're always in cuffs and bracers during transit, no exceptions. That's just stuff we'll go over later, but it's pretty basic stuff. You'll have our operations manual on your PDA by tonight – send me your preferred user name today when we're done here so I can add you to the network – and it'll explain all our policies, procedures and provide you with a map of the entire facility. It's a handy thing."

"Wow, that's one interesting view," I commented as we made our way across the fairly open room. To my left, there was a collection of privacy domes, nearly identical to the prisoner cells on the upper level. A few scientists moved between them, offering me a glimpse of the work they were doing at the station. Most of it was on large PDAs that reminded me of old computer banks, though I did see a centrifugal machine in one of the rooms.

The only reason I knew what centrifuges look like is because the rebels on Soma had stolen a few and tried to make a nuke once.

AIRS had gotten a bit ambitious after managing to snooker the UN into believing that they only wanted nuclear power for peaceful purposes and kidnapped two female Marines to try and "encourage" US cooperation with the UN resolution. They'd actually gotten a facility up and running before the Navy had decided that an orbital bombardment was the easiest way to discourage any further attempts at building a nuke. Unfortunately, the missing Marines were being kept in the facility. My unit had gone in and rescued them so the Navy could drop a twenty ton nickel-and-iron rod on the rebels. The squids had even waited until we were clear.

For values of 'clear.'

It had not ended well for the rebels. I'd heard that more than one rod was dropped. I'm not certain, since I was too busy running away. On the plus side, the rebels stopped trying to build a nuclear bomb.

I shook off the memories. On my right lay a few benches near the plasteel, which allowed someone to have a beautiful and unobstructed view of the lake. There were a few tubes filled with the liquid methane running across the room and feeding into The Well. They were more than large enough for multiple adults to swim through together, which I found quite a bit odd. They looked to be late additions to the structure and not part of the original design, though their seams looked flawless. For a moment, I started to wonder about the structural integrity of the station before I remembered that I hadn't gone to college and really knew jack-all about structural engineering. Or engineering in general.

I walked to the plasteel, paused, and looked out into the lake. It was peaceful, serene. The light from both Saturn and the sun was mostly blocked by the thick and dense atmosphere, but what did manage to break through created a golden effect beneath the liquid surface. Not enough to light the bottom of the lake, but there was more than enough to give the scientists inside the station a good view.

I sighed and put my hands behind my back. I stared out into the golden haze. One year. I had signed a contract for one year with the option to renew each additional year in expectation of being assigned to guard some dignitary on a war-torn world. I had anticipated a dangerous job, hard work which almost justified my exorbitant pay.

This though? This was practically a vacation. Outside of the slim possibility that the station could collapse upon itself due to outside atmospheric pressure, this was the safest job I had ever had in my entire life, and that included being a pizza delivery driver in my hometown when I was a teenager. Granted, I grew up in a big city and was poor, so the comparisons were a bit skewed.

I closed my eyes and took a deep breath. The horrors from Soma would never truly leave, but they were something I could learn to deal with, in time. Wounds leave scars, and scars can be ugly, but scars also made up the person I was. Scars also faded with time and became a more permanent part of a person the faster they learned to accept that they will remain.

I wanted them to remain. It would have been dishonorable to try and forget. I couldn't allow the guys in my unit to be forgotten just so I could hide my own pain. That was the sort of thing that makes a Marine forget the entire reason behind their enlistment, forget their purpose, and their oath.

I opened my eyes.

Something dark and shadowy flitted through the oily liquid outside the station, almost too fast for me to see. I jumped back and let out a startled yelp in surprise. I looked over at Gerry, who was looking at me with a smug expression on his face. Annoyed and slightly embarrassed, I leaned back in towards the plasteel so that I could look into the lake once more.

The dark shape returned, albeit moving at a much slower pace. I barely stifled a gasp as it drifted into the ambient light of the research station. At first glance, it looked like an Earth manta ray, with fins protruding from the side like wings. It was medium-sized, almost as big as a German Shepherd. At first glance it looked like an Earth manta ray, with fins protruding from the side like wings. Unlike a ray, each wing had small hands with three tiny fingers.

Its elongated body was more similar to a moray eel than a manta ray, however. It swam back and forth much like a snake on land, the protruding wings more for stability than anything. The creature was pink, almost brightly so, with varying hues of blue and purple running along the wings. The long tail trailing behind it seemed flatten at the end, like the fluke of a whale. I guessed it was shaped that way so it could be capable of sudden bursts of speed to hunt food or to escape some larger predator.

The face was something from the deepest, darkest horrors of a nightmare. Wide, like a manta ray, but no eyes. Instead, tentacles flailed at random before scooping towards the large mouth. No teeth, but a strange bulge on its upper jaw. I searched for the word. *Baleen, like whales on Earth.*

My suspicions were confirmed an instant later. The mouth closed, followed by a large pulse of liquid. The creature barely paused in its swimming as it began hunting for more food.

It was terrifying and magnificent all in one.

"I hope this gives you a small idea as to what we're guarding here now," Gerry said to me as I continued to watch the alien swim by the station. It was weird watching the being move through the methane, yet completely natural at the same time. "We've discovered something so big, so important, that we literally could be looking at the next step in humanity's journey to the stars."

"Holy shit," I breathed, watching the strange, horrible, and yet beautiful creature swim gracefully around in the liquid. "What the hell is that thing?"

"We call them krakens," a feminine voice behind me answered, "and they're as alien as they appear. Welcome to Kraken Mare."

CHAPTER FOUR

Nature is relentless and unchangeable, and it is indifferent as to whether its hidden reasons and actions are understandable to man or not.
–Galileo Galilei

Fifteen minutes later, I'd found myself with my new boss and the head researcher of the facility in another section of the station everyone called the Gallery. The name made sense; there were dozens of specially-designed tubes throughout the room, creating a labyrinth within what looked at first glance to be a standard observation room. Running throughout the room were more of the tubes filled with liquid methane, along with a few habitats. It was eerily beautiful.

"You're doing experiments here," I commented as I walked with the doctor and Gerry through the Gallery. Most of the krakens were slowly drifting through the liquid methane inside their specialized habitats, but a few had used their miniscule hands to pull themselves out of the watery substance and onto the rubbery, artificial beach the scientists had created within a few of the pressurized habitats. They were basking under a special lamp which emitted blue light. It reminded me of the turtle aquarium I had when I was just a kid. Albeit, this was an aquarium that could kill everyone in the station should it break open.

Introductions had been easy. Dr. Marie Marillac was the leading researcher at the station and someone that I would be dealing with on a semi-regular basis. She was a bright, bubbly person who was also easy on the eyes and possessed a brain that put anyone I knew to shame. I'd always considered myself smart but when dealing with the xenobiologist, I felt like a drooling toddler. I briefly wondered just how many of the contractors on the station had made a pass at the woman and figured it was most – if not all – of the single ones. I also was willing to bet money that their success rate was at about zero.

"Experiments, yes," Dr. Marillac agreed. "That's science for you." I chuckled at this. The woman was both smart *and* attractive. A dangerous combination.

"How do they breathe?" I wondered aloud.

"They absorb methane through their skin," she explained as we walked slowly through the Gallery. She stopped every few steps to look at one of the kraken before moving on. She was so engrossed in the science behind the aliens that I wasn't completely certain she remembered I was still in the room with her. "We believe that they are able to metabolize it. Our theory is that they emit small doses of xenon in a cycle, much like the carbon dioxide to oxygen cycle of plants on Earth. Of course, it's still a theory, but a fairly solid one. We've found trace elements of the gas in the methane lakes here."

"I...see," I said, nodding slowly. In truth, I really didn't understand, but I did know that what humans exhaled, plants inhaled, and vice versa. I figured that was what she was trying to tell me in her overly scientific way.

I paused and watched as one of the smaller aliens slid off the rubbery beach and back into the liquid. It drifted towards me slowly, as if it were sizing me up. It was creepy as hell the way that it seemed to scrutinize me. I tilted my head to the side and stared as the creature approached.

"How smart are they?" I asked, my earlier train of thought gone as I watched the small being hover in the tank before me. I still couldn't see any obvious eyes on the creature, but I could feel it looking at me, assessing me. *Perhaps the tentacles doubled as eyes*, I wondered. It was mildly uncomfortable to think about, considering that it also used the tentacles to eat with.

"We're not entirely sure," Doctor Marillac admitted. She moved to the other side of the habitat, her face slightly distorted from the liquid and clear-steel. Her eyes were intent upon the one which was hovering in front of me. "They're smarter than dolphins, we're certain of that."

"That's pretty smart, right?" I asked, struggling to dredge up long-forgotten memories of my youth. I had been an avid fan of the ocean as a child and had thought about becoming a marine biologist one day in the future. Of course, once I had realized just how poor my family was and that I would have to come up with a way to pay for schooling myself, I'd chosen to become a Marine instead, who would then pay for it. That course of action became a moot point when they drummed me out on medical. I suppose I could argue that I was halfway to achieving my childhood dream. Thanks to the new job, I could afford it now.

"Dolphins have been tested to have an average EQ – that stands for encephalization quotient, which measures your actual brain mass versus your body mass, and can give a pretty solid determinate of how smart you are – of 4.5," Dr. Marillac said as she traced a slender finger along the contours of the plasteel, her eyes distant as she watched more of the alien creatures swim into view. "This is very high. Humans average around 7.5. We're guessing that the krakens are around a high five, maybe even six. There's no way of knowing without years of more research, and we're rather reluctant to cut open a live specimen."

"I still think you should just do it when they die of old age," Gerry stated, moving to stand closer to the attractive scientist. I tried not to smirk at my new boss and what he was doing. It was obvious to anyone with a pulse and any sort of knowledge of human interaction that he was very interested in the woman. The good doctor, however, remained oblivious to his not-too-subtle advances. I nearly laughed out loud at the absurdity of it. The woman was all about her aliens and seemed to lack any knowledge of basic human courtship, or was even aware that Gerry existed. The poor bastard.

Dr. Marillac squirmed uncomfortably at Gerry's statement. It seemed to be a sore subject between them, and I guessed she would explain for my benefit. I was not disappointed.

"For some reason, their body mass decreases upon death. We're not entirely sure why. Plus, what if they're as smart as we are, and they see us cutting open their dead? I would be a little annoyed if someone cut open my dead grandmother, for instance. So far as we can tell, they're allowing us to study them from afar. The Well allows them to come and go as much as they want. They're not what you would call typical specimens, and they're definitely not pets. So cutting open one of their dead might ruin whatever potential relationships we might get out of this. If they're as smart as we think they are."

She has a point, I conceded, my previous humor tapering off some. I wouldn't want some mad scientist cracking open my grandfather's skull and looking at his brain just to see how it ticked. There would undoubtedly be more than one dead body in the room when I finally calmed down.

"How do you measure their body mass without actually touching them?" I asked. It was an interesting dilemma though I was pretty sure I already knew how they accomplished it.

"Laser spectrum," the doctor explained, which confirmed my suspicion. "It scans them when they bask beneath the blue lamps in the habitats. They swim in, sunbathe, and then swim away."

"Changing the light bulb when it burns out must be a bitch," I said in a low tone. The doctor must have overheard me because she smiled.

"You have no idea just how hard it is," she confirmed. "Takes half of a day. Fortunately, when a light bulb goes out, the kraken go elsewhere."

"Do they have some sort of habitat elsewhere? Or are they like sharks and just roam around the lake in patterns?" I asked her, my curiosity piqued.

"We don't know," the doctor admitted. "Analysis suggests that they can withstand an amazing amount of pressure, since they live in liquid methane. The lake goes deep, extremely deep in fact. They might have habitats down below, but we have no idea if it's something they built or something that they found in a cave or anything. We really don't know that much about them."

"And someone decided to build a station in a lake just to study them?" I pressed, amazed at the idea of someone dropping a massive station onto a planet from orbit to study something that looked like a cross between a manta ray and Cthulhu's love child.

"Not necessarily," she admitted. "I can't talk about some of it, as you know."

I'd figured as much and I knew when not to press. Part of the non-disclosure agreement I had signed when hired by the company covered any instances should I find myself around sensitive information and, accordingly, was not supposed to look too deep into it. It had been the same back when I was still active duty.

Still though, I had to wonder. If the scientists weren't on Titan to study the kraken, and there were prisoners aboard, then what were they actually doing there?

ᚦ

"Any thoughts?" Gerry's jovial attitude had changed once we had arrived in the guard quarters. He had shown me to my bedroom, which was bigger than some flats I had seen in New York City. Each contractor had their own room, albeit a sparingly decorated one. Still, it allowed for privacy, and privacy was rare for the average soldier. I was extremely happy to discover that I even had my own shower.

"Seems like an easy job," I admitted as I tossed my bag onto the bed. Someone had been kind enough to drop it off outside my new room. I took a quick look around the room and shrugged. "A bit overpaid for the assignment, if you really want to know."

"No vacation," Gerry reminded me. "No way out. You're pretty much stuck here for a year."

I shrugged a second time. "Must be rough for some. Me? I enjoy the solitude."

"I don't think you understand," Gerry said as he walked over to the small desk and pulled out the only chair in the room. He sat down and leaned back. His dark brown eyes bore into mine. "There is no escape from someone you don't like here. You have to see them every day. Every. Damn. Day. Sure, you can come back to your room. But even then, it's not like you can jet off to a vineyard for a day trip to escape from this crap. It's not as bad as living on a Navy ship while crossing the Threshold, but it's pretty bad."

I opened my mouth to say something but stopped. He was right, of course. Plus, I didn't have the experience Gerry did, so it would be pointless to say that I would be perfectly fine. Plus, I never really had to deal with being in a Marine Expeditionary Unit and stuck on a Navy ship for months on end as it traveled between worlds. A random quirk of my enlistment, one that I was both fortunate and remiss to have avoided.

Instead of arguing, I changed the subject. "How do the single guys cope?"

"Lots of downloads," Gerry said. "They always try to hit on the civilians we're here to guard, but that's not happening. We have female security contractors here, but there's a strict no fraternization rule that I vigorously enforce. When I catch them."

"That's rough," I pointed out. "Those must be interesting discussions when you do catch them."

"I think I've given the speech once or twice."

"That's a lot less than I thought it would be."

"You're single, according to the file I got on you," Gerry said. "Divorced?"

"Widowed."

"I'm sorry."

"So am I."

"What happened?"

I stared hard at the far wall, thinking back. It had been a long while since I had talked about Concy with anyone not related to me. That particular wound had not yet had time to scar over, but it didn't hurt nearly as bad now as it had five years ago.

"Long story."

"I've got time," Gerry spread his hands. "One of my jobs here is to make sure all of my employees are mentally suitable for this sort of work. Isolation and monotony tends to make the mind wander quite a bit, and that could take the emotions of anyone in the wrong direction. So…if you're up for it, I'm all ears."

"You remember when the People's Republic of Uganda fell awhile back, right?" I asked. It had been all over the news at the time, but public opinion – and public attention – had quickly turned towards other wars, different news stories. "When the Caliphate of Sokoto took over and all hell broke loose?"

"I remember. That was a hell of a messy civil war," Gerry nodded. "There were an estimated sixteen million killed or displaced? Still got some hotspots flaring up even now. The US and the UN have deployed peacekeepers there half a dozen times or so since."

"Yeah," I said. "Well, my wife was from Uganda originally before immigrating to the states when she was ten. Left quite a bit of family behind when her mother and brothers packed up at the outset of the war. They weren't rich, not by our standards at least, but they had money squirreled away just in case. Her mother was...a bit prescient when it came to predicting if and when a government was about ready to fall. She would have made one hell of an election analyst.

"Concy was...hell, I don't know. She was special. I was a scrawny bookworm who got picked on a lot. She was this beautiful, exotic girl who seemed to enjoy hanging out with me. She was assigned to be my lab partner in middle school and we hit it off. We both loved reading, and she knew more about the classic writers than I did. We went from friends to being in a relationship, a strong one. Got some weird looks but who cared, right? We were young, in love, and I had it all planned out. I couldn't get into college – no money, my family was fairly poor – so I joined the Corps. We married right before I left for Parris Island so she could get my health benefits. My parents weren't sure about it – not because she was a foreigner or that we were too young, but they thought that she would be too traumatized from the war to acclimate and that we were rushing into it, plus I would be leaving her alone so soon after we got married. My folks may have been poor but they sure as hell weren't stupid. They were just overly cautious when it came to me. Extremely protective.

"You have my files, so you know I was assigned to the Second Marine Division. I found base housing for us. Concy was prepared to move in with me when news came that some family she still had in Uganda were in some serious shit. Like, in danger of being enslaved or executed because they had found themselves on the wrong side of the Caliphate. When she heard, she completely lost it and flew home. She had to get them out before anything bad happened to them."

"Oh no..." Gerry's face was filled with sorrow and understanding. "She never came back?"

"She got caught in one of those religious dragnets where they whip women who are caught in public without their husbands or a male family member escorting her. They flipped out when they found out that she had come home from the US to save her family. They swore to make an example out of her. And they did." I closed my eyes. I hated crying in front of people. Five years after the fact and it still pained me to even think about her death. "I heard about it and almost went AWOL to kill all of the bastards. Had a CSM literally drag me back on base so I wouldn't be counted as AWOL. He beat the shit out of me too, after roll call. I couldn't deal with anything at the time. Shelved all the pain and emotion for later. Broke down once in the barracks and just let it all out. Almost ended everything by eating a bullet. Again, the CSM kicked my ass and got my head back on straight. Asked me what Concy would think of me if she'd found out I had tried to take the coward's way out. Made me stop, made me think. So instead of ending the pain, I focused all of it into being the best Marine I could be. Got picked up for special ops a few years later, then my unit was sent to Soma to quell the civil war there…and here we are."

"Damn," Gerry said as I watched sympathy and…something else fill his eyes. "You probably suffer more PTSD from that than you ever could from being on the run from AIRS rebels."

"That'd be a pretty good guess," I agreed. "It hurts, but it's not nearly as bad as it was. It's worse when I think about what could have been. If I focus on what we had, it's sad, but manageable. So I lock on to the good times, like high school and stuff. Summer on the lake. Going up to Wisconsin to go snowboarding. Things that remind me of living."

Gerry stood up from the chair. He stuck his hand out. Uncertain, I accepted it.

"You're going to be fine, John," Gerry told me in a firm tone. "You'll fit in well here. Duty roster will be sent to you via PDA later tonight. I'll give you a day to get adjusted before you start your shifts. Get some rest and some food. Those are two things that we can offer down here that beat anything you got on Soma, that's for damn sure."

Pretty sure the strangeness of this place beats Soma any day of the week, I didn't say as Gerry walked to the door. Instead, I said, "I'm glad I'm here. I think I'll fit in well."

"So do I," Gerry said and left the room. I waited a few moments before closing the door behind him. I leaned forward and pressed my head against the cool plasteel surface of the door. After a moment, I turned back and walked over to my bed. I shoved the heavy travel bag onto the floor. I crawled on top of the covers and didn't even bother to kick my shoes off. I was asleep in seconds, dreams of a smiling face looking down upon my own from the night of our wedding.

CHAPTER FIVE

It's a new dawn, it's a new day, it's a new life for me—
And I'm feelin' good.
–Nina Simone, "Feeling Good"

Gerry gave me some time to acclimatize myself to life in the station. Over the next week, I fell into a routine – I'd wake up, exercise in the gym, shower and shave, then report for my shift. Initially, I thought a twelve-hour shift would be dull and repetitive, but further exploration of the station changed my opinion. I discovered that the fascinating creatures who inhabited the lake and rose up from The Well made the time pass by quickly.

As intrigued as I was with them, it appeared that the creatures were even more interested in me. Multiple times while I was moving through the upper galley, I found that the aliens had banded together and were following my progress and using The Well to dive into the deeper levels of the station when I moved to a lower level. I wasn't entirely certain why they were interested in me, but some of the other guards had taken to calling me the "Kraken Whisperer."

It wouldn't have mattered so much if not for the inordinate amount of attention I received from the scientists because of all this.

"In all seriousness, John, do you not realize how important this development is?" Dr. Marillac asked me for the umpteenth time a month later as we walked through the Gallery together. Quite a few of the krakens seemed to be lounging about in their specialized pods, basking in the artificial lights. The area had been designed as a lounge for the scientists, but the discovery of the krakens had turned it into dual-purpose section.

I had tried to simply shrug off the scientists at first, but Doctor Marillac was insistent. I'd finally given in and allowed her to pester me and ask me seemingly pointless questions. I had been reticent about answering but eventually I started replying in more than one syllable words.

"They recognize you, John, and actively communicate with one another that you're here," she said as she folded her arms across her chest. She looked at me with a look that was a strange combination of annoyance and excitement. "This development puts their QE at potential human levels."

"Don't crows do the same thing?" I asked, trying to deflect her interest. The scientist was undeterred, however.

"Not like this. Crows call out for each other with distinctive cries," she explained. "The krakens don't communicate that way. We thought their wings changing in color tone was indicative of a language we hadn't deciphered yet, but now we're thinking that it's body language and their real language is more empathic and they can detect this in others. It's the only explanation to how they call their brethren outside The Well to come into the facility and look at you."

"Empathic...telepathic?" I stared at her and shifted my feet uncomfortably at the idea of aliens in my head. I scratched my chin to hide my unease as I recalled some book I'd read a few years ago. "No. Empathic is being able to feel...emotions, right?"

"Correct." Dr. Marillac clapped her hands together and smiled broadly. She seemed immensely pleased with my apparent grasp of what she was trying to explain. "We're beginning to gather enough evidence to prove that they are both sentient *and* empathic beings, which we can bring forth to the UN for official recognition in accordance with UN Resolution 9012. Can you imagine it, though? Aliens, real aliens!"

"The UN is going shit themselves," I muttered as I thought about the various geopolitical power struggles within the UN and the impact such an announcement would make. "I bet most of the countries will veto it, since the US and her allies have funded almost all of the research here."

"No, I was thinking of the fact that we've scoured the known regions of space for signs of intelligent life, and it's been in our own backyard the entire time," Dr. Marillac said, her tone slightly deflated.

"Oh. That too, yeah."

"I never understand you soldier types," she threw her hands up in the air in exasperation. "You march around with your assault rifles—"

"A tranq gun is hardly an assault rifle…"

"—and your battle armor—"

"The impact absorption shirt is nothing more than an extremely thin layer of pillow to prevent me from getting punched hard enough to damage my internal organs…"

"—and when the greatest scientific discovery in the modern era is found, all you can think of is how a global cooperative of nations is going to try and shut us down," she complained. "Just such a typical attitude of a warmonger."

"Hey now," I looked at her, surprised at the outburst. While excitable, I'd never seen the doctor angry before. Nor had she ever shown any sign of being anti-military. Goes to show you that you never really know someone until they get worked up. She blinked and looked away, confusion in her eyes.

"I'm sorry," she apologized. "I have no idea where that came from."

"It's okay, ma'am," I said in a neutral tone. I rubbed the bridge of my nose, thinking. I did not need the lead scientist at the best job I'd ever had pissed off at me. I also didn't want to lose this job. Though I was pretty sure that I had not done anything wrong, I needed to make certain things remained on the up and up. That meant I had to make a sacrifice. "If you like, I can spend some of my downtime in the Gallery with the kraken soon."

"You don't have to," Doctor Marillac shook her head. Her tone, though, told me all that I needed to know. Interacting with the kraken would make all of the scientists on the station happy and would give them more time to research the alien creatures. More time to test their hypothesis, and potentially create the greatest scientific achievements since the splitting of the atom.

Plus, it would probably keep Doctor Marillac from going off on me again, which was even better.

"It's fine, ma'am," I told her in what I hoped was a completely convincing tone. "I have plenty of downtime to spare."

"I do apologize for my attitude," the scientist looked back at me. Her eyes were alight with excitement, though her face was contrite. "I've been feeling a little under the weather lately. Headaches and such. It's making me irritable."

"I'm off shift in four hours, ma'am," I said after a quick glance at the digital clock on the wall. It was set to match UN headquarters on Earth, which was set to UTC–4. *Or*, I thought as I mentally converted the numbers, *two in the afternoon*. "I'll be at the Gallery around 1800 hours, ma'am."

"I do appreciate this, John," Doctor Marillac smiled at me. Her eyes clouded briefly as she thought about it. "That's six in the evening, correct?"

"Yes, ma'am."

"Perfect!" she clapped her hands once more. "This will be a terrific scientific opportunity! I can hardly wait!"

"Neither can I," I lied.

Women can be downright terrifying.

♃

I changed up my route a bit to make the Gallery my last stop, about thirty minutes before shift's end. I hoped that whatever mental phone tree they used would have a head start, and maybe I could get away sooner.

I had to admit that while the scientists drove me nuts, the kraken were pretty interesting. Watching them feed was a bit disconcerting to see, but their swimming and playing evoked a subtle memory of my own childhood playing with friends. Of course, that led to other memories that were more bittersweet than anything else.

The Gallery was quiet. It was early still, and I had expected someone to be in the room when I arrived, but it had been surprisingly empty. I sat down on one of the benches in the room and watched as two of the kraken brushed against the station, their alien fingers touching the plasteel as they passed. They pivoted and swam back, their bodies changing colors as they moved. A varying array of pinks and purples covered their underbellies, changing rapidly back and forth. I chuckled as one of the kraken turned a deep blue for a moment. I could almost imagine a couple arguing about something and the man getting put in his place. I laughed at the idea of my dad trying to back his way out of an argument with my mom and failing miserably.

"Good luck with that, buddy," I told the kraken who had turned blue.

Both kraken suddenly stopped swimming and turned towards me. For the barest of moments, I felt as though the aliens were staring *through* me, peering into the depths of my heart and soul. I shivered and looked away, trying to appear as it the kraken's movements had not bothered me in the slightest.

I was fairly certain I wouldn't have fooled anybody in the slightest had they been there.

"Stop it," I whispered as I watched the kraken out of the corner of my eye. "That's creepy as hell."

My PDA chirped. Saved by the bell. I glanced down at the screen—it was Poole. I think. It could have been Lockhart.

"John," he said. "Report to Control for prisoner transport."

"Transport? I haven't been trained on that yet. Besides, shift ends in less twenty minutes."

"Won't take long, and you gotta start sometime," Poole (or Lockhart) said, before being shoved out of the way by Lockhart (or Poole). "Consider it oh jay tee, rookie." He was replaced by the first guy.

"Knock that off. You two are making me dizzy." *On the job training*, I translated internally. *Well, it could be worse. People could be trying to kill me with artillery.*

Twin grins filled the screen. I sighed and made a silent promise to get their names tattooed on their foreheads once the contract at the station was up.

"Roger Control, will be there as soon as I can. Out." I clicked off and stowed the PDA. I could still feel the two Kraken watching me. I met their gaze and gave them my best All-is-right-because-I'm-A-Marine grin. "Duty calls. You two play nice." I pointed at the kraken I'd designated as the husband. "And trust me, buddy, just take out the trash. And tell her she's got a nice butt or something. Chicks dig that."

I would've sworn the alien gave me a thumbs up in reply.

It only took a few minutes to get to Control, most of the time taken by the elevator ride. I stepped out and walked towards the desk. One of the Things stood up as I approached. Behind him was Neil Frandsen, another guard that everyone else called Bigfoot for some reason. I'd only spoken to him in passing since he typically wasn't in my shift rotation. He seemed like a decent enough guy.

"I'll go with you to show you the ropes, rook." On the PDA, I could only see faces. In person, Poole's name tag was visible. I sighed with relief. No more guessing games today, thank God. "Don't worry, you're starting off with Holomisa. We'll work you up slowly to the more…difficult inmates."

We started towards the holding area, Poole in the lead. Bigfoot followed behind. I took this to mean he had the heat today.

Protocol stated one guard per shift carried a firearm, concealed, as well as the standard issue tranq gun. The designation rotated with each shift, and the same guard never carried twice in a row. A message on the PDA prior to clocking in would send the designated guard to the armory to pick up the firearm.

"How difficult is difficult?"

"Well," Poole said, scratching his goatee, "let's see—most of them aren't too bad, just the usual bullshit that comes with prisoners. Wheeling, dealing, trying to get something they don't have. That would be…" He ticked names off on his fingers. "Wohl, Hernandez, Jones, and Aviotti."

"And the others?"

"Flynn and Dupay are surly, to put it mildly, but fairly compliant for the most part. The occasional outburst, but loss of a privilege or two for a while brings them back in line." He paused, frowning. "Gentry and Jou make me nervous. With those two, I feel like it's only a matter of time before something happens."

"Oh?"

"Yeah, I've been doing this a while, back home I did a rotation in Leavenworth. I've seen the type before. Always probing, looking for something they can use. Information, patterns, weaknesses of any sort. Be careful around them. Gentry will try and get your goat, make you slip up and reveal something about yourself. He'll use that to mess with you. My advice is to just keep your mouth shut and follow procedure."

"And Jou?"

"He's more physical. Don't move him without a partner. He'll resist without making it obvious, you know? Passive resistance, when it's someone that big, could cause some problems." Poole checked his PDA and jerked his head down the corridor. "We gotta go, they're expecting us." We moved on. "With Jou, he'll make it difficult to restrain him, but nothing overt. He's strong, though. Very strong."

I nodded, making mental notes. My ego scoffed at the idea of anyone getting the better of me, but I knew deep down that Poole was speaking of lessons learned from experience. I would heed his words carefully.

I had a list of all of the prisoners and their backgrounds uploaded onto my PDA, but I hadn't quite gotten around to reading them yet. I'd been on rotation since I'd arrived and had been putting it off. I made another mental note to go over them later after my shift ended. If I was going to start doing transport work, now would be a great time to know more about the prisoners.

"What about the last one? Bastille, right?"

"Baptiste. And quite frankly, he just flat-out scares me. He's just as polite and calm as Holomisa, but, I don't know. There's something in his eyes that just seems off. I've never met anyone like him before, and we had some pretty bad mothers back home."

We arrived at the first cell on the block, which belonged to Captain Holomisa. I looked at Poole, uncertain. He gave a reassuring grin.

"Just follow my instructions and observe for now," he said. "You'll get a chance later."

"Got it."

"You ready?" Poole's thumb hovered over the button.

"As I'll ever be."

The wall went clear. Holomisa looked up from his book, nodded, and marked his place. He stood and approached the door, turning around and clasping his hands behind his back. His movements, while slow, were deliberate, and didn't seem to be challenging us or mocking in any way. Just someone making sure we knew he was complying, no ulterior motive.

"Nothing up my sleeve…" I muttered. A quick smile flashed across Holomisa's face. I gave him a funny look before I shook my head. I wondered if he could read lips as well. It wouldn't surprise me.

Poole triggered the lock, and the door slid into the floor. Holomisa took one careful step backwards and stopped. Poole carefully snapped the cuffs on the captain's wrists, then bent to attach the leg restraints. Bigfoot stood to the left of the prisoner, hand on his tranq gun in case something went wrong.

"Ok, Captain, you may turn around and exit your cell."

Holomisa did so, and then surprised me. He spoke.

"Ah, Lockhart, it is good to see you again."

I did a double take.

"Can't fool you, can I?" the older guard said, chuckling. "Thought the name tag would throw you off this time." He shot me a look and grinned. "Captain H here is batting a thousand. Only one on the station that can tell us apart without a cheat of some kind."

My brain did a quick somersault, reassigning a name to the person I was standing next to.

"Shall we, gentlemen?" Holomisa nodded in the direction of the elevator. I found myself taking a step involuntarily, momentarily forgetting that I was the one with the authority here. I flushed at Poole's — Lockhart's, damn it — grin.

"Don't worry, rook, he has that effect on everyone at first." To Holomisa, he said, "Introductions, first, Captain. Captain Holomisa, this is John Manning, recently in from Soma, and recently out of the Marines." Holomisa gave a small bow in my direction. "Manning, this is Captain Emery Holomisa, formerly of the US Army."

"Captain, your reputation and career precedes you," I said. "I wish we could've met under different circumstances."

"Likewise." A slight smile crossed his lips. "Soma? Surely you have some interesting stories."

"Just one, Captain. And don't…"

"…Call you Shirley?" A toothy grin came and went quickly.

"Uh, yeah." I couldn't help but to grin back. "A fan of the classics, I see."

"I have absolutely no idea what you two are talking about," Lockhart said, shaking his head. "Let's head down before you guys start in on the war stories."

All in all, Holomisa was a model prisoner. He quit talking as we started walking towards the elevator; however, I had the feeling it was so we wouldn't become distracted and could perform our duties properly. Respect for our position, regardless of the situation. It was comforting, in a way, and somewhat inspiring.

Jesus. I've known the guy less than five minutes and I'd follow him into Hell.

I forced the thought back and concentrated on what I was supposed to do.

The doors closed, and I tensed. If anything were to go down, this would be the place to do it. Natural leader and hero or not, Holomisa was still a prisoner, and one that was damn difficult to keep that way.

Thirty seconds later, the doors opened to the research deck. I had never been down this far yet, so I was immensely curious to see just what went on in the most restricted area on the station. I was not to be disappointed.

The larger entry room was barren save for a few more tubes for the kraken to swim in. There were not windows of plasteel here, only the sturdy walls which blocked anyone from looking out or in. Oddly enough, there didn't appear to be any of the aliens in this part of the station. I'd seen them everywhere so far, so it was a bit strange to not see any here. I chalked it up to circumstance and walked Captain Holomisa into the room.

Dr. Marillac turned as we stepped out, PDA in hand. Her face was devoid of any emotion, which I figured was her "professional scientist" look. She nodded at Lockhart and jotted down an entry on her PDA.

"Prisoner H-6 has entered Research for his prescribed treatment session," she said into the mic. "The time is five-five-six pm Central Standard Time. Treatment will be handled by Doctor Isaac." She turned to the scrawny scientist next to her. "Doctor Isaac, if you would, please."

"Good evening, Captain," Isaac said, stepping forward. The young doctor carried his PDA in one hand and a strange-looking device in the other. "If you'll come with me, we'll get started."

Holomisa nodded and followed the doctor, Lockhart and I falling in at his side. Bigfoot silently took up the rear once more. The procedure room looked like most of the exam rooms I had been in, with a few computer screens, an IV stand, heart-rate monitor, etc. A small wheeled table held a tray with assorted surgical instruments arranged neatly on a blue napkin. Dead center of the room was dominated by a large chair, over which was suspended a large machine. The various needles, probes, and invasive-looking gizmos gave it a very sinister appearance. All in all, the whole room gave off a "Marquis de Sade, D.D.S." feel.

Only far less comforting.

"The captain is always on his best behavior while here, rookie," Lockhart said as we approached the chair. "But some of the others may give you some pushback. We'll do this by the numbers for your sake." He stopped next to the armrest, facing Holomisa. "Captain, please turn around and back up slowly, until your calves are against the leg rest."

Holomisa complied, again moving slowly and deliberately.

"John, please attach the restraints on the leg rest to the captain's ankles."

I ran the heavy leather straps around Holomisa's legs and buckled them tight.

"Captain, please be seated." Again, the captain did as he was directed, hands still cuffed behind him

"Now release one cuff and attach it to the armrest." I did as instructed, closing the cuff around the D-ring bit into the chair. "Now take your cuffs and repeat with the other arm." I did. Lockhart gave a quick grin. "Thank you, Captain."

Holomisa gave a small nod and closed his eyes as the chair began to elevate and recline. I heard the door open behind me and turned.

The next shift had arrived. I had only met the two guards briefly, a few minutes here and there the week before. The larger, one Joseph Capdepon, was a barrel-chested Texan whose huge beard barely contained his constant grin. Good-natured guy, from what I could tell, but did tend to bitch about the lack of beer. Specifically, St. Arnold's, from back home in Houston. The stuff must have been nectar to the gods or something with his constant lamenting and moaning about not having the beer.

Johnny Minion was smaller, but he was just as wide as Capdepon. He carried it well, and I knew from the gym that he wasn't soft. He was quiet, but I had been warned by Gerry about his fondness for practical jokes. He was constantly making the odd comment which bordered that line between inappropriate and hilarious, which made ample opportunity for the prankster to continue his merry little villainous ways.

The evilest trick (or would that be the best prank?) he had done to date was to swap out the records for one of the female guards with Gerry's. Our boss was undoubtedly surprised to be informed that he had missed his yearly pap smear from the automated insurance call from headquarters and he needed to get it done if he wanted to avoid a lapse in medical coverage, thank you for choosing Bell Life Insurance. Even Gerry, once things had been cleared up, had found it hilarious.

Johnny had still been forced to pull night shifts for a week, though, so it was arguable who had the last laugh. Plus, April had been less than amused when asked about scheduling a proctology appointment by said insurance company.

Efficiency at its best.

"We'll take it from here, John," Joseph said. "Bigfoot, you're on tonight? Good. Hey Manning, aren't you supposed to be off?"

"Yeah, just learning the ropes." I glanced at Lockhart pointedly. "We good?"

He nodded, and I followed him out into the main room. Dr. Marillac was waiting for me.

"John, you're off now, right?"

I suppressed a heavy sigh. I'd completely forgotten about my earlier promise in the excitement of learning something new for the job. "Yeah, I am." I faked a smile. "Gallery?"

"I'll tell the others."

The elevator ride was again, quiet. Lockhart clapped me on the shoulder and threw me a sympathetic look as he exited at Central, but did nothing to help me out of the current situation. That rat bastard.

The Gallery was much busier this time — it seemed like any xenobiologist scientist type that wasn't eating or sleeping had gotten the word I'd be there. Unfortunately, the kraken hadn't seemed to have gotten the memo. As I walked in, everyone in the room turned, expectant looks on their faces. I gave a half-hearted wave.

"Hey everyone…" I guess I expected some sort of answer, a "Hi John!" or something. Something besides the sound of about ten people tapping on their PDAs at once. It was disconcerting to hear nothing but heavy breathing and incessant tapping. Dirty, even.

"Everyone ready?" Dr. Marillac asked the group. Ten heads nodded simultaneously. It was extremely unnerving, like watching a group of cats watching a mouse. "Excellent. John, please call the Kraken."

Jeez, Doc, way to put a guy on the spot. I felt my face flush as I moved closer to the plasteel. I looked out but I couldn't see any of the kraken about. Of course, there was always the possibility that they were out hiding in the shadows. The doc did say that they liked to play a lot.

"Okay guys," I muttered. "Anytime you want to come by, that would be great." I felt all eyes on me, and gave everyone a sheepish grin. "Heeeerrreee alien fishy things." Not a chuckle. I swore I heard crickets chirping. All that was missing was a stray tumbleweed rolling through the room. The scientists were not a humorous lot. "Uhm… I really don't try to call them, they just kind of show up when I'm around. Usually."

"Well," Dr. Marillac said with a barely concealed glare, "I guess we'll have to just make ourselves comfortable and wait."

I sighed. It was going to be a long night.

CHAPTER SIX

Dreaming or awake, we perceive only events that have meaning to us.
–Jane Roberts

I found night time at the station to be my favorite time while on duty. The scientists usually quit their research projects and disappeared into their own quarters just before dinner, rarely coming out into the common area to mingle with the guards and the maintenance crew. Most of my fellow coworkers tended to spend the majority of their downtime in that area, which left the remaining levels a quiet place for someone who preferred solitude. Someone like me.

Gerry had been right when he warned me on my first day at the station: finding any true alone time was difficult at the best of times, especially if one did not want to spend all of their free time confined in their private quarters. The security manager had been prescient and always seemed to speak with a solid voice of experience. The more I got to know him, the more I respected him. He was a solid boss, which is just about what anyone could ask.

The really nice thing about afterhours on the station was the dim lighting. In order to attract the kraken, the station lights were set to a hue which we really couldn't see. It was just enough, though, to cause some of the other guards' eyes to search around the room, unconsciously moving to avoid the light but simultaneously being attracted to it. More than a few of my fellow guards wore contacts to help block out the shifting light. I was one of the fortunate who weren't bothered by the changing-light spectrum.

To conserve power, most of the lights on the levels where there weren't any living quarters went to half-power at night. Save for vital levels of the station, at least. Central stayed at full power throughout the night, but the lights in the prisoner cells were dimmed to levels low enough to allow them to sleep. They didn't seem as bothered by the light-spectrum variations as my fellow guards were. Or if they were bothered, they never complained, though they did bitch about everything else.

It was weird. Despite escorting the prisoners down to Research on the rare occasion at the beginning or end of my shift, I knew very little about them. Sure, a few were quite chatty and tried to strike up a conversation, but mostly their talks consisted of insults or provocative comments. It's amazing just how creative someone can get with their veiled threats when confined to a small room for most of the day. Some of them were so depraved that I had to wonder just how they made it past the psychological evaluations all military personnel were required to endure before their enlistment began.

The only one I felt that I had any grasp of was Emery Holomisa, which was funny because he hardly spoke at all. Out of all of the prisoners we held, he never insulted us, never talked back and never tried to argue his way out of the mobile restraints we used while escorting them to and from Research. He just wanted to do his duty and be left alone, something that I both understood and was able to appreciate. I had been the same way once while the shrinks were trying to mess around with my head, though he had much better patience than I had ever been.

Part of the reason that I'd done well at sniper school—other than a near-supernatural ability to hit a target from just about any distance—was my preference to work with as few people as possible. In high school, I'd hung out with friends and was never considered anti-social. Not one of the cool kids, sure. But I had enough friends that it never occurred to me that I might want something else. It was something I hadn't known about myself until sniper school, when I'd been paired up with a spotter and send out on the Survival Course for six weeks.

Sniper training has evolved over the past hundred years. Marine Force Recon snipers used to only deal with regular recon training. With the advent of space travel and colonization of alien worlds, we had to deepen our training and techniques, to try and find that balance between specialization and generalization. It became tougher to be a Marine, and even more difficult to make it through Recon training. To do this, lots of training regiments were created to weed out the weak. One of those was simply known as the Survival Course.

Some mad scientist/bored Gunnery Sergeant with too much time on his or her hands had come up with the idea that Marine Force Recon training had to be tougher than everything else in the history of the world. Combined. After deciding that Navy BUDS (Basic Underwater Demolition School) had been too easy, a mash up of Recon training, the BUDS and SERE (Survival, Evasion, Resistance and Escape) schools came about and morphed into what most of the brass named the Marine Corps Survival, Reconnaissance, and Tactical Course. Those of us who made it through just called it the Time of Major Suck.

Ninety percent failed to complete the first Time of Major Suck. Instead of making it simpler, as other branches of the Armed Forces had done in the past, the Corps decided that it was too easy and made it…tougher. Gone were the random food drops to keep Marines fed. If you wanted to be Recon, you had to find your own food. Lost? Should have brought a map, or stolen one. Lack of food? Suck it up, Marine. Water? Urine is sterile, you whiner. Drink up and stay alive.

Needless to say, the last week of the Time of Major Suck is a bit of a blur to me. On the other hand, it's the primary reason I survived my unwanted and unasked for field trip on Soma.

It was still early in my shift as I wandered the levels of the station, doing what the rest of the guards called a "leak and peek" check. I had originally thought that they were messing around with me when they told me about it. Harass the new guy and all that, so I ignored it. I got royally chewed out by Gerry on my third night after finishing my rounds well ahead of schedule. After he explained precisely what a "leak and peek" check was, though, I made damn certain to take my time and do exactly as I had been told.

The station was pressurized to keep the air inside breathable. It was what kept us alive. A series of locks and pressurized vaults allowed for the shuttles to arrive in the hangar, and another set let the deep sea research vessels depart into the lake and explore the surroundings. Throughout the remaining parts, the plasteel and carefully sealed joints kept the inhabitants of the station safe.

The "leak and peek" check basically meant that a guard had to wander all over the station and listen to any strange sounds, anything miniscule to something like air escaping or hissing, and even a bubbling, boiling water sound. The guard also looked for any sign of dampness in the outer passageways. Sensors covered the entire station and were wired into Control in case something catastrophic happened, but sometimes the sensors missed things. That was why idiots like me walked the halls looking for trouble.

Strangely enough, my boss mentioned that if I could hear the boiling water sound then I was probably already dead. I would like to think that he was just messing with the new guy, but the odds were pretty good that he wasn't.

The Gallery was dimly lit and quiet, as I'd expected. I briefly scanned the room for any signs of life, but even the kraken had disappeared from the viewing tubes for the evening. While the inquisitive aliens were almost always watching the scientists, the only other guard besides me that they paid any attention to was the boss, Gerry. Which meant that once the scientists left, the kraken disappeared into the mysterious depths of the lake.

I logged my inspection of the large space on my PDA and moved around the edge of the room, looking out through the plasteel and into the lake. I could see tiny, almost microscopic flashes of fluorescent light moving about. The plankton had startled me the first time I had seen it, though the explanation was easy. Much like lightning bugs of Earth and the parietal bugs on Soma, the fluorescent was designed to attract mates. It was eerily beautiful, much like everything else on this moon.

I stopped and watched the show for a few seconds before moving on. As much as I enjoyed it, I had a job to do.

I turned the corner and spotted Post Three, one of the five security checkpoints strategically placed throughout the station. They protected the restricted locations throughout the base, places like Research and Control where the few civilian maintenance workers could not go. I felt it was a bit redundant to have that many posts for only thirty civilian workers but it wasn't up to me.

Justin Balyeat and April Voecks were on duty tonight at Post Three. Justin was a pretty bland guy who was a bit of a nerd like me, except his interests ran more to the math side than mine. He was taller than I was and better built, but I liked to think that I had better hair. He was pretty reserved, too, rarely displaying his emotions for anyone to see. I never really understood how he got into private contracting, since he was one of the rare few who didn't have military experience. His room was actually next to mine so I could have just gone over and asked, but we didn't interact much for some reason. It's not as though I was trying to avoid him or anything. We just never really talked once we were off duty.

April, on the other hand, had a crass sense of humor that I greatly appreciated and was fairly gregarious. She was one of the few non-civilian females on the station and, because of this, was the center of attention for a lot of the single guys, as well as a few of the married ones. She never seemed to show any interest in any of them, though, and particularly enjoyed shooting down their attempts. Watching someone crash and burn while trying to hit on her was a form of entertainment most of us never seemed to tire of. Her husband back on Earth must have been one hell of a guy to keep her loyalty, I figured. She was a former pararescuer, a special operations unit that worked to save pilots when they were shot down in hostile territory. It was a tough group to get into by any standards. She was, by any definition of the word, a total badass.

"Hey Manning," April greeted me as I approached their post. "How are things on this lovely fall evening?"

"I guess that's the nice thing about being on a station where you don't see any seasonal changes," I observed as I stopped at the desk. "You can tell me it was winter and I'd believe you."

"Benefits of the station's isolation," Justin stated as he held out a PDA. I pressed my thumb on the screen for a few seconds until it chirped. Logged, I leaned against the desk and glanced at the clock. It was just past midnight, standard Zulu time. I wondered for a moment if my mom had made enchiladas for dinner. The idea made my stomach gurgle hungrily.

"Benefit?" I asked and gave him a curious look. I told my stomach to shut up.

"You're still aging the same as if you were on Earth, since we still use Earth time and calendar here," Justin explained. "No matter where in orbit we are in relation to Saturn, we're still on

HQ's seasonal calendar, which means Chicago. Not like if we were on, oh, Soma or something, where we had to try to match the calendar to the planet's orbit. It'd be kind of stupid to try and match the calendar of the station to the moon's orbit when we never even see a seasonal change."

"Point," I conceded. Having three months of August on Soma had sucked hardcore. Especially when the average temperature was three degrees higher than Earth's, and the humidity levels were five times greater on average. It was like the Deep South, but worse. Much, much worse. "Never really thought of it like that."

"Quiet night, like always," April said as she rubbed her face with her hands. "I hate the night shift. Too damn slow for me. Why'd you volunteer for it?"

"I like the quiet," I admitted. "Not to sound rude, but I don't have to deal with a lot of people this way. The prisoners are asleep, and the scientists aren't begging me to interact with the krakens for more research while I'm on duty."

"It's nice," Justin agreed with me. "But the occasional change of routine? I wouldn't complain."

"Bitch whine moan," I chuckled. "Paid as much as we are to do nothing? I almost feel guilty."

"I don't," April grinned. "I jumped into hot LZ's eighty-six times during my hitch while making a little over minimum wage. You can offer me more money than I make right now to do this and not a shred of guilt would ever touch my soul."

"Amen, sister," I said, impressed. I knew she had made a few combat jumps, but not that many. "All right, I'm off to Post Two. Leak and peek watch is as exciting as competitive lawn growing. Catch you guys later."

"See you at 0500," April said and waved. Justin merely grunted in my direction as I walked off.

The distance between the posts was enough that we needed our comms to stay in contact. The station was *huge* by civilian standards and featured lots of varying hallways and rooms throughout that made traversing it slow. I'd gotten lost a few times my first week at the station and endured some ridicule from the others, but eventually I was able to figure it out.

Five minutes later, I was nearing Research when I felt the air around me suddenly grow colder. I paused and looked around. I couldn't hear anything unusual so I began to mentally go through my checklist. The air recyclers of the station kept the temperature at a balmy 72 degrees at all times, and there was almost never any sort of fluctuations. A change in air temperature usually meant that one of the recyclers was on the fritz. A simple fix but a common problem on a station this size. I scowled and brought up my PDA. I typed in a few commands before I began to speak.

"Post Three, this is Manning."

"Go, Manning," April's voice came back almost instantly.

"One of the recyclers needs to be repaired in hallway four, delta level," I informed her. I rattled off the numbers which were stenciled on the wall where I was at for her to reference the precise recyclers I was talking about. "Just picked up a cold spot. Run a diagnostic to confirm."

"Cold spot in hallway four, delta level," she then repeated the numbers back to me. "Running diagnostic test now to confirm."

"Thanks," I said.

A moment later she came back on the PDA. "John, readings in the hallway says that the temperature is steady and the same as the rest of the station. All recyclers show green and are running within parameters."

"Well that's bull," I muttered. "Negative, Post Three. It's decidedly cooler in this hallway. Feels like it's fifty degrees or colder here."

"I'm showing everything to be green, John," she countered in a disbelieving tone. "You running a fever or something?"

"Not that I'm aware," I said, puzzled. What the hell?

"Do we need to send a maintenance crew down there?" April asked.

"No, I don't think so," I said after a moment of thought. If I were running a fever, I would be sweaty, so I checked my forehead with my free hand. No sweat. I scowled. I stayed quiet and listened, but I couldn't hear anything out of the ordinary. The gentle hum of the recyclers remained steady, and I couldn't hear anything that remotely sounded like an air leak. "It's probably nothing. Thanks for checking, April."

"No problem. Post Three, out."

I tucked my PDA back into my pants pocket. Methane needed to be both cold and under extreme amounts of pressure in order to remain in liquid form, and Titan had both in spades. I listened carefully but heard nothing that sounded like water bubbling. In fact, the entire hall was eerily silent. I rubbed my exposed arms as goose bumps began to rise. I held up my PDA and tapped into the environmental scanners remotely. According to the sensors, the temperature was normal. I scowled and slapped the stupid machine before I tucked it back into my pocket. I didn't care what the sensors said. It was *cold*.

A tickling sensation ran down my spine. It was a feeling which I'd come to dread while out in the depths of the wilderness. The hair on the back of my neck stood up and goose bumps, which had nothing to do with the temperature, raised on my forearms. My gut churned. This was too familiar.

I was being watched and I didn't know by who.

I glanced up and looked for the security cameras. They were scattered throughout the station and were constantly monitored by the guards back at Control. For a brief instant, I thought that maybe I was being watched electronically but dismissed that notion almost immediately. Whoever was spying on me was closer than the cameras, which was impossible. There was nothing in the hallway that anyone could hide behind and nowhere to hide in, like a utility room, and the space between the walls and the recyclers was too small to fit anyone larger than a child. Yet the sensation remained. It was bizarre, and it was starting to freak me out a little.

Movement flickered in the corner of my eye. I whirled quickly, my hand dropping to where I would normally have had a sidearm. Guards didn't carry actual firearms, though, merely tranquilizer guns. Handy but not something I wanted to trust with my life.

It didn't matter, though. There was nothing there. I let my eyes slide slowly across the hall, though I never took my hand off of the tranq gun. No movement, no sign of whatever I thought I had seen, nothing. *Had I lost my mind*, I wondered as I continued to scan the hallway. *Had I finally snapped?*

"Jesus," I muttered under my breath. I was getting myself all worked up over nothing. It was all in my mind, my brain filling in gaps of what my eyes couldn't see. My imagination gone wild was a far simpler solution than anything else. I made a mental note to talk with Gerry after my shift ended. Maybe I needed to swap shifts with someone for a few days? I rubbed my tired eyes as I turned around.

An apparition of some sort was standing in the hall, facing away from me. I almost screamed but managed to keep my composure, though I still went for my sidearm…which was worthless against something like this. The sweat on the back of my neck was icy cold, my palms were clammy. I was staring at something that wasn't supposed to exist. *Couldn't* exist.

I fumbled for my tranq gun but the nerves in my fingers seemed to be numb. I couldn't feel the release catch for the holster.

Ghosts aren't real, I thought as I struggled to keep hold of my sanity. *Ghosts can't be real!*

Ghosts aren't real, and yet there was one standing right in front of me. It was facing away, looking out into…what? I didn't know. I couldn't even imagine what the ghost was thinking. Or if they even did think. It was too much. I had to be hallucinating…

…but I wasn't. I knew I couldn't be hallucinating. Which meant that the ghost before me was real. Who could it be, though? Had one of the workers died during construction and was now doomed to roam the halls? Or was it something else entirely? And why me? Why would the ghost show itself to me?

The ghost turned and my heart stopped beating in my chest. I knew every single angle of that delicate face, the curve of her lips, the shape of her eyes. I recognized the curious tilt of her head, the slight quirk of her smile, the laughter which was yet to come. I was intimately familiar with everything about her even though I had only seen her in photos taken years before.

A man never forgets his first, last, and only love.

"No," I whispered as I stared at her. I took a step back. "This is a trick. My brain is playing tricks on me. That's all. That's all this is."

John…

"Oh fuck no!" I screamed and looked away. "No! I'm not going through this shit again!"

KRAKEN MARE

After a minute of silence, I looked back .She was still there, watching me, a strange expression on her face. It was filled with sorrow, but there was something else on the edge of that. It was almost as though Concy – *no, just a ghost, not Concy,* I told myself – looked guilty.

How can the dead look guilty? I wondered.

John…danger…

"What are you talking about?" I asked in a hushed whisper, terrified that if I spoke too loudly that she would leave or, worse yet, stay. I can't explain why I thought this, it was just there, in the back of my mind. A lingering doubt. "What do you mean?"

Danger…comes…

"Comes from where? What are you talking about?" I knew I was babbling but I couldn't help it.

From…within…below…

Below? From the bottom of the lake? Was there something at the bottom of the lake that was coming for us? I was confused, frightened, and in a hell of a lot of pain. Pain of the heart, of the soul. A deep, dark depression, something I had thought I'd left behind years before, welled up. It threatened to overwhelm me, to drag me back down into that never-ending abyss.

Was I hallucinating? Had I finally snapped and gone crazy? Tears blinded me. The hall wavered in my eyes as my vision blurred. I knew I hadn't snapped, not yet in any case. But I didn't understand any of it. What did she mean? I hastily wiped my eyes with the back of my hand. I had to know. I had to—

She was gone. The hallway was back to normal temperature. The lights were no longer flickering or acting oddly. I leaned against the wall, emotionally exhausted, barely able to contain the soul-wrenching sobs which threatened to tear me apart from the inside out. My heart threatened to tear itself in two for the second time in my life, and I slowly slid down the wall until I was seated. I pressed my head against the cool surface of the wall and closed my eyes. I began to count, slowly, by threes until my breathing began to return to normal. My racing heart slowed and the old, familiar dull ache in my soul faded. I opened my eyes.

There was no sign of anyone in the hall with me. I could hear nothing but the steady, gentle pulsing of the recyclers working in

- 62 -

the ducts below. I couldn't smell anything other than my own stale sweat and fear. I bent my head down and pressed it against my knee. I was alone and nobody would be able to see a thing.

I let the last remnants of the festering wound in my soul pour forth. The pain was almost welcome. It was long past overdue.

CHAPTER SEVEN

The past is our definition. We may strive with good reason to escape it, or to escape what is bad in it. But we will escape it only by adding something better to it.
-Wendell Barry

I didn't tell anyone what I had seen in the hallway. I'd finished my shift and immediately made my way to the gym where I could beat up on a punching bag while I sorted through my jumbled emotions. It took long enough that by the time I'd finished punching, all the muscles in my shoulders were numb and I could no longer feel my hands. I was exhausted and needed to go to bed, but I was almost afraid to. I wasn't sure how my dreams would turn and, given how raw my emotions were, I decided to forgo for the time being. Catnaps would suffice, I hoped.

Gerry could tell something was wrong when he saw me come into the gym. He wisely left me alone while I hit the bag. After I'd returned from the showers carrying my dirty workout clothes, however, he pulled me aside.

"What's on your mind?" he asked as soon as we were away from the Things, who were sparring and tossing each other around with what looked like Judo throws. Gary and Kelly were good people, but other than our usual interaction during my shift, we rarely spoke. Plus, I liked to hit things. They liked to throw them. It made working out together awkward.

"Bad shift," I admitted. I grabbed my workout bag and tossed my shorts and shirt inside.

"Coworkers?" he prodded some more. I shook my head.

"Just…too much time alone with my thoughts," I said. I looked up and saw that he looked fairly worried. I tried to set his mind at ease. "You think I might be able to swap to daytime hours for a week or two?"

"Bigfoot's been bugging me to go to nights, so it shouldn't be a problem," Gerry said, referring to our lone Canadian on the team.

I'd gotten to know Bigfoot much better over the past few weeks. He also one of the tallest operators I'd ever run across, which had led to the origin of part of his nickname. Like me, he was trained as a sniper, only the majority of his action had taken place a long time ago on battlefields I'd never heard of. He was nearing mandatory retirement age for the company, which put him in some exclusive company. He also sported one of the most impressive beards I had ever seen and, after seeing him naked in the gym shower more often than I cared to, I came to fully understand how he earned his moniker.

Some mental images never went away, no matter how hard you tried to mentally scrub it with bleach.

"Thanks," I said.

"Anything else going on?" he pressed.

"No, not really," I lied. I was a little ashamed of lying to my boss, but what the hell was I supposed to do, admit that I was either going crazy or that I'd actually seen a ghost? I liked my job too much for that much honesty.

"Good," Gerry grunted. "By the way, Doc Marillac is looking for you. Said you haven't been down in a few days. Go on down and spend some time in the Gallery at least. Let the scientists poke around and ask stupid questions."

Shit.

"Yeah, fine," I grumbled. Gerry chuckled softly. I gave him a look.

"I'll come with you, Kraken Whisperer," he smiled. "At least then I can spend time with, uh, watching the kraken interact with you."

"Yeah, sure," I snorted, amused by his lame attempt at hiding his affection for Doctor Marillac. He was an extremely easy person to read. "Kraken."

�

Watching Gerry try to flirt with the doctor was very similar to observing someone strap a jet rocket onto the ass of a penguin to try and make it fly. He bumbled his way through the start of the conversation, managed to find some footing once he quit trying to impress her and be himself, and finally made her smile a few times. He succeeded, but the bruises to his ego had to hurt. They'd hurt me, and I was a not-so-impartial observer. Fortunately for him, Doctor Marillac seemed just as inept as he was at flirting and reading the signs of interested parties, so they sort of canceled one another out.

Concy would have found it adorably sweet and offered tips for next time. I thought it was funny as hell, and planned on mocking my boss mercilessly once we were in the clear.

For the time being, however, I left him and the doc alone as I wandered through the Gallery. As much as I hated being bugged by the doc and her merry minions, I enjoyed the Gallery and the alien creatures which seemed drawn to it. The kraken were out and about, though not nearly as many as I'd seen a few days before. The six or seven in view were active, flashing their wings in varying colors of red and black. I took a seat on one of the benches which looked out into the lake and watched the aliens swim quickly by, diving, twisting, and turning in dizzying patterns.

After a few minutes of watching them, I realized that there *was* a pattern to their swimming. I leaned closer and stared, intrigued. I could see the pattern repeating over and over again but I had no idea what it meant.

"Mating ritual?" I muttered under my breath. It was something I would mention to the doc. After, of course, Gerry was done trying to flirt with her. The last thing I wanted to do was to interrupt a potentially good thing.

Watching the kraken dance in the liquid methane lake, my mind began to drift back to my first date with Concy. I hadn't even realized it was a date until she'd grabbed my hand while we were walking to the movies. I'd gone from cocky and self-assured to drooling idiot in the span of about three seconds, which had to be a record of some sort.

I'd been fortunate. My dad had taught me that it was better to be silent and thought an idiot than to open one's mouth and remove all doubt. If it had been anyone else, I would have seemed to be the strong, silent type. Since Concy had already known me for five years before our accidental date, however, she had known just how nervous I was and didn't laugh too much.

I had already loved her. I just had not realized it until I saw our fingers intertwined.

I didn't remember the movie we saw. Nor where we went to dinner afterwards. The only thing I could remember were her eyes, bright and assuring, and her hand held gently in mine. Oh, and the lecture I got from my parents for missing curfew. Granted, they hadn't grounded me for being late once I told them all about the date. However, that had led to the *other* lecture about being careful and birth control and things I was really, really uncomfortable hearing about from my mom. My dad had simply watched me squirm under the constant barrage from my mom and smiled. At least I know where I get my sense of humor from.

Nobody at school had understood. They'd known about our friendship, since we had been inseparable before we'd started dating. Their minds hadn't been able to make the transition, though, and whispered rumors floated around school. Concy just laughed at them, but I was ready to murder everyone when I started hearing the accusations. They were ugly, hurtful, with the barest hints of truth, which were far more than enough to make everyone believe that I was taking advantage of the "poor immigrant." I'd gotten into more than a few fights over that and would have been expelled had Concy not put a stop to things.

I never figured out exactly what she had done, but one day the rumors suddenly stopped.

My mind drifted back to the present. The kraken weren't swimming around as frantically as they had been before. They were drifting through the lake now, occasionally spinning their bodies to reposition themselves within the loop. Instead of hues of black and red, their wings were more demure pinks and soft blues. Melancholy, I supposed. It fit my own mood.

I leaned forward. The kraken were mimicking my mood. I'd seen it before but I hadn't really put two and two together. How could they know…unless the doctor was right and the aliens could sense human emotion? I grew excited as the implications of it all began to set in. That meant that the doctor's theories were correct and the aliens were intelligent.

The prospect of it all was exciting. Here was the proof that the doc, hell, the entire human race, needed. Proof that aliens could communicate beyond our level, that they could be more than we were. A terrifying thought, but a slap in the face to the idea that humanity ruled the known galaxy uncontested.

I paused. What they were doing was direct evidence that they had empathic abilities, at a minimum. If they could sense my mood and mimic it, could they sense others moods as well? Evidence suggested just that. But if that were the case, just whose emotions had they been repeating when we had first arrived? Who on the station was in a mood that would cause the kraken to be black and red, colors we traditionally associated with anger and despair?

The question and subsequent internal debate was enough to make me keep silent when Gerry reappeared thirty minutes later, Doctor Marillac in tow. His grin alone led me to believe that more than just some harmless flirting had occurred. *Maybe he had managed to get to second base?* I thought. That would have been a surprise.

I winced as a headache began to form near the back of my skull. I rubbed the sinus cavities on both sides of my face, hoping to relieve the pressure before it could really hit. I'd had a few migraines in the past couple of weeks and recognized the early signs of an impending one. Other than popping a prescription pain pill or a nasal stimulant, there was little which seemed to counter them.

This is going to be a bad one, I thought as closed my eyes. The throbbing pain grew, pushing at the very edge of my tolerance threshold. The gray was closing in on my mind. A wave of nausea washed over me. It threatened to toss my lunch all over the polished floor.

Just as quickly as the migraine appeared, it was gone. I rubbed the back of my neck and slowly opened my eyes. The lights were bright but not painfully so. I was thankful for that, at least. Still, the random migraines were starting to become a nuisance. I shook my head. Migraines sucked.

"Soooo…?" I let the question hang in the air as the duo stopped a few feet before me. Gerry's grin never faltered.

"She agreed to let me take her out to dinner once we're back on Earth," Gerry proclaimed triumphantly. Doctor Marillac squirmed uncomfortably and frowned at him.

"There were some stipulations," she reminded him. She looked at me oddly. "You looked as though you had something to say when we walked in. What was it?"

I opened my mouth to say something but paused. Did I? I couldn't remember. The migraine had taken a lot out of me, and all I wanted to do right then was go take a nap, workout be damned. I thought about it as I stared at the kraken outside, who all seemed to be watching the duo with no small amount of interest.

"Nope, nothing I can think of," I said. Doctor Marillac gave me another strange look.

"Well, just because I agreed to one date with you, Gerry, doesn't mean we're a serious couple now," she reminded my boss. The admonition didn't even begin to faze the grin still on his face.

I chuckled. Whatever it was that I had forgotten, it couldn't have been too important.

CHAPTER EIGHT

The secret of your future is hidden in your daily routine.
-- Mike Murdock

Routine. It was the standard for any military personnel, it's what helped drill the basics into any soldier or sailor. Routine is what kept a lot of us sane when we were off-world somewhere with nothing to do.

All branches of the military had a routine of some sort. Wake up, exercise, shower and shave, formation, then daily tasks until lunch...all were part of the routine. It kept the mindset of the soldier focused, even if it had been years since that individual had finished basic training.

Routine on the station was the same thing, though on a much different level.

The next few weeks were much of the same for me. Transport a prisoner down to Research, stand outside while he is poked and prodded, then escort him back up. It was mind-numbing, dull, repetitive, and did much to take my mind off of what had happened to me in the hallway.

What had happened to me in that hallway, exactly? The more I thought about it, the more firmly I become convinced that I had suffered from some sort of PTSD break. Nothing else made any sense to me. Ghosts aren't real, science had proven that conclusively. Of course, that brought up another potential problem. If I actually was suffering from an episode, would that hamper my job performance?

I thought about talking with Gerry and explaining the situation but dismissed the idea as quickly as it had appeared. I was sure he was already concerned about my mental state. The last thing I needed to do was to give him a reason to get me off-station, and a crazy guard in a place where there was no escape was most definitely a Bad Thing.

I was still convinced that time and more punching bags would help me out more than a shrink armed with prescription pills and a strait jacket. I just needed to keep my head on straight. The best way to do that was to keep working, keep doing my job. Focus on something that would keep my mind off of the past. The doctors would have said I was avoiding the situation. I wouldn't have said that they were wrong.

Besides, everything I'd ever heard or read about said that ghosts only haunted the locations where they died.

"Hey, Doctor Isaac!" I spotted the young scientist walking as I exited the chow hall. I had spoken to him in passing a few times down in Research but other than that I had little interaction with the kid.

He was the youngest scientist on the station by far and he seemed to be the most comfortable with interacting with us fellow human beings. I guessed his age to be in his mid-twenties, maybe. His haircut and styling made me think younger though. His body language and general attitude suggested a maturity that was hidden behind layers of carefully applied personal appearance masks. Still, he was easy for me to deal with, most of the time. Compared to the other scientists, at least. He still gave off the vibe of an extremely awkward college student once in a while.

"Oh, hi John," he said as he turned and saw me. "How're you doing?"

"Good, Doc," I replied. "Where you headed?"

"To the Gallery, then on down to Research," he said as I caught up to him. He carried multiple PDA's in his hands. He saw my questioning look and grinned. "Doctor Marillac. She likes to keep each patient's information on a separate PDA."

"That's weird," I muttered. He chuckled.

"That's nothing," he said, "You should see how Doctor Furter dictates to his PDA. He looks like he either needs to use the bathroom or he's dancing…"

"First a jump to the left…" I said in a sing-song tone. The young scientist shot me a confused look.

"I'd heard you were weird, but I just figured that was the guards giving the new guy a hard time."

I inwardly sighed. Nobody respected the classics anymore. Tim Curry would have wept manly, transvestite tears.

"So what's new down in the dungeon?" I changed the subject as we walked up to the Gallery. It was located on the floor above the mess hall, and a lot of the guards and scientists both took the stairs instead of the elevator. I found it a good way to help burn off that extra dessert I always seemed to stuff my hole with. I was blessed with a fantastic metabolism, but I didn't see why I couldn't help it out as often as I could.

"Dungeon? Oh, down in Research," he shrugged his shoulders. "Mass transference."

"Huh? What's that mean, Doc?"

"Jelly," he tried to explain, "and please, call me Isaac. The doc is Doctor Marillac."

"Ah, like the Corps," I grinned. "Last names make it easier."

"What? No," the scientist gave me a strange look, "Isaac's my first name."

"Why do they call you Doctor Isaac then? Wouldn't it be Doctor...what's your last name?"

"Szymaniewski," he answered, "but since nobody seems to be able to pronounce it correctly, I've gone by Isaac since I was an undergrad student."

"Chi—" I stopped myself and grinned, "yeah, I could see how that could be a problem. Isaac it is."

"See? Easy."

"So what did you mean, jelly?" I asked, bringing the topic back to what he had mentioned earlier.

"Jelly?" he asked, confused.

"Mass transference and jelly?" I reminded him.

"Oh, right!" he said. "I'm testing a theory about mass transference right now—well, when I get back down the Research, at least—and the best way to think about it is something pliable and filled with jelly. So I figured the cafeteria would have some jelly, but not tonight. So I need to work on my theory with artificial gel, like ballistic gelatin. I'm gonna check the armory tomorrow and see if I can borrow some to see if mass transference and modifications are possible in a controlled test."

"Uh…" I was lost. Fortunately, he was one of the few scientists on the station who spoke mortal.

"Think of a baby teething ring," he explained, "you know, the ones with the jelly inside?"

"Yeah, okay."

"Now take that ring and squeeze it," he continued, "and the jelly leaves the part where you just squeezed. On the other side of the ring, more jelly has appeared. In layman terms, you just caused mass transference."

"Uh…okay?" I was confused a bit. "All I did was move the jelly to one side."

"Yeah, well, you can't just get rid of the mass." His brow furrowed. "I mean, it has to go somewhere."

"Aha!" I exclaimed, pleased that I finally understood. "I transferred the jelly to the other side! Mass transference! Very clever, Doc."

"Who said Marines were as dumb as a box of rocks?" he laughed. I scowled at him.

"Me use rock, crush puny big egghead," I growled in mock-seriousness. In truth, that was one of the funnier things any of the scientists had managed to say since I'd arrived. The kid may not appreciate the classic movies, but at least he had some semblance of humor. The others seemed to have had any shred of humor beaten out of them.

We arrived in the Gallery and I spotted Gerry and Doctor Marillac talking near one of the larger plasteel windows which looked out into the lake. A few of the kraken were swimming just within range of the lit area outside the station, but surprisingly there weren't any within the interior tubes at the moment. The ones outside were watching Gerry and the doctor, but I could see in their color schemes that they weren't exactly happy about something.

"Doctor Marillac, ma'am," Isaac bowed his head slightly in greeting. I waved awkwardly. There was no way I would bow my head to anyone, Pope included. Okay, maybe the Pope.

"Yes, Doctor Isaac?" the scientist's tone was crisp and formal, precisely what I had grown to expect from her. It seemed that while she was in the presence of the other scientists she was in full boss mode.

"The PDA's for this evening's patients, ma'am," he said and handed her the five tablets.

"Thank you, Doctor," she said as she tucked them under her arm. She looked at Isaac, whose gaze was shifting back and forth between the doctor and Gerry. He slowly began to grin. She frowned. "Is that all?"

"Oh, yes ma'am, sorry ma'am," Isaac babbled, chagrined. He dipped his head again and disappeared back the way we had arrived from, moving as fast as he could without actually running. I would have laughed at him but I felt a bit sorry for the kid.

"John, I'm going down to Research to continue our testing," she said as she turned that steely gaze upon me. I swallowed nervously and nodded. "I was wondering if I could ask you a few things about your interactions with the kraken last week while I'm on my way. We've noticed a few things that I would like to confirm."

"If it's okay with the boss here." I jerked a thumb towards Gerry, who shrugged.

"You do what you want on your time," Gerry chuckled. "I'm on my way down to Research as well. Can I escort you?"

"You don't have to…" Doctor Marillac's voice trailed off. She shook her head and smiled serenely. A light being flicked on wasn't nearly as abrupt. *That was bizarre,* I thought. "Actually, I would enjoy that."

"Really?" Gerry asked, dumbfounded. I was a bit surprised myself. He had been trying to get the doctor to pay attention to him since she had agreed to their date once they were back on Earth and she had never given him any indication that she noticed him. I hid my sudden grin as best as I could.

"Sure, why not?" Doctor Marillac asked. "I enjoy your company."

Well then. I had a sneaking suspicion that Gerry's chances of getting to know the good doctor in the biblical sense sooner rather than later had just increased drastically. I wasn't sure why the sudden change occurred, I was just happy that it did. Gerry was a great guy.

"So I heard you started doing prisoner transports," Gerry said as the three of us made our way down to Research. I let them enter first before me and queued the elevator to go down. While I hadn't really planned on going to Research initially, it was a better option than letting the doc poke and prod me with questions up in the Gallery.

"Yeah, last week," I replied as the elevator dropped us deeper into the station. "Started with Captain Holomisa, then assisted a transfer from Research with Aviotti. Fairly routine."

"It gets harder," Gerry promised me. "Jou is a pain in the ass if he passively resists, and some of the others make you work for it. Just remember to not hesitate or seem unsure. They feed on that."

"That's what Thing One—I mean, Poole said," I said, nodding. I paused and thought about it for a moment. "Wait. Is he Thing Two?"

Gerry chuckled. "Who knows?"

We were halfway down the hall to Research when the elevator dinged behind us. I glanced over my shoulder and spotted three guards escorting Gentry down to his next appointment. I frowned but continued onwards. I watched Gerry draw himself a little closer to Doctor Marillac, and this time she didn't shy away. I smiled a little. Gerry was a patient and determined man. I applauded his efforts.

The main door to Research slid open. I stopped and waited as Brendan, Joseph and April moved Jou down the hallway. It was wide enough for all of us to pass without too much difficulty, even the next set of guards escorting another prisoner towards Research. I recognized Werner, one of our German guards, leading Gentry and two other guards down the hall in our direction. I looked back at Gerry.

"Never seen two of them out together before," I stated. "Pretty interesting."

Gerry had a look of confusion about him that made me mildly uncomfortable for a moment.

"We typically don't," he said, scratching his beard before shrugging. "The scientists must have run over with Jou."

"It happens," Doctor Marillac admitted as we watched Werner and his two guards walking Gentry down the hall. She shook her head a bit. "Though it doesn't happen very often."

I felt a definitive change in the atmosphere as Jou and Gentry drew closer. I couldn't put my finger on what it was, however. It did remind me of something I'd experienced in the past. My eyes slid over the guards and watched their movements, but their attitudes seemed to be fine. They appeared to be solely focused on their tasks.

Which left the prisoners. I stared at Jou, since he was far bigger than Gentry and would probably break the skinny prisoner in half by simply looking at him. The big man was sweating, which wasn't too uncommon with him. Still, for a man in a climate-controlled hallway that wasn't precisely warm, he was sweating quite a bit.

Maybe he's been doing his passive-resistance thing today, I idly wondered as my gaze shifted to Gentry. I nearly froze in my tracks.

Gentry was tensed and ready for action. It screamed *danger!* to me when I spotted the way he carried himself. It was like a puma on the prowl, preparing to attack, focused solely on his prey. His eyes were locked on to Jou. I took a step forward and began to open my mouth to warn the other guards almost as fast as I processed the sight in my mind. Unfortunately, I was too slow.

Gentry's war-cry was feral and challenging, the piercing shriek digging into my skull. It was so sudden and sharp that Werner lost track of his prisoner for a split second. It was all Gentry needed.

He kicked back and down sharply, driving Werner away from him. A second sharp movement allowed him to maneuver the feet bindings around. Legs freer now, he elbowed Werner in the gut, the force of the impact knocking the air out of the man and driving him away. Gentry let loose another crazed howl and locked in on Jou.

Gentry charged Jou and slammed his shoulder into his ribs. The larger man went down with a grunt as Gentry drove a knee into his side. April and Werner tried to pull him off of Jou, who was yelling and screaming for help. One of the chains slipped off and Gentry suddenly was no longer hobbled. Free from his lower shackles, Gentry kicked April in the shin, which caused her to yelp in surprise and pain. She slipped and fell to the ground, which blocked Werner from pulling the smaller prisoner off of Jou.

It suddenly became a scrum as more guards piled on top of the enraged Gentry, who was kicking and yelling to no avail. Gerry pulled Jou out from beneath the mound of people and shoved him against the wall.

"Stay there!" Gerry bellowed and looked back at the dog pile, which was beginning to get under control. Gentry was pinned down on the floor, his arms held behind his back as a second set of cuffs were applied by April. Gentry struggled again and she rabbit-punched him in the kidneys repeatedly. He quit struggling after eight or nine blows. I winced but kept Dr. Marillac away as she tried to protest the rough treatment. Gentry would probably be pissing blood for the foreseeable future.

"Those are my patients!" she complained as she tried to push past me.

"They're our convicts, first and foremost," I reminded her as I gently held her back. "Relax, Doc. If we kill them it's even more paperwork. Just let us do our job."

The doctor was clearly shaken by the events but did her best to hide it. She stopped struggling and watched as Gentry was hauled to his feet. Ling attached the handcuffs to the lower shackles with a chain. Crude, but an effective way to ensure that the prisoner could not move quickly. I wasn't sure Gentry was going to be moving fast even without them, thanks to April. That woman had a vindictive streak a mile wide and had tagged him a few times that were borderline sadistic. I admired her a little bit.

I looked over at Jou, who was watching the proceedings with wide eyes. I almost felt sorry for the guy until I remembered that he had raped and killed seven women while he had been in the Navy. Any sympathy that might have been there went flying out the airlock. I started to look away but stopped after seeing something strange out of the corner of my eye. I gave the prisoner a closer look.

There.

It was smooth, I'll give him that. If I hadn't been looking directly at him the exact moment he had made his move, I would have missed Jou stealing the master key card from Gerry completely.

I quickly stepped over and confronted him. "All right, Jou, jig's up," I growled and pushed the surprised prisoner up against the wall. He looked at me with a strange combination of alarm and annoyance. He'd underestimated us and he knew it, but there was no way he could admit to it. It took a big pair of brass ones to pull off what he was trying to do. He needed to be both calm, cool and collected.

He failed. Miserably.

"Don't know what you're talking about," he tried to argue. I didn't have the time nor patience to deal with him so I kept him pressed against the wall.

"Just give it back. I don't want to get physical, but I did miss out on a good scrum," I rolled my shoulders for emphasis. "I'm all ready to go, and I've got friends."

"You're fucking crazy," Jou blurted, fear thick in his tone. I smiled grimly. I had the bastard.

"You sold that fight well, Jou," I snarled as I yanked the passcard the convict had stolen out of his pocket. I flipped it over and passed it back to Gerry, who looked at it in surprise. He took the passcard and slipped it back into his pocket. Gerry looked at Jou, appeared to be extremely frustrated. I pushed harder on Jou's chest. "Almost got away with it. Too bad you just got your ass kicked for nothing."

"Fuck off," Jou spat angrily. I smirked.

"Stupid twit," I spun him around and pressed him against the wall. I began to frisk him but found nothing else. I looked over at Fritz, who was staring at me with a dumbfounded expression. "The fight was just a distraction. They planned this. Almost got away with it as well."

"Jesus," Fritz muttered. He moved past me and grabbed Jou by his white shirt. He hauled the beefy convict down the corridor. Leigh and Chun followed close behind. I nodded at Gerry and walked back over to where Dr. Marillac stood. The expression on her face was a mixture of shock, horror and confusion. I couldn't blame her. I had barely caught the move by Jou myself.

- 78 -

"Just remember, Doc," I told her in a low tone. "They are convicts first, patients second. Never forget why they were incarcerated in the first place, or how they used your research and need for volunteers to keep from being hanged for their crimes. As much as they help you discover whatever it is that you're looking for, they'll just as soon kill you. For fun."

⚶

It wasn't until I was in my room that night, half-asleep on my bed, when it hit me. I quickly pulled out my PDA and queued Gerry on the comms. He was available so I pinged him to contact me at his earliest convenience. He responded to my ping almost immediately.

"What's up?" Gerry asked. I could hear how tired he was over the comm. "Got lots of paperwork to do, thanks to those chuckleheads. That was a good catch on the card swipe, by the way. I don't know how I missed it."

"Thanks. I have a question for you," I said as I rolled back onto my bed. "Do the prisoners interact with each other often?"

"They don't interact with each other at all," Gerry said. "Other than passing one another in the hall, and even then that rarely happens. Why?"

"Well…" I hesitated. I was the noob and I didn't want to sound like a complete moron. The last thing I needed at my new job was to be known as the guy who reported everything out of the ordinary and caused his boss more work and bigger headaches. I decided to think some more about it before I came out and asked. I changed my mind and decided to just voice my concern instead. "Oh, I don't know. That just felt weird, you know? That entire fight?"

"First fight I've had here," Gerry answered. "I think we're going to go over procedures to ensure that something like that never happens again. Maybe a route going to Research and a different one going out? Hmm…you know what? You're task for the next few days is to come up with viable alternate routes so the prisoners moving from Research and their cells never cross paths. Think you can handle that?"

"Uh, sure, I guess," I replied. *Damn it*, I didn't say. Rule number six I learned while in the military: never volunteer yourself. Besides, I hated route mapping. It had been one of my least favorite activities while in the Corps. Still though, I *was* a bit overpaid for a glorified security guard. I could at least try to help out my boss. "I'll draw something up and have it to you by Saturday."

"Good deal." He closed the comm on his end, leaving me alone with my jumbled thoughts. I tried to picture the station, hallways leading to and from Research, and how to transport the prisoners without their paths crossing in my head. My mind, however, kept coming back to the one unanswered question in the back of my skull.

How had they managed to plan and stage that fight if they never speak to each other?

CHAPTER NINE

The law's the law, but people are people.
— M.L. Stedman, *The Light Between Oceans*

The station-wide alarm caught me with a fork full of the Chef's Special halfway to my mouth. I was on my feet and running for the door before the last remnants of my bite hit the floor. Old reflexes died hard.

Halfway to the first checkpoint, the alarm stopped. I kept going, waiting to hear the all-clear message from the desk guards to come through on my PDA. I pounded down the stairs towards Control as fast as I could manage, but still no word of an all clear. My annoyance at having my dinner interrupted by some drill began to change to worry. I sprinted down the hallway and passed one of the passage tubes that the aliens used. I noticed that none of the tubes held any of the kraken within. I slowed my pace to a jog and checked my PDA. Still nothing about an all-clear. As I rounded the corner, I saw why it hadn't come yet.

Control was empty, both guards who were scheduled to be on not evident in any shape or form. Not good. I slowed down but kept moving, hoping this was all a big malfunction, and everything was five by five. My hand drifted down to my belt, where the tranq gun I was required to carry while in uniform rested. That hope sank as I approached the cell block.

A prison break. It was, outside of explosive decompression and the station sinking into the lake, our biggest worry. Given as to how squirrelly the prisoners had been lately, this turn of events simply confirmed my suspicions. Especially considering the staged brawl in the hall from the other day.

The cells were all open, save the last, Holomisa's. Made sense, given the mutual animosity and the typical "us versus them" mentality of the convicts. Holomisa may have been a prisoner, but he simply wasn't one of them. The guard's duty desk was empty, another bad sign. I ran through the roster in my head. *Kirby and Brendan should've been on tonight, so where the hell were they?*

Something flew by my ear with enough force to strike the wall ten feet behind me. I dove for the desk, trying to get it between me and what was coming next. Rolling to keep low, I got behind it just as the next projectile hit the spot I'd just left. It splattered noisily on the desk and knocked over a display monitor.

The Kirby question was answered – he lay face down on the floor next to me. No obvious signs of blood, which was comforting. There was little time to check on him more, though. I had more important things to worry about. Like how I was supposed to do anything with a stupid tranq gun against someone who was flinging…*something* at me.

I risked a look over the top of the desk, the console a Christmas Tree of blinking lights and warning screens. I ducked down again as something moved in the corridor leading to the living quarters.

"That you, Manning?" A familiar voice called out. *Jou. That fucking bastard.* He sounded like he had a mouthful of marbles, his words punctuated with a loud snuffling noise. It was a sound that the human mouth was not designed to make. "Yeah, that's you. I can smell your fear, Jarhead."

"I'm impressed, Jou." I moved slightly, trying to find the emergency seal button without exposing myself. "You used words with more than one syllable." There, about six inches in front of me. "Wanna try something more challenging, like, 'Expeditionary?'"

"I'll tear your heart out, motherfucker!" I could sort of see him now—my taunting had irritated him enough that he had come forward slightly and into my line of sight.

"That's four, very good." Another projectile splattered against the plasteel above my head. "Shit!" It sounded gross, whatever it was. I grabbed the stool that Kirby had been sitting on and hurled it towards the big prisoner, aiming for a spot just in front of him. He flinched, taking a step back into the hall. I slapped the emergency seal button and watched as an elastic bubble closed around the area.

In theory, it protected us from outside elements in case of a hull breach. In truth, it probably just prolonged our suffocation and terror at the idea of dying while forcing us to wait for help that would never arrive. There was no way that the Navy could get down and evacuate someone if they were trapped within one of the bubbles if something happened to the station. There was one thing that I figured it could do to help me out, though. I was counting on it blocking the hallway, preventing Jou from coming any closer and murdering me.

Sure enough, the bubble completely sealed the hallway and blocked anything from getting to and from the cell block. From this direction, at least. The back way out of the cell block led to a stairwell, which allowed for passage between Central and the rest of the station – except for Research, of course.

For now, however, Control was as secure as it ever was going to be.

I knelt down and checked Kirby's pulse. It was strong and steady, which surprised me. In fact, other than the large bruise on his forehead, he appeared to be in good shape. He would have one hell of a headache when he woke up, but otherwise, he was unscathed. I spotted another unmoving form on the exposed side of the desk. I shot a quick glance down the hall but there was still no sign of Jou. I shifted around and recognized Brendan.

I'd found Kirby alive. The same could not be said about poor Brendan.

The kid had his throat torn open from ear to ear. Before that, though, he must have put up a fight. His hands were bruised and crusted with blood, and he had cuts up and down his arms. A massive pool of blood was under his body and was beginning to leak into the ventilation grates beneath the security post.

Brendan had died, and he had been brutalized in a way that made me more than a little sick.

It saddened me to see the life of someone so young be taken so abruptly, but it also made me feel more than a little pride in the kid. He'd been a Marine, though he had only been in for a single tour before getting into the private sector. However, once a Marine, always a Marine. I would make his death count for something.

I dragged his corpse back behind the desk for safety. I was reasonably confident in the ability of the bubble to stop Jou, but not entirely. If it fell while I was in an exposed position, I wouldn't last very long in a stand-up fight against the giant.

"Central, this is Manning at Control," I said as I turned away from the duo, pressing the comm button. "We've got a security breach in the prisoner's cells. Mass prisoner break has occurred. Initiate lockdown protocols."

Nothing. I frowned.

"Central, this is Manning. Come in. Anyone on this net?"

Silence.

"Well, damn," I muttered. The protective bubble must have been preventing me from contacting Control. I didn't think that could happen but I wasn't an engineer by any stretch of the imagination. It was entirely possible that the bubble blocked the comms, an oversight that had to be some kind of safety violation. Not that it mattered, since I seriously doubted that the Health and Worker Safety Commission would drop by at that exact moment.

I peeked over the countertop, looking for Jou. The massive prisoner was nowhere to be found.

"Jou?" I called out tentatively. "You mind telling me what you're doing? It's not like you can get off the station or anything. Just surrender peacefully and we'll see about working this whole thing out." *After I get done beating your ass, that is.*

Still nothing. I frowned. Maybe he was smarter than he looked, either keeping quiet to ambush me when I released the bubble, or he had done the more sensible thing and was run for his life. I drew the tranq gun and checked the charge on it. Four shots left. I hoped that would do.

I hit the red button again and the bubble dropped. I aimed and waited nervously for Jou to reappear, hands sweaty despite the relative cool room. A prisoner on the loose defined a bad day for any guard. Eleven of them…that was nightmare fuel.

I wiped a palm on my pants, trying to get rid of the greasy feel. Still nothing. Fighting impatience, I recalled the mantra that my training sergeant had beaten into my head, *Rash actions lead to dead Marines.* A few deep breaths helped, the last one coming out as a growl.

"C'mon Jou, I don't have all fucking day."

I risked another peek. The hallway remained empty. Jou was gone. *Dammit. Think, Marine. Think!*

I glanced down and took a closer look at what Jou had been throwing. Whatever it was, it was red, oozing…*Oh Christ.*

Anatomy wasn't one of my strong points, but I knew a heart when I saw one. I was pretty sure the other thing was a liver. *But whose?* I looked back at Brendan and shivered. *That was a hell of a lot of blood, but…*

Time to move. If there were any staff members in their quarters, I had to keep Jou from getting to them. Kirby didn't have a sidearm on him, but maybe…*Yes.* Hard to see when Jou had been standing there, someone's feet were now visible in the hallway. Not a scientist, from the look and design of the boots. It was a guard, and probably a dead one. I approached slowly, tranq gun at the ready, feeling like I was hunting a pissed-off rabid Rottweiler with a rolled-up newspaper.

Still clear. There was no sign of Jou. I knelt down next to the body, one eye on the hall. A quick glance told me who the poor, dead bastard on the floor was. Dale Fletcher. Good guy, had an ex-wife and a few kids back on Earth. I hoped against hope that Jou hadn't noticed what poor Fletcher had on him.

Fate was on my side for that singular moment.

Today had been Fletcher's turn with heat. It was a bit shocking that Jou hadn't searched the body, but I wasn't going to complain. I unbuckled his shoulder rig, trying hard to get a grip through all the blood, shuddering as something slimy and solid slipped over the back of my hand. I repressed a shudder. Now I knew where Jou had gotten his biological missiles.

"Poor bastard, you never saw it coming." I took the holster, extra magazine, and his tranq gun, working quickly to get it all situated on my person. Out of habit, I checked the mag and racked the slide. It was oddly comforting, the weight and feel of a real weapon as opposed to the lighter tranq pistol. I couldn't help the sigh of relief as I raised it. "Yeah, baby."

Tranqs were a handy way of keeping order with the prisoners. The tranqs often caused the recipient to wake up with the migraine from Hell, and since we rarely offered amenities to someone who earned a tranq shot, it was a debilitating thing to recover from. Of course, that assumed that the tranq didn't fizzle or something worse, like not work. Training dictated using a tranq gun as a second-to-last resort.

The last resort was at hand, and nothing fit it better than something a little more lethal.

I took stock of the situation. I knew precisely how many hostiles were out there, though not where. I had an unknown number of guards alive, presumably. The supervisors were unaccounted for, but that didn't necessarily mean anything. Gerry could have slept through the blaring emergency alarm, the riots, the gunfire and the splattering of body parts throughout the station.

Right, and I'm the Space Pope.

I checked my comm again but nobody responded. I pulled up my PDA and looked to see if I was even receiving any signal. The PDA wasn't picking up any signal, which told me quite a bit. Internal comms were down, as was the networking system. My PDA should have been able to pick up some sort of signal otherwise. That's the basic way Wi-Fi worked. I dug through the settings of the PDA and found the secured channel, which acted as a hidden signal broadcaster for each and every PDA within a limited space. Granted, "limited space" was about five hundred yards in every direction, but it was used more as an emergency beacon than anything else. The secured channel should have picked up the other PDA's in the station at the very least.

So why wasn't anybody responding?

A few guesses flew through my head, all worse than the last. Deep down we're all pessimists.

With the station on lockdown for the time being, the elevator tube was out of the question. I would have to risk the stairwell, which would limit escape options should I run into Jou or any of the other escapees running amok on the station. Not an ideal situation but the only one in front of me at the moment.

"Wait," I muttered as a small blip suddenly appeared on my PDA. It was a ghost-like image, showing me that another PDA was close. Two floors down, to be precise. It disappeared seconds later but I already had the location fixed in my mind. It was near Doctor Marillac's private suite, or in it. I wasn't too certain about which, but at least I knew that *someone* on the station was up and about. For how long, though, I couldn't say.

I quickly made my way to the stairwell, staying in cover as best as I could the entire way. I knew that if one of the prisoners caught me out in the open, I'd be forced to use the handgun, which would probably be heard by anyone and everyone. That would tell the enemy precisely where I was. No, I had to use stealth for as long as I could. Gunshots would only draw unwanted attention.

I slid open the door to the stairwell and stuck my head inside. The air was cold but safe, though the air blowing up from the bottom of the shaft prohibited me from hearing anything other than circulating oxygen. On the plus side, it meant that nobody could hear me as I made my way down the metal stairwell.

I paused as I reached the proper level and peeked through the small window before I stepped inside. The lights were dimmed but still bright enough for me to see that the coast looked clear. I tried to peek around the edge but I couldn't see in either direction. If someone was lurking around the corner waiting to clobber me, I wouldn't know it until they hit. Time to be preemptive.

I yanked the door open and dashed into the hall, then tucked into a roll. I came up from the acrobatic maneuver with my gun trained on the stairwell. Nothing. I pivoted on my heel and brought the gun around. Still nothing. I had control of the level.

Relief flooded through me. I still held the handgun at the ready, but I was no longer in immediate danger. I could relax and take a deep breath, so I did. I wiped a sweaty hand on my pants. I needed to find some tactical gloves or something to help absorb the moisture. I hate when my hands sweat. It was a nasty, disgusting thing. Women especially don't like it.

I made my way down the hall. I wasn't too familiar with the level, since it wasn't on any of my usual paths for leak-and-peek check. It did resemble base housing a bit, minus the usual wear and tear one would expect from a government facility. I had a feeling I knew what the area was used for, but I wanted to make certain. I brought up my PDA and checked.

Once more, I applauded my foresight. If I hadn't downloaded the schematics of the station and relied on the cloud storage like everyone else, I would have been up the proverbial creek without any sort of propulsion device.

Sure enough, it was one of the berthing areas for guests and VIPs whenever they arrived on the station. It was rarely used, which made sense for the good doctor to use it for her own personal space. She did like her privacy, after all. I wondered if her ego and desire to reign over all her little minions caused her to isolate herself accordingly. It would have made sense, actually, her staying away from the little people.

I shook my head to clear my thoughts. I sure could be a dick at times.

A muffled sound came from the door a few meters down. The fleeting sense of control I had felt earlier disappeared, all nerves back on full alert. Jou was here somewhere, likely trying to hide until I left the area. I moved carefully, my head on a swivel as I passed the first two doors. I stopped at the source of the noise and recognized the sounds from within. A knowing grin began to spread across my face before I remembered what, precisely, was going on in the station. The office belonged to Doctor Marillac and, judging by the sounds coming from within, she had finally decided to fully get to know Gerry. In a biblical sense.

In case I haven't made myself perfectly clear– sex. They were having sex. Noisily and vigorously, if my hunch was correct.

I knocked, softly but firmly. What sounded like grunts, groans, and a wet smacking noise continued. It was weird and I hated to interrupt them, but there was a crisis on hand. I sighed. If we lived, Gerry was going to kick my ass for this.

"Guys," I said, feeling a flush spread across my face. Interrupting people in the middle of bumping uglies embarrassed the hell out of me. "Hate to be a bother, but we've got an emergency situation here."

More muffled sounds of exertion, followed by a wet smacking. Loud moans. I rolled my eyes. This was ridiculous. I knocked harder.

"Doc, Gerry? We have a mass breakout. Inmates at large." I looked around quickly, not wanting Jou to catch me with my pants down. Speaking of pants down… "Gerry, I need you out here."

I tried the keypad on the door, but Doctor Marillac was high enough up on the pecking order that my 'master override' code didn't work. So much for the master override code being the all-mighty great and powerful.

"Fine, dammit, you two have fun, we'll be out here trying to keep violent..." The door slid open, and I found myself face to face with Doctor Marillac.

Blood, wet and dark, dripped from her face. One hand slowly smeared what was on her lips as she stared at me. Through me. Her eyes were unfocused and wild, her pupils dilated large enough that I couldn't tell what color they originally were. I think her eyes had once been a warm brown shade. Now they were empty pools of black. There was no life there. I'd seen looks like that before, on fellow Marines who had simply seen too much. It was pretty damn creepy.

"What the fuck? Doc, what happened?" I lowered the pistol slightly as she continued to stare, eyes blank and unfocused. I took a small step back, just in case. "Are you okay?"

Still no answer. She blocked enough of the door to make it impossible to see into the room behind her.

"Gerry! You in there?" Dr. Marillac turned and walked back into the room, looking more like a zombie than a biologist. Her steps seemed stiff, as though someone were operating her remotely. Alarm bells began to go off in my head. Something was not right here, not in the least. The blood on her face was the most obvious clue, but there was more going on here than I knew. I followed her inside before the door could close again but kept my pistol trained on the center of her back.

"Ma'am, I'm going to need you stay in here, with the door locked until we get this taken care of." I kept moving into the main room, a combination kitchen and office area. The bedroom, from what I could tell, was a smaller section in the back of the apartment. No door, just a blank space where two walls met, allowing me to see the foot of a bed.

A bed with Gerry's boots, covered in blood, were situated on top of it. Next to those on the floor was Gerry's body. Rather, what remained of it.

Someone—I assumed the culprit to be Doctor Marillac—had ripped open his throat and let him bleed out on the bed. I could faintly see bite marks all over the poor bastard's body, as well as more of him than I ever needed. His body had been worked over by a true sadist. I nearly gagged.

The pistol came back up, this time aimed directly at Dr. Marillac's head. Cold fury coursed through my veins. I'd seen a lot of bad things in my time, but rarely had I seen this sort of cruel attack on someone I respected and cared about.

The situation on the station had gone from dangerous to flat-out terrifying.

"Doctor, I need to know what's going on, right—"

In one fluid movement, Dr. Marillac spun, crouched and sprang, fingers curled into talons. Surprise sent my first shot wide, the bullet boring into the wall above her desk. She hit me harder than I thought she could, knocking me solidly on my ass. Her fingers closed around my throat as she pulled my face towards her snapping teeth.

I jammed my forearm under her chin, using what little leverage I had to keep her at bay. It bought me enough time to bring the pistol up and fire into her ribs. Her body jerked as the bullets tore through her, the pressure on my Adam's apple loosening enough for me to get free. I rolled, slamming Marillac to the floor. The last shot went between her eyes, splattering pink and grey matter across the imitation Persian rug.

I scrambled back, panting, until I reached the wall of her quarters. The gun in my hand trembled a little, which didn't surprise me. I'd killed before, obviously. It was part of my job. A sniper doesn't fight, a sniper kills.

I'd never killed a civilian though. Not like this, not this way.

For a moment, I thought that Chef's Special was going to paint the walls of the doctor's quarters, joining the now-deceased duo's blood. That greasy, roiling sensation in the pit of my stomach was both familiar and unwelcome. I swallowed a few times to keep from losing my lunch and slowly dragged myself back to my feet. I was a bit unsteady but otherwise unharmed. Physically, at least. Emotionally, I was something entirely else.

I refused to look at the doc. That would have been bad. Instead, I ejected the magazine in my handgun and checked the count. I had five rounds left, plus the two extra mags I'd pilfered from Fletcher's corpse. That could theoretically get me up to the armory, which would probably still be secure. If there were any guards in the area, we could link up and push back to retake the station.

That thought made me pause. Had we lost the station yet? For some reason, a small voice in the back of my head suggested that we had. I hoped that my intuition was wrong. I took a deep, calming breath. I needed the proper mindset for what was to come. Assuming, of course, that my intuition was correct.

I started to go back over the base's standard procedures in my head. Securing the cell block was out of the question, given that 11 of the 12 were out and roaming the station already. Comms were still down, which screwed the next three steps. Eventually, I'd have to go and get them back up and running, or find someone who actually knew how to do the technical stuff. We had a maintenance crew on board who were contracted to do the technical repairs of the station, but I hadn't really seen them around much. With the comms down, there'd be no easy way to get the contractors to—

My train of thought screeched to a halt.

Where the hell was everybody?

I pushed the thought away—I'd have to assume I was on my own for now. I walked into the bedroom. Gerry's eyes were wide open, face frozen in surprise. Dr. Marillac had torn out his throat, then started on the fleshy part of his chest.

"Damn, Gerry." I moved closer, trying to avoid the blood pooled on the floor and around his body. "Hell of a way to go. I'm sorry I wasn't faster getting here." I holstered the pistol and gently closed his eyes.

I carefully adjusted his shirt, checking his breast pockets as I covered the wounds. He wasn't wearing any pants, and I couldn't see any sign of them. If Gerry followed the new protocols that we had drawn up, though, I shouldn't need to search for his pants. I felt around in his shirt. *His keycard should be...here.* I wanted a backup plan, in case my codes didn't work at the armory.

I was in luck. His keycard was precisely where it should have been.

There was nothing else for me here, Gerry hadn't been armed when he'd come back with the Doc. I pulled the sheet off the bed and over him. I walked back to the front room, keeping my distance both physically, and mentally, from Doctor Marillac's corpse. The door opened as I got within range of its sensor.

Bringing me face to face with Jou.

One would think that a guy as big as Jou wouldn't be all that fast. They'd definitely be wrong.

Before I could react, his fist connected with my nose, rocking me back. Stars exploded in front of my tearing eyes, effectively blinding me. The punch was so hard, so vicious that I could have sworn my hair hurt from the blow. The second punch took me hard in the gut, my breath rushing out of my lungs with a strangled groan. I struggled to breathe as I hit the floor. I tried to inhale but my diaphragm was not following instructions, so I lay on the floor, gaping like a drowning fish as Jou loomed above me.

Jou's hand closed around my ankle, dragging me out into the hallway with ease.

"Boss says he wants you alive." His deep voice rumbled slowly from within his chest, as though speaking was costing him more effort than hauling me around. "So I can't kill you. Yet."

I gasped in my first full breath in what felt like hours, my vision clearing as oxygen filled my lungs. I was behind and slightly to his left, my right ankle in his left hand. Smart, actually, it kept me from getting any leverage to deliver a solid kick. It did, however, let me get the pistol clear of the holster.

Jou turned at the sound, his unnatural speed allowing him to get a hand over the muzzle as I pulled the trigger. He barely flinched as the bullet tore through his palm, ripping the pistol from my grip and tossing it behind him. I was helpless as he slammed me into the walls, only staying conscious through sheer willpower and keeping my chin tucked down against my chest so I wouldn't get too concussed.

As the blobs of color faded from my vision, I watched as he held up his damaged hand. The hole closed as a sinister grin spreading across his face. His voice penetrated the ringing in my ears.

"Boss says alive, not undamaged." He resumed dragging me back towards the stairwell. I stopped struggling in a vain attempt to conserve my energy. Jou didn't seem to notice nor care. My shoulder caught the emergency door as it started to close, but by that time I was beyond petty pain. Or at least, so I thought. I was dragged painfully up the stairs, each metal step slamming into my spine and the back of my head. Jou seemed to be in a hurry, and he was kicking my ass without even doing anything.

Two floors up. Eighty steps. Eighty hard shots to the body. If I wasn't pissing blood by the end of this, it would be a miracle. Jou's bone-crushing grip on my ankle was unrelenting. My shirt had gotten pulled up a bit while going up the stairs, and I could feel a burning sensation up my back as I was dragged across the carpeted floor.

Rug burn. Great. Talk about adding insult to injury.

I assumed he was taking me to the cells. If I had any hope of getting the situation back under control, much less surviving this experience, I needed to break free before we got there. At least I still had the tranq guns. Whoopee.

The non-lethal weaponry used lasers to form an electrically charged plasma channel, delivering a miniature lightning strike to the target. Against normal people, the resulting shock and miniature sonic boom incapacitates them, with minor splash damage to anyone within a few feet. The tech had been developed in the 21st century, for use against crowds, but development over the last few hundred years had made the application smaller, and more precise. It still wasn't a good idea to use it any closer than five feet away, or you'd find yourself pissing your pants and drooling along with the intended recipient.

I was well within 'danger close' range, if not 'danger stupid.' No matter what, the moronic thing I was about to do would have to be timed just right.

The tranq gun cleared the holster with as much noise as I could make, counting on Jou to react the same way he had before. I wasn't disappointed, bracing for impact and tightening my grip. Aiming while hitting the wall was difficult, but the design of the weapon allowed for a fairly large margin of error. All things considered, my luck was better than I thought it would be, his second swing brought me in front of him, and faster. He was trying to put me out cold for good this time. I pulled the trigger as the muzzle swung in the general direction of Jou's shoulder.

My luck held, the point of impact was far enough away that I only felt a slight tingling in the sole of my foot. Jou involuntarily released his grip on my ankle, effectively hurling me down the hallway in front of him.

I skidded across the floor, drawing a quick bead on Jou's legs and squeezing off two charges before he could come running after me. It seemed to work, more or less; one shot was supposed to take a normal human out of the fight. In Jou's case, it just seemed to make whatever it hit go numb for a second. His knees buckled sending him to the floor. I got my feet, making a break for the detention area. With a little more room to move, I may just have a chance.

Oh, good, now I'm back where I started, I realized as I dragged up and out of Fletcher's remains. *Now what?* Jou's roar told me I needed to come up with something fast. One charge left in the tranq gun. I checked Fletcher's. It had two.

Movement behind me. I whipped around, leveling the pistol, hoping beyond hope the non-lethal rounds would be effective against the new threat. I dropped it immediately as April and Bigfoot entered.

"John, what's going on?" April's voice was tense, but not panicked. "Whoa, what happened to you?"

Another bellow from the hallway, followed by heavy footsteps.

"Jou happened," I said, "All prisoners at large except Holomisa. Kirby's wounded, Brendan, Gerry, Fletcher, and Doc M dead. Jou's coming this way. Fast."

April nodded, drawing her tranq gun. Bigfoot followed suit.

"Hell," he said, "Three of us should have no…"

Jou appeared in the entrance of the hall. I blinked several times at the sight. The prisoner, always large and muscular, seemed somehow bigger, but shorter. As though he had shrunk and grew more muscles, which should have been impossible. Legs like tree trunks, arms the size of my thighs. He smiled, rolling his neck and flexing. His smile was not pleasant and promised an inordinate amount of pain in my near future.

"You think you can take me?" His laugh, sinister and cruel, bubbled up from inside his massive torso. "Two pussy ass Marines and a split. This'll be fun."

April and Bigfoot cut loose with tranq fire, the shots sizzling as they ionized the air. 1.8 million volts of electricity coursed through the convict's body, enough to down a full grown horse with ease. His clothing smoldered and his chest muscles twitched slightly, but he remained standing when he should have been on the ground, drooling and twitching. Jou looked down at the four distinct impacts on his chest with a chuckle, apparently more amused than incapacitated.

That did not bode well.

"That tickles," he said, picking up Fletcher's body. "My turn."

Bigfoot dove as the corpse flew towards him. April wasn't quite fast enough. Fletcher's head struck her squarely in the chest, knocking her to the floor and stunning her. Bigfoot, kneeling behind a small desk, fired again as I raised the muzzle of my pistol. I knew the tranq shots wouldn't do much, but maybe they could distract Jou long enough for me to come up with a better plan.

"First, I'm going to tear you apart, old man. Then I'll deal with you, Manning." His smile widened. "Then I'll have myself some fun with the split."

"Over my dead body, convict!" Bigfoot stood, tossing his now useless tranq gun away. He pushed up his sleeves and began to crack his knuckles. It would have been impressive as hell had I not seen just how massive Jou had become.

"Kinky, but I like it." Jou stalked towards the older guard, rolling his shoulders. In his excitement, he didn't notice me moving to flank him. Bigfoot gave me a slight nod.

I threw a quick glance at April. Her eyes were closed; the impact seemed to have knocked her cold. I hoped. Bigfoot squared up, fists in a classic boxer's guard.

"Golden Gloves champion, three years running," he said. "Think you got what it takes, boy?" Jou stopped, spreading his arms wide.

"Take your best shot."

I made my move. Launching myself onto his back, I slid one arm around his neck and flexed. It was like trying to choke out a statue, but harder. Jou's neck muscles were like iron. Jou roared loudly, more in surprise and anger than anything else. I brought the tranq gun up to his temple, whispered a prayer, and pulled the trigger.

Remember what I said about danger stupid? That move defines it.

The stun blast hit him hard, stopping him dead in his tracks. It also had the side effect of stunning me. I hit the ground hard, twitching uncontrollably, barely able to focus on what was happening.

Jou stood there, mouth open and eyes wide as Bigfoot launched two strikes into his gut and solar plexus, followed by a solid uppercut into Jou's jaw. The crack of bones breaking was loud enough to be heard from my position.

"No snappy comeback?" Bigfoot said, grinning, "Oh, right, hard to do with a broken jaw."

I was getting some feeling back into my extremities, but still couldn't get the muscle spasms under control enough to move. I watched helplessly as Jou shook his head, bellowing.

My mouth moved, soundlessly, trying to force air through my lungs to shout a warning. Bigfoot got an arm up just in time to block Jou's haymaker, but missed the follow up hook. The punch caught him in the cheek, whipping his head hard to the left. Jou's next punch took the old Marine in the same spot, forcing his neck around further.

Bigfoot hit the ground, his head twisted at an unnatural angle. He didn't move.

"No!" April's shout got both Jou's and my attention. Closing ground quickly, she threw herself at the larger man with abandon, the collapsible baton in her hand a flickering blur of motion. Jou, moving fast, blocked most of the strikes; however, the ones that got thru his defense caused him some trouble.

It suddenly hit me. Jou had somehow increased his muscle mass, but had sacrificed something else to do so. It's why he appeared shorter, and why Bigfoot was able to break his jaw so easily. Bone density, internal organs, and lots of stuff in your body that can be sacrificed for some short term gains, at least in his limited mental capacity. He most likely hadn't thought about exactly what he was giving up, just what he thought he'd need to put me in the cell.

Mass transference... something whispered in the back of my mind.

What the hell? Since when was my subconscious talking science behind my back?

April was still fighting, able to dodge most of Jou's punches and grabs, but she was tiring, quickly. She stepped back, avoiding another whistling haymaker from the brute, but fatigue caught up with her, and she hooked an ankle. The stutter step to catch her balance was the opening Jou needed. His fist locked around her free hand, twisting and squeezing it back towards her shoulder. A wet sounding snap an instant before her scream told me he'd dislocated her elbow. Jou had left himself open, however, and the baton smashed into his wrist. His grip relaxed, and April staggered back out of reach.

"April," my voice sounded like steel wool on aluminum, escaping my throat as a gasp. I could barely hear it, much less anyone else. I tried again. "April!"

"What?" her voice, strained and tight, still carried the rage she had shown earlier. Her left arm hung limp at her side, swaying gently as she bounced on the balls of her feet. "I'm busy!"

"His bones are brittle."

Jou's face showed his realization of his error as April's grew more determined, focused. I watched her push through the pain in her elbow, a mental transformation that was a sight to behold. Estimating how long it took him to recover from my first tranq bursts, and to perform his physical change, I hoped he didn't have time to make any more "adjustments." April came in hard and fast on Jou, cracking the baton up his damaged arm, whirling and striking his lower extremities like a snake before pushing back up and driving the tip of the baton into the nerve cluster at the inside of his thigh, keeping him off balance and unable to block without opening himself up to more punishment.

I looked around, finally able to move without as much effort. The pistol Jou had tossed earlier lay about five feet away. I stretched, agonizingly slow, forcing my arms and legs to do my bidding. Four feet. I rolled onto my stomach, my feet weakly scuffing the floor as I tried to find purchase. Two feet.

C'mon Marine! Move your lazy ass! Concy's voice echoed in my skull. One more foot…

April's second scream, a raw sound of rage and frustration tinged with horror, came from behind me. I snapped my head around in time to see Jou, laughing triumphantly, lifting her by the neck with his good hand. He flexed, forcing her scream to fade into a wet gurgle. The fucker was crushing her throat.

Six inches, I stretched my fingers toward the butt of the 10mm, lunging with everything I had. The hard plastic grip felt cool in my hand as I tried to roll onto my back, making it as far as my side before losing momentum.

April dangled from Jou's hand, her weak kicks and punches failing to do any damage as she fought for air. I raised the pistol as Jou gave her throat a final squeeze, shaking her like a rag doll.

"You need to stay alive just a little bit longer, frail. I have a promise to keep to the old man." He smiled again as he tossed her to the floor, stomping down hard on her thigh. Her mouth opened silently, only a faint gagging sound emerging.

The spasms still had me. My fingers could barely grip the pistol, causing the sights to bounce around crazily. I didn't have an angle. Jou brought down his foot again, this time snapping April's remaining femur. She thrashed violently, trying to gain some type of hold with her good arm, managing to turn slightly in my direction. Jou met her with a solid kick to the torso, curling her into a fetal position.

I focused, gathering all the strength I had in my traitorous muscles. Only one chance.

The 10mm slid across the floor, some stroke of luck bringing the grip in line with April's good hand. She brought it up, pulling the trigger as it lined up on Jou's knee. At point blank range, the bullet tore through the weakened bone and cartilage, spraying gore behind him. He dropped, just in time to meet two more rounds to the chest.

The last thing he saw was the barrel, now at eye level, belching flame and death. Brains and bits of skull exploded from the large exit wound, landing on the white floor amid a mist of pink. Jou fell back, finally still.

April dropped the gun, slumping with a wheeze. The effects of the tranq gun had subsided, finally, enough to let me get to my knees and crawl towards her. I could tell, though, that there was nothing I could do except comfort her. Two major bones broken, bruises forming on her windpipe, and me with no medical training that would be of any help. Comms were still down, too.

Where the fuck were the maintenance weenies?

"...ck that guy." April's voice couldn't get above a raspy whisper. I got close enough to take her head in my lap, carefully, trying not to hurt her.

"He's down for good, April," I said, "Try to relax, ok?"

She gave a tight-lipped smile, clenching her jaw against the pain, failing as a cough racked her body. Blood poured from her mouth. Shit, Jou must've broken a rib on top of everything else, possibly puncturing a lung.

"Got the bastard," she said, eyes closing. What breath she had left rattled on its way out, bloody froth bubbling forth from her lips. It was the last one she took.

I sat there for a moment, gently stroking her hair before easing her head to the floor.

♄

April's death shook me up far more than I would have ever admitted publicly.

It was weird, really. I watched Bigfoot die. I'd stumbled onto Gerry's half-eaten corpse, and killed the woman responsible. That one would give me nightmares eventually. I'd even been forced to pick some of Fletcher's gore out of my hair on my way through the station, which had been disturbing on a new level. None of their deaths affected me the way that April's had, though.

It made sense, when I managed to think about it. It's why killing Doctor Marillac bothered me so much. I had a protective streak a mile wide, especially when it came to women. Call it what you will, but any man who loses his wife at a young age would feel that way. Hell, any man should feel protective towards a woman. It's in our DNA, as they say. Protect the family. Defend the tribe. It's encoded into us genetically.

What the hell was going on here?

I didn't know. I didn't understand how Jou had done...whatever it was. Change his body? It was outside the realm of everything I understood about biology, which was admittedly very little. I knew which parts were the squishy parts, and where to put a round from a good distance away. The way Jou had changed was like nothing I had ever seen or heard of, except for in science fiction novels.

My thoughts drifted back to when I had sparked up my friendship with Dr. Isaac. He had talked about something similar once, I'm almost certain. Shape changing but mass staying the same or something. Or loss of mass?

Damn it, I don't remember! I mentally screamed into the silence.

Relax, came that familiar, soothing tone from the back of my head. *If you're stumped, look elsewhere for the answers.*

Shut up, subconscious.

It did have a point, though. I didn't have the answers, but I knew several someones who might. I had to find them first. They also needed to be alive for me to get my answers. Which meant I had to find someone who had managed to get somewhere and hide from the carnage that the escapees had created. Someone who was both agile enough to avoid them, smart enough to run from them and young enough to not give up.

Son of a bitch. I knew the one person I needed.

I just needed him to be breathing and still alive. Conscious and coherent would be an added bonus. The odds of that being the case were not very good, if previous experience suggested anything. Still, one could hope.

CHAPTER TEN

Only two things are infinite, the universe and human stupidity, and I'm not sure about the former.
-Albert Einstein

I checked the last place a scientist should go to in an emergency on the station first: Research. Unsurprisingly, that's where I found him. That was the good news.

The bad news? I found him at roughly the same time that Hernandez did.

The svelte former paratrooper had Isaac cornered in the hallway leading into Research. The kid was plainly terrified and was almost in tears as Hernandez toyed with him. The prisoner's face contained far too much glee in Isaac's fear. I'd seen malice before, many times. I'd seen anger and rage. This, though, was something far scarier. It was a look filled with sick, sadistic pleasure. It was the visage of a true psychopath.

I had to do something, and in a hurry. Isaac wouldn't be able to withstand any sort of physical assault from Hernandez. He was a good kid, but the poor guy was built like a runner. A long distance runner at that.

Hernandez was, well, *changed.*

The prisoner looked emaciated, as though he hadn't eaten in months. His eyes were sunken into his skull, his arms had almost no meat on them whatsoever. It was a terrifying change from the man who should have been the picture of health, which was precisely how he had looked earlier that morning when I had taken him down to Research.

Had it only been twelve hours since then? It was amazing how time seemed to change when everything went to shit.

Hernandez pushed Isaac against the wall and held him there with one hand. He leaned closer and put his mouth next to Isaac's ear. He began to growl in a low, guttural tone. I strained to listen.

"You smell strange, like fear, but smart, very smart to fear," I heard him say. Jesus, the guy had totally lost it. I had to stop him before he did something to the only person I knew who could tell me precisely what the hell was going on with the prisoners.

"P-please," Isaac stammered.

"We have to hurt you," Hernandez hissed and bared his teeth. He pressed them against Isaac's exposed throat. "You hurt us."

"Hernandez!" I called out in an attempt to distract him. Damn it, too many good people had already died. I didn't know if Isaac was a good guy or not, but he was a saint when compared to guys like Jou and Hernandez. Plus, I still needed Isaac. He had answers. "Let him go!"

Hernandez moved his mouth inches away from Isaac's neck. "Boss wants them both alive. We have to hurt them though. But the boss wants them alive. If we eat their fingers, will they live? Yes, they will live. They will hurt. They will live. Boss will be happy. We can be happy."

Holy fucking shit…the bastard had absolutely *lost* it.

"They won't be happy though," Hernandez continued to argue with…well, himself I think. I couldn't be certain about it. "Do we care what they want though? No, only what the boss wants. Care what the boss wants. Are fingers even tasty? Probably very crunchy. But tasty? Like chicken? Do we know? Only one way to find out, we guess."

He snagged Isaac's hand and raised it towards his mouth. I had to make a choice, and I only had two rounds in the magazine left. They had to count, and did Isaac really need all his fingers?

I shook the fugue state from my mind. That was a dark train of thought that I shouldn't even begin to contemplate. I needed Isaac unharmed and fully functioning, and had little use for the escaped prisoner. That made the decision very easy, once I put it that way.

The pistol cleared the holster and was aimed at Hernandez's hip in smooth and practiced motion. I didn't hesitate and pulled the trigger. It broke clean and the round punctured precisely where I had aimed, shattering Hernandez's hip. The prisoner slumped and cried out, enraged and in pain. His turned his head and looked at me, his eyes wild.

"Boss wants you!"

"I don't have time for you or your boss's shit," I replied and put the second – and final – round right between his eyes. Blood splashed out of the exit wound and Hernandez fell to the floor, clearly dead. I kept the pistol trained on him, just in case someone else was watching from where I couldn't see. There was no point in letting the casual observer know I was out of ammo, lacked a fully charged stunner and was pretty much unarmed at this point.

Isaac looked down at the dead prisoner, over at me, then back down at the body before he let out a terrified scream.

I slapped my free hand over his mouth and motioned for him to be quiet. His eyes were wild but he managed a weak nod. I held up three fingers, then counted down to one before I slowly let go of his mouth. He started babbling the moment my hand was clear.

"Thank God you showed up! I think he was about to kill me. Or hurt me, I don't know. He was rambling like a man with only half his brain on the task. I think he was distracted, but at least he was alone. I'd just finished my shift when the alarm hit, and I figured this place is pretty secure, even if it's at the bottom of the station, so I'd ride out whatever was going on from down here. The doc would kill me if the research was compromised. Well, she'd write me up at the very least. She—"

"Shush," I ordered. "Take a deep breath. Count backwards from ten. In Latin."

He looked confused but noticeably calmer. "I don't speak Latin."

Another classic movie quote wasted on the ignorant. However, he wasn't babbling any longer, so I chalked it up as a win. I moved on.

"I need to know something, and I need to know it now," I said and grabbed the scientist by the shoulders. I shook the man hard, harder than I meant to, but I needed answers in a hurry. "What the fuck were you really doing in your experiments down here?"

"C-can't s-s-say," Isaac stuttered, terrified once more. "S-she'll f-fire me!"

"I'll shoot you if I don't get some answers!" I roared, losing patience with him. I was serious, too. The guy could still talk without a knee. Well, if I had any ammunition left at least. I wasn't going to tell him that, though. Intimidation only worked if the person thought you had something to intimidate them with. An empty pistol made for a decent bludgeoning tool, and maybe a paperweight, but that was it. "Fired or shot. Choose quickly!"

"Plankton!" Isaac blurted out. "Methanotrophic plankton!"

"What the hell is that?" I asked angrily and let go of the young researcher. The man leaned back against the plasteel, shaking. I wiped my sweaty palm off on my pants.

"Methane-based life-form that the kraken feed on," Isaac said as he began to rub his arms.

"Explain it to me, all of it," I said as I holstered my sidearm, my anger dissipating rapidly. My hand lingered near it, though, just in case I needed to threaten—excuse me, *motivate* him once more. "Explain it slowly."

Isaac sighed. "Methanotrophic life forms are something we've found on Earth in the past. Think of it as a tiny life form that lives on eating methane. Pretty handy to have around if you don't want methane levels to get too high. Cattle farmers started cultivating them for the gut of their livestock in the late twenty-first century to cut back their emissions. It had a two-fold effect. First, the cows produced less methane without harming themselves. Secondly, it produced a higher quality of meat."

"Yeah, that's why beef products cost more than pork," I said nodding, remembering something I had read about after I had shipped off to Soma. It was a brief news piece about potentially shifting beef exports from Soma, which would be cheaper than raising them on Earth. The only reason it had stuck in my mind is because I'm a huge fan of hamburgers. "I get that. But how does—?"

"I'm getting there," Isaac interrupted. The young, cocky, self-assured scientist was back. Good. I needed him to explain it all to me, in a hurry. "There is plankton here that the kraken eat. Methanotrophic plankton, to be exact. The kraken thrive, and they're hyper intelligent. They're as smart as humans, without a doubt. But how? How did they become so smart? We couldn't figure it out until Dr. Marillac suggested that, like humans, an evolving diet created a more evolved brain. So it must be something they eat became the theory. But since they only eat one thing from what we can see…"

"The plankton," I scratched my head, annoyed. Some weird stuff was going on here and I needed to figure out just what it was, as well as just how screwed we all were. "Same as whales on Earth."

"Close," Isaac acknowledged. "The initial experiments indicated that Dr. Marillac's theory was plausibly correct. The possibilities of an expanded universe opened up. We began to wonder about the health applications for this. Alzheimer's? ALS? PCD? We could cure them. Now, and forever. We were excited. We would have done some animal testing but when the UN charter came down we had to find something else, since animal testing is currently banned. And we found…volunteers."

"The prisoners." My eyes widened involuntarily. I knew that this place was a research facility, and some of the testing going on swam in a grey area of legal mumbo jumbo, but I hadn't thought that they were actually trying to play God. Perhaps I should have, though. I'd known enough of the minor details that turning my head would have been easier. No, check that. It was easier to play ignorant than face the ugly truths I would have discovered if I'd actually looked at things. I swallowed and shook away the self-recriminations. There would be a time for that later. "What did you do to them?"

"We thought we were helping," Isaac insisted in a reluctant voice. "Each and every one of them suffered from some sort of terminal neurological disease. Even Captain Holomisa suffered from early onset Parkinson's. The cellular structure of the plankton showed remarkable prowess in rebuilding damaged brain cells and rewiring the damaged neurons within the brain. So, uh…how to explain this…"

"Just say 'sciencey stuff', wave your hands like you're doing magic, and keep going," I said and waggled my fingers as an example. "I don't have time for a dissertation."

"Right, okay," Isaac exhaled. He mimicked my hand gesture. "We did sciencey stuff and fixed them."

"Okay, fine, you fixed them." I looked away from the young scientist, my mind on overdrive as I tried to figure out just what had gone wrong. "You used the plankton, did sciencey stuff, and now they're healed. Now tell me what happened after. How did the prisoners change? How did they manage to physically change? How are they capable of some things that should be impossible?"

"The human mind is a vast and untapped tool," Isaac stated, his tone more excited and lively, "and the body is its vessel. We have such potential and we don't know how to harness it. So Dr. Marillac wondered—okay, we all wondered —that if the plankton can cure diseases, what can it do to a healthy, engaged neurological system that has already been exposed to the curative properties of the plankton? What depths of the mind can we plumb? Can the human brain evolve before the body?

"So we pushed onwards. Every neuron in the brain we made better. Every synapse fired faster, new neurological pathways were created, damaged and aged ones repaired, cells rejuvenated—not cloned, but literally remade. We found a way to block addiction in the dopamine receptors by simply tweaking them a bit. That means we've cured addictions of all sorts. We've barely cracked open the quantum entanglement theorems that could reside in the folds of the brain itself to help enhance memory storage and retention, but the possibility is there for something huge, something amazing. We have so much more to do.

"But...the question remains. What did we do to their bodies? Think of it this way: the brain controls the body. What if we gave the brain absolute control over the body? I mean absolute, one hundred percent control over appearance, bone structure, muscle density..."

"Impossible," I muttered. "That's just—"

"Insane?" Isaac's chuckle was dark. "Yeah, in hindsight, maybe we should have slowed down. But at the time...wow. All of the research subjects exhibited varying behaviors and body modification. Gentry, who had been chronically overweight his entire life and needed waivers to get into the Navy to begin with, went the extreme other direction for long periods of time. He changed from morbidly obese to rail thin. Because he can't simply rid the body of mass, he made his bones denser so that his weight stayed the same. Then he simply tightened up his loose skin by rearranging them at a cellular level and could direct the excess mass wherever he wanted. It was a dietician's dream. Baptiste showed remarkable improvements in his motor skill functions, reversing years of neural degradation thanks to ALS, and even Holomisa exhibited signs that his overall body was improving. He could regulate—"

"Can whatever you did to them give them… I don't know, some kind of psychic abilities?" I cut him off. I didn't have time for this. I'd already figured that something along those lines had occurred. Jou, for starters, had done exactly what he had described.

"In theory, I suppose," Isaac answered with a shrug. "Never really thought about that, but the human brain is a very strange thing. Who knows what goes on in it all the time? There would have to be something in the root DNA which would be unlocked by the treatments, though. Psychic abilities could be something as small as empathy, for example. Behavioral science is not—"

"That could explain how they got out of their cells," I growled, cutting him off again. I didn't mean to be rude but all of us on the station were running out of time. "They probably whammied someone into letting them out." Isaac's face went pale at that.

"Wait, they're out of their cells?" Isaac asked. I nodded, distracted by the thought of mind control. Could someone have put those dreams into my head? My thoughts drifted back to the now-deceased Doctor Marillac. She had moved awkwardly, like a puppet on strings. Had someone been controlling her?

"Yep, they're out," I answered as I thought of the implications of mind control.

The odds of my survival were not good.

"Oh God," Isaac whimpered. "I thought you'd gone rogue or something."

"Not yet," I replied. "But I'm getting real damn close."

"Where's Doctor Marillac? She has to know! She *must* know!" Isaac began to look frantically around the research level. "There are protocols for this."

"She's dead," I answered in a harsh, cold tone. "And yeah, I know the protocols. Why do you think I have a firearm and not a stunner?"

"She's…dead? What? How?" Isaac was shocked and horrified.

"I put a round into her head after she ate my boss."

"What? You…*killed* her? How could you? Why?!"

"She ate Gerry."

"Ate...how...?"

"Later," I said and looked around the research level. It was dimly lit and empty of all the other scientists. Nobody else from my shift was down here. I needed to get Isaac somewhere safe before heading back up to Control. I could only hope that the layered prison cells held them to the west side of the station. If they managed to get past more than half of the security posts, then all hell truly would break loose.

The decision came easily to me. I grabbed Isaac by the back of the shirt and hauled him away from the plasteel. "Right now my job is to keep you alive. Worry about all that other shit later."

"We're on a moon where everything can kill us!" Isaac's eyes were as wide as plates. "Air. Lake. Planet's surface. Everything! Where are you going to find safety here?"

The scientist had a point, as much as it bothered me to admit it. Inside the station was as safe as anywhere on this moon. Outside for any amount of time meant death, from either methane poisoning or the atmospheric pressure scrubbing the flesh from our bones before we would feel the pain. Theoretically, at least. Still though, I wasn't about to be the first volunteer to test that one.

It was a tough position for anyone to be in. It still didn't quite top the list of bad places I've found myself over the years, though. Which either says a lot about my career choices, or my decision-making abilities.

"Let's get to Central first," I decided after running through our options a few more times in my head. "Control's a lost cause, but Central might still be up and running. We'll worry about the dying part later."

CHAPTER ELEVEN

"Science has made us gods even before we are worthy of being men."
–Jean Rostand

I was shocked to find that Central was not only manned, but that both Thing One and Two had survived and taken control of the backup station. They had been equally surprised to see the two of us alive and relatively unharmed. Well, okay, Isaac was uninjured. I was nursing too many injuries to count. The Things looked like hell warmed over, but I was pretty sure my blood-and-gore covered shirt and pants trumped them both. Isaac's pristine lab coat and well-groomed appearance was a stark contrast to us all. I wiped some blood on his sleeve.

I'll admit it, I felt a rush of hope at finding the twins alive. The thought of trying to get the situation under control with only Isaac for help was depressing. Granted, we weren't out of the woods yet– the odds were definitely against us, and we'd probably die trying. But hey, company!

Once I had Isaac safely tucked away in the corner and quiet, I turned and began giving orders to the Things, who apparently had been waiting for someone in charge to show up. Unfortunately, they only got me.

"Got the comms back up, but I've locked them out for now except on the emergency channel," Poole told me as soon as I got Isaac out of the way. "Wi-Fi is back up but weak. Not sure why. General overhead PA system is back online as well. Someone did a number on the comms system but we're good now. One of the maintenance people must have gotten into the system and fixed it."

"Seal off the access tunnels and make certain that the elevator is disabled," I said, staring at the monitors. Nine of the twelve tracking devices were showing cell breaches and movement. The last—Captain Holomisa's—showed that he was still in his cell, though the containment field had clearly failed. I recalled what

Gerry had said and nodded to myself. *Treat a man like a man and he will act as such. Treat him as an animal...* "Sound off the alarm to upstairs. The Navy has to know. Where is everyone else? Last thing we need are hostages."

"Posts One and Three are not responding," Poole replied as he hastily complied, punching in various commands into his control console. "Two, Four and Five are secure."

"Damn it," I growled. Post One led to The Well, and Post Three led to the civilian quarters. Neither news was good, but hostages could make things even more dangerous than they already were. I had already suspected Post Three was down, since it would have stopped anyone from making it to the Doctor Marillac's quarters. Some bad news was worse than others at this point, though. Of course, I had no idea why Post One would be down. Other than The Well, there was nothing down that way except for some maintenance areas that contained very little. "Have you heard from anyone who is a senior supervisor yet? What about Joseph?"

"No sign of Gerry anywhere that I can see," Lockhart answered, his worried tone matching Poole's in a nearly-identical manner. "Voecks' comms and vitals aren't registering, and I'm showing the same for Capdepon. You see Gerry out there?"

"April and Bigfoot are dead," I swore under my breath. I didn't have the heart to let them know that their boss was definitely dead, nor did I want to get into details and specifics. Admitting that Gerry was getting some from the scientist before she tore open his throat with her bare teeth would be horrible for morale. Plus, I didn't want him to be remembered that way. "Gerry's secure with Doctor M in her quarters"

"On the plus side, it appears that the prisoners aren't trying to make a break for the hangar just yet," Poole informed us. "Both transport shuttles are locked down and only I've got the codes to unlock them. There's no way they'll know who did it, either, so once they figure that out, they'll want to negotiate. Then we'll own them."

I had a bad feeling about the plan but couldn't see a better alternative. I doubted that we would ever "own" them, so to speak. They'd been two steps ahead of us from the moment the jail break had begun. I doubted they would slip up this soon. "Fine. Let's focus on shoring up our defenses at the posts who are still responding. We have twenty-two guards in the facility and fifteen scientists. We've got to find someplace secure to establish a safe zone from where we can fight back from."

"Don't forget the maintenance crew," Poole reminded me.

"How many are there?" I asked.

"Two dozen, but they're wiped," Poole stated. I stared at him, shocked.

"They let *wiped* do maintenance work?"

"They're reprogrammed to only do their assigned tasks and go to their berthing," Poole said in a defensive tone. "It's part of their sentence."

"Yeah, I know," I sighed, defeated. I'd read about that, somewhere, but had completely forgotten about it. It wasn't as if I saw much of the maintenance crews around anyway. Their mental reprogramming limited their communication skills as well as their decision-making. They were almost as good as autonomous androids, but were far cheaper and easier to maintain.

"How did they get out, anyways?" Lockhart asked as he punched in orders, "The prisoners I mean. Those spheres are supposed to be indestructible."

"It only takes one to escape and let the others out," I said. I thought back to my first tour of the facility. The cells had certainly seemed rather tough back then. Now, though, I wasn't so sure. Not after seeing whatever Jou had turned in to. Plus, my gut was telling me that something far worse was going on. I just wasn't ready to admit it yet. "Give me a confirmation on the elevator being disabled."

"Done. There's still the emergency stairwell, though," Lockhart reminded him. I swore again in memory of being dragged up those damned stairs. If I ever saw them again, I'd firebomb something. "Plus The Well," Lockhart added. The layout of the station was proving to be a tactical nightmare.

"The Well is suicide." I paused, then added, "I think. None of the DSRV's can make it *up* The Well, right?"

"They're too big," Lockhart confirmed. "They can go down and out, but not up. It's a designed funnel."

"Okay, I've got two ideas for that safe zone you were looking for," Poole announced suddenly. "The scientist's living quarters are on the way to the hangar. There's two ways in and out. The main entrance is defensible, and the back way means that any attacker would have to move all the way around the station and through the hangar to get in. This is good, except that it's nowhere near the armory. Anyone who isn't carrying is screwed."

"What's the other option?" I scowled. "I don't like the idea of being unarmed and trying to protect a bunch of civilians from a bunch of escaped convicts."

"Unarmed?" Isaac piped up, surprise in his voice. "You've got the pistol you threatened to shoot me with!"

"Really?" Lockhart raised an eyebrow in my direction. I shrugged.

""I'm out of rounds," I admitted to all present. I focused my attention on Isaac. "I wasn't going to shoot you."

"Sure seemed like you were," he groused.

"The Observation Deck," Poole interjected, getting the conversation back onto the rails. "It's only got one way in and out, which could mean a death trap. But it's also above the hangar, and the hangar is probably the best protected place on the station—outside of the cells, at least. Plus, the Armory is closer."

"Not the best comparison," I said, still scowling. I mentally ran through the schematics of the station. "Damn. Damn it all to hell."

"What's up?" Lockhart looked at him.

"The Observation Deck is the safest place and easiest to secure." An idea began to form. "We control Post Two. I think. That leads to the hangar and the Observation Deck. Send out a coded alert to everyone who has checked in. Post Two will be our rally point."

"Rally point?" Poole asked, surprised.

"Yeah, a rally point."

"A rally point usually means that we're rallying to somewhere," Lockhart stated.

"We are. Or rather, we will. We have to take back this station. We'll start from Post Two. Civilians will be safe in the Observation Deck."

"I don't know…" Poole's tone was filled with doubt.

"Worst-case scenario, the civilians die last because there's nobody left to protect them." I rolled my eyes and let out a heavy sigh. "C'mon, it's not as if we have a ton of options here. Outside of nuking this place from orbit—and considering that this place was *dropped from orbit*, I seriously doubt a nuke will hurt it—our only options are to take back the base or run. My knees ache and I'll probably have a bad back one day, so you can understand why I hate running. Plus that means leaving civilians behind. Helpless, mostly innocent civilians. Nowhere in my NDA or contract does it state that I am to abandon my post and leave everyone else to die if the feces strikes the rotary impeller. So that means we take back the station. From Post Two. Any more questions?"

The duo was silent. I gave Isaac a curt nod before I gave my orders to the Things.

"Good. Code that message. I'll be back."

"Where are you going?" Poole asked as he began to relay information through Central's hub. I grabbed one of the PDA ear buds that we almost never used and popped it in. As expected, the device was the wrong shape for my ear and a dull ache began almost immediately. However, in a situation like this, it was worth the discomfort. It would allow for me to remains hands-free at crucial times.

"Someone's got to go check the Armory and see what type of weapons we have. Might as well be me." I pointed to the screen. "Looks like the way is clear. No better time than the present."

♌

The path to the Armory remained remarkably clear the entire length of my harrowing yet short walk. I was fortunate to have the Things in my ear, since they could keep an eye out and warn me about any impending danger. It was still a psychological ordeal, though, one I didn't want to repeat anytime soon.

I spotted the door which led into the Armory. There were no guards posted, which wasn't too surprising. I was a little more shocked that none of the prisoners had tried to take it yet. Then again, thinking back to what I had seen Jou turn into, they probably didn't even need the weapons the Armory provided. I keyed the door to the Armory and stepped inside, making sure it closed securely behind me. That done, I looked around.

Ok, I'll admit it, I wiped away a tear of sheer joy. A manly tear, dammit.

Guns. Guns everywhere. So many guns, and neatly arranged on the racks, a shopper's dream come true. The image made me wish I was Jou's size and strength just so I could carry more. I moved through the storage area, muttering to myself.

"All I'll need is this rifle, really. And these pistols. That's all I'll need." I started strapping on holsters, slinging the carbine across my back. "And these magazines. The rifle, these magazines, and these pistols. That's all I need. And these flash bangs. I shouldn't need anything else. Just the rifle, magazines, pistols, flash bangs, and this baton. Oh dear God in Heaven, is that a bullpup .50 caliber submachine gun? Fuck me, it is. That's it. That's all I... Ooh, body armor!"

The fight with Jou had rattled me a bit. This, naturally, led me to start quoting every damn movie I'd ever seen. It helped me both get my brain back on track as well as prepare me for any surprised which may come up. I hated walking into a situation blind, and the random banter with myself helped calm me down a bit. Besides, who knew what the other prisoners would be able to do? Lift a shuttle? Leap tall buildings in a single bound? No, that was too insane. There was a point where enough was enough.

Was I at the breaking point yet? I couldn't be sure. Better safe than sorry. I went for more weapons.

"Okay, that should be good. Rifle, pistols, magazines, flash bang grenades, and the baton. Leave the bullpup? Yeah, yeah, better leave the bullpup. That's all I need. Shouldn't need anything else. Wait...are those breaching charges?"

"John," Lockhart's voice came over the earpiece. "Who are you talking to?"

"Just thinking out loud." I clanked a bit with each step. "There's a couple of packs here, I'll load them up with small arms for you guys."

Several more pistols and ammo went in the backpacks, along with a roll of duct tape. There's always duct tape. I juggled things around until it was reasonably balanced out. Beggars can't be choosers.

I looked back down at the breaching charges. An evil thought came to mind.

"Hey Lockhart, you there?"

"What's up?"

"How's the fire suppression system in the hangar bay? It's a Halon-type of system, right? Just like the ones they use on Navy vessels?"

"Uh...why?"

"Better question: can we turn it off?"

"Why?"

"Actually, can we safely activate the Halon-3303 and dump it all into the hangar *after* I do something and get to a safe area?"

"*Why?!*"

"I have a really stupid idea," I admitted, "but if it works, then it's not stupid. Right?"

"What the...?"

"Relax," I interrupted in the best soothing tone I could possibly manage given the circumstances we were in. "The worst thing that could happen is that I kill us all."

�

I'll be the first to admit that I don't always think plans completely through when I suggest them to others. It's a flaw in my mental process. I get so focused on the aftermath of the plan that I don't really consider what others think of the implementation of said plan. I also have a bad habit of forgetting to share all of the details of the plan with others, which leads to situations.

"This plan is borked," Lockhart grumbled as he took the submachine gun I offered him. He cleared the chamber and inspected it briefly before nodding in satisfaction. He grabbed one of the many magazines I had pilfered from the Armory and slammed it home. He still was pretty pissed, though. "You want to do *what* with our fire suppression system?"

"It's easy," I tried to explain in a comforting tone. "We use the suppression system to knock out anyone in the area where we trigger it. The locale with the best suppression system in a contained environment is the hangar. Ergo, we lure those psychos up to it and then knock them out with the Halon. Backup plan is we blow them up and vent the hangar of all oxygen, which gets rid of the flames and keeps the station from melting from the inside."

"That doesn't sound easy," Poole picked up complaining where Lockhart left off. "It sounds overly complicated and extremely dangerous."

"You're pocketing grenades while bitching about safety, Gary," I reminded him. "You really don't have much of a leg to stand on here."

"Well, I can't have just one…" he muttered in a low voice. I shook my head and tried not to sigh out loud. It was difficult.

"So how are you going to lure them up to the hangar anyways?" Lockhart asked as he grabbed a handgun and loaded up for bear. He gave me a sideways look.

"We can remotely lock the Observation Deck from here, right?" I asked. Seeing his confirming nod, I continued, "We lock the scientists in their berthing areas and make a general announcement over the PA about escaping in the shuttles. The escapees will rush up there to steal the shuttles and get off the station."

"That…could actually work," Lockhart admitted. While there was some doubt still in his tone, I could see that he was warming up to the idea. Poole was a harder sell, though.

"You're assuming a lot," he said, "and you're assuming that they'll come along like little mice for the cheese fairy. What if they suspect it's a trap?"

"It's mice and the Pied Piper, and that's why we have guns." I patted my bag of goodies. As bad as the situation was, I felt that we were beginning to get the upper hand at last. Too many had died already, and there would be hell to pay, but we were finally getting a handle on things. Relatively speaking, at least.

"How are you going to keep them from getting too suspicious?" Lockhart asked me.

"We're going to make the channel secured, but since I'm almost certain that one of them has a comm unit on them, we'll broadcast over it for all the other guards," I said.

"But what happens if the guards believe the call and go there as well?" Lockhart pressed.

"I don't know, shit," I exhaled heavily and thought for a moment. That was something I hadn't really thought about. "I'll worry about that if it happens. Anybody else check in yet?"

"One of the maintenance wipes, when directly ordered," Poole answered, "and some scientists. I'm sending you the list now."

"Guards?"

"Not yet," he said, though I could see in his eyes that he wasn't expecting anyone else to report in despite his use of the word "yet."

I had to agree with the unspoken sentiment. If the other guards hadn't reported in by now, they were never going to report in at all. So far as we could tell, the three of us were all that was left of the security force from Xanadu.

Welp, that's going to create some high-paying openings in the job market, a dark and sinister voice whispered in the back of my mind. I grumbled and told my subconscious to shut the hell up. I grabbed my bag of goodies and slung it over my shoulder.

"Take care of him," I nodded at Isaac.

"Will do," Lockhart stated

"We'll be waiting for the signal," Poole added helpfully.

I exited Central and slowly made my way up those godforsaken stairs. Six floors up might not sound like a lot to anyone in reasonable shape, but I had gotten my ass kicked twice already, was carrying enough explosives and ammunition to give Honduras pause, and had already suffered through a pretty shitty day. Don't judge me.

When I wasn't being dragged up them forcefully and having my kidneys slammed into the edge of every step, the stairs weren't actually all that bad. I probably could have hit them more often than anything in the gym, been left alone by my fellow guards and gotten a pretty good workout to boot. Plus, the stairwell was a few degrees cooler than the rest of the station. That would have been a nice benefit.

Yeah, yeah, I know. Hindsight and all that.

And I was lying about the stairs. They sucked, as always. Single story is the way to go, people.

I reached my destination level and took a deep breath. I triple-checked the safety and the magazine on the submachine gun before I paused to say a swift prayer. I might not have been the most religious of men, but even I'll admit that I'll ask for help whenever I needed it. Buddha, Flying Spaghetti Monster, God…all usually work on the side of the angels, and I could use all the help I could get.

I had a slight flashback to Soma. I shoved it away. I might have been outnumbered once again, but there was no way I was outgunned. There would be no bastard with a comm to call down an artillery strike on my position this time. I was facing, at most, nine hostiles. Compared to Soma, this would be a cake walk.

I pushed the door open and quickly checked the right before swiveling around and pushing fully into the hall, the barrel of the machine gun turning left. My eyes scanned the immediate area. Nothing. I let out a sigh of relief. Score one for the good guys. I wasn't going to die just yet.

The corridor was nearly dark, with only the emergency lights up and running. It created some weird shadows and dark holes which set my teeth on edge. I was tempted to empty a full burst into each and every one of them but I stopped myself. I was saving all the ammo for legitimate threats. I didn't need to expend any to soothe my shattered nerves.

So I turned to my usual reaction to shitty situations: I began to mouth off.

"Of course the lights are dimmed up here to create a spooky fucking atmosphere," I complained in a low voice as I carefully made my way down the corridor towards the hangar. "Why the fuck not? It's not like I'm not living through a horror movie already." Each step I took was cautious, each breath was measured. Every second was painstakingly long and I could cut the tension in the air with a knife.

"Let's see, the bad guy is going to pop out of one of these doors with a knife while wearing a bloody hockey mask and hack me with a machete," I continued, all the while my eyes scanned the corridor. "Or drop down from a ventilation duct, like that one, with acid dripping from his alien-like jaws and eat my face. Better still, they'll pop up right behind me even though there's nowhere for them to hide. In retrospect, that seems more likely."

Yeah, we all project our fears in different ways. I've mentioned this before and I'll probably say it again. Besides, you try walking down a super freaky corridor sometime while hunting for men who were both hardened killers and shape-changing psychopaths. It's not an easy thing to process. When you do, tell me how you coped.

I have my ways, you have yours.

I caught a blur of motion out of the corner of my eye. Before I could even blink, something heavy slammed against my left and I was tossed aside like a ragdoll. The submachine gun flew from my grip as I landed heavily onto the corridor floor. I slid a few more feet before coming to a stop near the stairwell door. My neck and shoulder ached from the impact, but the adrenaline was pumping and fear fueled me. I was back on my feet with one of my myriad of handguns up and pointed at my attacker's head in moments.

Someone was standing in the shadows, waiting. I couldn't quite make out who it was, but I wasn't taking any chances.

"Back off, convict," I growled. I was going to remain under the assumption that it was one of our escaped prisoners until proof showed otherwise.

"Manning...oh, I hoped it'd be you," a frightening voice came from the darkness.

Shit. I recognized that voice. It belonged to Charles Gentry, one of our most problematic prisoners. He was a sick and twisted individual who loved to play mental games with the scientists and guards alike. Why he had ever been allowed to participate in this scientific study was something all of us guards had debated over. My theory was that he had some senator bent over a barrel somewhere and had also knocked up his daughter. Nobody else bought that theory, but it seemed solid to me.

"Gentry, hands behind your head and face the wall," I demanded. I really didn't want to shoot him, not just yet. If I killed him out here and one of the others were around, I'd never be able to set the trap properly. Digging out escaped convicts from within the confines of this station, each of whom were dangerous as hell, was not something I could afford to do. We simply didn't have the manpower for it, not any longer. It had to be one shot to get them all.

"Let me come into the light, Manning," Gentry hissed.

"What the hell…" I whispered as the tall, lanky ex-soldier moved out of the shadows and into the dim light fully for the first time.

I'd gotten my love for classic movies from my mother. I'd seen just about every movie that she considered a "classic" multiple times. Granted, what she termed a classic, I would later discover, most "real" critics of classical film considered to be campy at best, all the way to downright horrible. So I'd seen movies that most of my friends had never considered, which included hundreds of horror movies. Horror movies which depicted aliens, zombies, and everything else that used to scare the crap out of kids.

That movie list also included *Nosferatu*.

Apparently, Gentry had seen that one as well. If he hadn't, then it was one hell of a coincidence that he looked just like Max Schreck.

His skin had turned a pasty white, which was a stark contrast to the darkness behind him. He had hair, once, but now it appeared to have disappeared, along with his wide chest and muscular arms. His arms were elongated and his elbows just looked wrong somehow. His ears were pointed slightly and his eyes appeared to be sunken deep within his skull. His mouth was twisted and broken, and there was a strange glint in his eyes. I was used to his crazy, but this was just too much.

He had changed himself into a freaking vampire. What a cliché. A terrifying, nightmarish cliché. My throat tightened for a moment as the fear took hold. I couldn't speak, could barely even breathe.

No. Not this time.

I swallowed and the tension eased. I would not be cowed by this wannabe. I would not be petrified by this convict. Besides, Max Schreck had been far scarier than this ass clown.

"Gentry! Turn around, get down on your knees and put your hands on your head!" I demanded, my voice thundering in the sterile metal corridor.

"Or what? You'll shoot me?" Gentry's mocking laugh sent chills up and down my spine. My fingers tightened on the pistol grip.

The prisoner took another step forward, his eyes locked onto mine. "I'd like to see you—"

I fired four times in the span of a single second. Every shot struck the creature that had once been Gentry solidly in the chest, the .45 caliber rounds erupting in small geysers of blood behind him. Spent shell casings landed on the floor. The creature looked down at the wounds clustered in a two-inch area right where his heart was. He scowled and shot me an irritated glare.

"Ow... Nice grouping, though," Gentry said in a voice which somehow managed to convey both annoyance and envy. His jaw, reminding me of a snake, unhinged, while his teeth... Jesus, *his teeth*!

Now pointed and sharp, they fit well within his newly formed mouth. I took a small step back, keeping the pistol level, unable to stop watching his continued transformation.

Gentry's fingers began to elongate, tips sharpening into claws. Snapping my attention back to his eyes, I watched as the pupils narrowed into slits and began to lighten. The color progressed from dark brown, to yellow, finally settling on a deep shade of crimson. He ripped his bloodied white smock off his body, exposing his chest. I watched in awe as the gunshot wounds closed, leaving only a slight blemish on his now alabaster skin. A very disturbing look for a man who appeared emaciated.

"Fine, tough guy. You want to play?" Gentry ran a finger through the still wet blood before raising it to his lips. He sucked the blood off noisily. "Then let's play."

As the Things would say, my original plan was borked. It was time to improvise.

Diamonds may be a girl's best friend, but grenades are definitely a Marine's. I grabbed two off of my belt and tossed them at Gentry. He darted to the side and out of the way as they bounced along the floor. I moved as well, though not in the anticipated direction. I charged forward, following the grenades as they rolled down the corridor.

The secured doors to the hangar was ten feet away. It would take me two seconds reach the doors, two more to enter my master code, two for the doors to open and then about one and a half for it to close behind me. The timer on the grenades was roughly six seconds. There was no way I would make it to safely before the grenades went off.

Of course, I wasn't exactly planning on making it to safety in time.

One.

I made it past the grenades, my bag of goodies slamming painfully into my spine as I sprinted down the corridor. Apparently, everything inside had shifted around and what had once been neat and orderly was now chaos. It didn't matter. Pain could be ignored temporarily.

Two.

I skid to a stop at the door and began to punch in the master override code. I could have used Gerry's keycard but that actually took longer, since the computer had to verify the card and double-check to ensure that the card had clearance for the area. The master override skipped all those procedures and simply opened the door.

Three.

I hated that I was a slow typist. Why the hell did anyone use actual keypads anymore, anyways? Holographic keypads had been out and on the market for the last fifty years. Who decided to save a few hundred dollars on a multi-trillion dollar super-secret military research station anyway? Fucking bean counters.

Four.

The code was accepted. The door unlocked and the pressurized chamber blasted air past my face as a crack appeared in the middle. A whiff of metallic and oil hit my senses. The door began to slide apart.

Five.

I heard a loud *pop!* as one of the grenades went early. I winced and mentally swore as blue smoke began to fill the corridor. I heard Gentry grunt in surprise somewhere on the other side of the smoke.

"What the hell?"

Six.

I stepped inside the hangar and pushed the button for the doors to close. The second grenade popped then, spewing orange-colored smoke into the hallway. No fragments peppering the hallway, no concussive explosion. Just boring old colored smoke.

Surprised? Gentry sure was. The AN-M2 Smoke Grenade had been used by the Marine Corps for centuries as a marker for deployed troops, concealment, and signals for aircraft pilots. Different colors signified different things and were coded thusly. I had assumed that Gentry was as mistrusting as he was psychotic and used that against him, tossing the smoke grenades instead of the real things. Sure, the smoke grenades were hot to the touch, and the smoke they generated could potentially suffocate someone in an enclosed area, but dangerous? Hardly.

I'd basically given Gentry the proverbial middle finger by popping smoke and avoiding conflict on his terms.

I had a plan, and I was sticking to it, damn it.

"Manning!" I heard Gentry scream through the orange-and-blue colored smoke. "You dirty, sneaky motherfu—"

The doors slammed shut, cutting him off. I panted as I typed in a new code to change the master override, just in case he'd seen what I had typed in. The keypad beeped twice and turned green. I locked the controls out as well, to be absolute certain. For what I was about to do, I needed time, and I needed the convicts to break into the hangar to kill me when I was ready for them.

I now had time. Not a lot, but enough. I commed Central.

"How we looking?" I asked.

"Good so far," Poole (I think) answered as Gentry began to pound on the secured doors. I could faintly hear him screaming at me, though I couldn't make out precisely what he was saying. Probably things about goats and his desire for them to consent to his sexual needs and desires, undoubtedly.

"Ready with the secured PA announcement?" I checked as I dumped my bag of goodies onto the hangar floor. Inert C-4 tumbled out, as well as the carefully packaged blasting caps and their respective detonators. I had a while and I wanted to make certain I did this correctly. Practice makes perfect, and I was way out of practice.

"Ready to give the word as soon as you tell us."

I began to set charges all across the hangar, making certain that each explosive was near something highly flammable. I wanted one hell of a fire, and also to take a few of the bastards out at the same time.

I wanted a chain of explosions in a descending order, but other than rigging a charge and blowing it up, I knew next to nothing about sequenced explosions. My best bet was to convince them that the explosions had failed and I was trapped. If they thought I was trapped, they would grow cocky. It was almost guaranteed.

"Start the broadcast," I said ten minutes later. I strung the last detonator to my master line and walked it back to the shuttle nearest the door. They would definitely see me in the cockpit, looking panicky and frightened. They would undoubtedly swarm the shuttle, eager to kill, ready to murder all survivors and make their way off of the station.

Yes, one must chum the water to bring about the sharks. It just sucked that I had to be the chum.

I waited patiently with one ear on the supposedly secured broadcast to the Observation Deck as I readied the detonator. I left the main door to the shuttle open but ready to be closed at a moment's notice. I needed to maintain the illusion of being helpless and ready to bolt, even if it meant that I would possibly get screwed hard if something went wrong.

Minutes passed. Nothing. I began to sweat profusely in the stifling heat. The one place where it was constantly warm in the station was the hangar, since it contained two pressure-sealed locks which led to the dangerous environments of Titan. Since the methane outside was so cold that it could freeze anything, the locks cycled in warmer air and pumped out the methane whenever the outer locks were opened. Since the warm air rose naturally from the generators near the bottom of the station anyway, it was all dumped into the hangar.

Which basically meant I was waiting for my possible death in an oven. Go me.

I finally heard shouting outside of the door where I had made it past Gentry. It sounded loud, angry and not very human. I almost whooped aloud in glee. There were more than two voices out there, and they all sounded like they wanted to get inside and murder me. This was getting better and better.

After much struggling and shouting, the escapees managed to pry the doors to the hangar open and step inside. I counted them off as they entered. Wohl, Jones, Aviotti, Flynn, Dupay, and coming up in the rear was Gentry. They all wore little to no clothing, and their bodies seemed as malformed and changed as Gentry's had. Jou had been subtle compared to these guys. Aviotti looked like he was going for the demonic look, while Wohl reminded me of a scarecrow. Dupay had grown hair all over his body and fangs. The convicts were scary and crazy, and I told myself that I was doing the universe a favor by killing them all. They had been men before, hiding their bestial natures behind a mask of humanity. Now though? They'd dropped their masks. It made what I was about to do all the easier.

I counted them off again and frowned. Baptiste was missing. Damn. I'd hope to nail all of them in one fell swoop.

Still, beggars couldn't be choosers. I would make do with what I had.

They began to holler and shout at me as they ran towards the shuttle. I quickly activated the automatic doors and sealed the ship. They skidded to a stop as a whole and eyed me suspiciously. That was a good idea, given as to what I was about to do to them, but it was already too late.

"Come on out, Manning," Gentry shouted from the rear of the pack. The others were grinning hungrily. "We just want to…talk things over."

Right. Space Pope, et cetera, et cetera.

"Screw you!" I shouted back after I flipped on the ship's external comms. Eloquent, no?

"Manning, if you don't open this shuttle and let all the scientists off, we're going to kill everyone slowly," Gentry promised with a hideous and ghastly smile. The dude was beginning to both piss me off and creep me out. I readjusted my mental ranking of Nosferatu and moved Gentry up the list of Things That Creep Me Out. Still not at the top, but he was closing in quickly.

Gentry continued to shout obscenities at me as well as threats but I had had enough. They say that the best sex oftentimes is surprise morning sex. Unless you're a convict in prison, that is.

"Surprise buttsex, motherfuckers!" I screamed and clacked the detonator in my hand. Yes, I'll be the first to admit that I'm extremely screwed-up individual.

My C-4 charges exploded, creating a wall of fire and heat which slammed into most of the convicts. A few were killed outright from the blast, though most appeared to have suffered only minor burns and some broken bones from the explosion. Fire began to rage as a few oil cans which had been haphazardly strewn about were lit. My strategically placed. My strategically places charges had done the trick, though. It had dazed and disoriented the surviving convicts for long enough that when they recovered, those that survived wouldn't guess that the force of the explosions had missed on purpose.

"Come on," I hissed as I watched the fires burn. The convicts began to get back up onto their feet. Murderous looks were being sent my direction in the shuttle. If looks could kill…well, let's just say that the phrase "glaring daggers" would have been the gentlest of ways they would have killed me. "Come on…"

Suddenly, a loud siren went off in the hangar. The convicts looked around in confusion as yellow lights began to flash, slowly at first but increasing their pace with each passing second. Everyone on the station who was not a prisoner knew precisely what that meant. Thirty seconds. That was all they had to get out of the hangar as fast as humanly possible. Unfortunately for the escaped prisoners, they never received that safety briefing.

It was an oversight I'm sure would be rectified in a few years, give or take a millennia.

All of the doors in the hangar slammed shut. The lights continued to flash but the sirens stopped their howling. I looked at the escapees with merciless eyes. Their thirty seconds were up.

"Enjoy Hell, you sons of bitches."

Halon-3303 was a nasty piece of work that had been created by some mad scientist on Earth thirty years before. It worked as both a fire suppressant and a fuel elimination system, which was handy for some of those fires which could kill an entire ship in the depths of space. The suppressant system worked as a traditional extinguishing system, smothering the fire with a cold foam and eliminating oxygen from the area, which removed two of the three basic needs of a sustained fire. However, older suppressants oftentimes ran the risk of the fire reappearing, especially when the fire had a fuel source. Something like cloth, wood, or anything else that was biodegradable. Fires that had been thought extinguished would rekindle, placing the ship in danger anew.

Enter the aforementioned mad scientist, who decided to imbue the suppression system with a nanite which would eliminate anything biodegradable trapped within the foam itself. This would ensure that all three elements of the "fire triangle" would be eliminated, making certain that the chance of a fire reappearing would be absolutely nil. Many ships and stations had been saved thanks to the new Halon-3303 system. Best part of all? The nanites eliminated themselves and the foam once there was nothing else biodegradable within the foam. Cleanup was a snap for maintenance crews.

Unfortunately for the prisoners who were out in the hangar, they did not know what Halon-3303 was about to do to them. The human body, after all, is biodegradable.

The Halon foam exploded from the rafters of the hangar, the thick, grey stuff landing on every piece of exposed equipment. It stuck to everything, including the escaped convicts. They looked around at one another, their faces masks of grey goop and foam. I could almost feel the palpable confusion in the room.

I looked away for the next part. I knew what was to come would be gruesome. I had enough nightmares already; I didn't see any need to add to them.

The convicts all began to scream simultaneously as the nanites within the foam began feasting on their exposed skin, clothing, and hair. Everything that could possibly be biological was eliminated in rapid order. The screams ended as abruptly as they began as the nanites chewed through bone and vital organs. All of the prisoners were the walking dead, even if their minds didn't quite know it yet.

I never did look. I mean, I could imagine what it had looked like, but I didn't actually see what happened. All I know is that when the all-clear siren sounded, the only evidence that there had been people in the hangar moments before was a few pieces of plastic and their slippers—that was odd—that all of them had been required to wear when walking to and from their cells.

I popped the door to the shuttle. I coughed and waved away smoke as I looked at the carnage I had wrought. Or rather, lack thereof. Minus the damage to the hangar itself, I really hadn't hurt much of anything. It would have been humorous if I'd been a screaming, raving lunatic. As it were, the reminder of what I had done just grossed me out a little.

The Halon system had done its job, sucking all of the oxygen out of the hangar as it doused the fire with suppressant. The system had cycled out all the nasty stuff that would have killed me if I hadn't been tucked safely away inside the shuttle and oxygen was pumping through once more. The foam had all disappeared, ensuring that I would survive another five minutes. Still, the smoke made my eyes water and burned my lungs a little. No fire suppression system was perfect, after all.

Whatever. It was a win, and as far as I could tell, there was now only one escaped prisoner that was still alive. He also happened to be the one I hadn't seen during all of this, nor heard a peep about.

Baptiste...where in the world could you be hiding?

The doors to the hangar opened as I approached. I looked up in surprise and stopped dead in my tracks. Standing before me in all his twisted, psychotic, vampiric glory was Gentry. He grinned, his mouth stretching wide over his malformed face.

"Missed one," he said and slammed a fist into my chest.

The body armor I had put on earlier while in the Armory probably saved my life. Combined with the impact absorption shirt I was wearing underneath and it only felt like I'd taken a shotgun full blast to the chest instead of being impaled by a freight train. I flew backwards a few feet and landed on my ass. I lay there for a moment, gaping like a fish as I struggled to breathe.

Over my gasping for air, I could hear Gentry approaching. His footsteps were loud in my ears for some reason. I rolled onto my side and winced as I managed to get some air into my lungs. That punch had hurt worse than when Jou had hit me. For some reason, I also got the feeling that Gentry had pulled his punch a little bit.

Not much, but enough to keep me alive...and make me suffer longer, I guess.

"That was actually pretty cunning," he said as he delivered a kick to my ribs. I slid another few feet back away from the door, and my escape. He continued to rant, "I almost got caught in the Halon system. Army guys might not know what the siren was for, but any former Navy personnel would. You sneaky little bastard. You're just about as psycho as we are."

I wish I could say I had a clever retort and a snappy rejoinder, but my ribs hurt too much to even whimper in pain. The spirit was there but the flesh, unwilling. It really sucked, too. I had some good ones saved up.

"Was that all you could plan though?" he asked again as he circled around behind me. Another kick, this time to my kidneys. I groaned through ragged breaths. Between him and Jou, I was going to be pissing blood for a year. I hoped like hell the medical insurance I had from the company covered a dialysis machine. "Lure us in, blow shit up, let the Halon clean up the mess?" He paused in his rant for a moment and knelt down beside me. His blood-red eyes bored into mine. "Actually, that's not a bad plan. Hard to prove murder when there's no body. Wish I had thought of it."

"Fuck..." I managed to spit out. He grinned, showing me his sharp teeth.

"No thanks," he replied and hauled me to my feet with one hand. He slapped me across the face. That stung, but at least on my feet I could breathe again. Bonus points for that. "I prefer mine to be a little more on the younger side."

He pivoted and tossed me across the hangar and out into the hall where our fight had initially begun. The air was still thick and heavy from the smoke grenades I had used to distract him with earlier. That was weird. The air filters should have cleared the smoke out in minutes. Lazy-assed maintenance workers.

I managed to crawl to my knees, which was a mistake. He reared back and kicked me so hard that I convulsed. I slammed into the wall, which broke open one of the air filter panels. I don't think I'd ever hurt that bad before in my life. I may have even peed a little. I couldn't be certain, since just about everything below my chest tingled and felt slightly numb. Even my hands tingled a little.

Did that bastard just snap my spine or something? I wondered as he grabbed the back of my body armor. I desperately reached out and grabbing some of the tubing which ran inside the panel. It slowed him down for barely a moment before he jerked harder. The hose ripped out from the panel and began to gush onto the ground. Steam began to rise and the oxygen sensors on the walls of the corridor began to beep.

What the hell?

I weakly kicked backwards at Gentry, a futile gesture which made him laugh. He rewarded my efforts by slamming my face into the wall a few times. I was fortunate that he didn't break anything important. I could feel my lower lip split, and there was some moisture on my upper lip. I tasted it and recognized my own blood. Awesome. Maybe he had broken something after all.

"You've stopped fighting," he said in a gloating tone from behind me. My vision was blurred from the repeated head bashings, but I could just make out the rising steam from the broken tube I had accidentally ripped out earlier. I blinked my eyes clear and watched as the liquid continued to spill out onto the floor.

Something in the back of my mind clicked. I knew what it was, and what I had to do. I could only hope that my body was up to the task.

It was growing harder to breathe. I wasn't sure if it was my ribs being kicked too much or the steam which was filling the corridor. I took as big of a breath as I dared and held it. I briefly wondered if Gentry even noticed or if he was too caught up in kicking my ass. Only one way to find out.

I reached out and carefully snagged the hose, my ribs screaming in protest. Being very careful not the get any of the liquid on my skin, I aimed the broken end directly at his exposed legs. It splashed against the skin and crystals began to form immediately.

Gentry howled in pain and tried to step back, only his legs had quit working. His feet had fused themselves to the floor. I aimed the spray from the hose higher and nailed his junk. His inhuman scream nearly shattered my eardrums, but I continued to hose him down.

For some reason or another, an engineer had decided to cool the station with liquid nitrogen during the design process. I was not about to look a gift horse in the mouth, however. I was going to make the most out of it.

My lungs burned and my head began to swim as my body cried out for oxygen. I refused to give in and kept pumping the nitrogen all over Gentry's form. It took nearly a full minute before I had him precisely where I wanted him: immobile and helpless.

Call me a sadist for continuing to dump the liquid nitrogen on him. I dare you.

I pitched the hose aside and crawled away as best as I could, gasping for air along the way I had held my breath for over a minute, which was longer than I ever had before. With bruised ribs, no less. All while lying dangerously close to a liquid that would have killed me if I hadn't noticed the oxygen alarms in the hall. Someone up there loved them a Marine.

Oorah.

I lay gasping for a few more minutes before I dug for my PDA. It had managed to survive the beatings I'd taken so far and with the Wi-Fi up and running I was able to tap into the maintenance section. I quickly put in a request for extra oxygen to be pumped into the corridor while the emergency cutoff for the liquid nitrogen finally kicked in.

Somebody in Maintenance was on and followed my orders without question. Score one for mindless efficiency, I guess. Yay team.

I rolled over onto my back and clutched my bruised ribs. I gingerly inspected them as best as I could through the body armor but I couldn't feel anything broken. I'd gotten extremely lucky. I touched my nose and grimaced as a fresh wave of pain washed over me. Okay, maybe not so lucky. My split lip was nothing new, since that seemed to happen even in dry weather all the time in the winter. Being punched hadn't helped, but at least I had a lame excuse other than forgetting to put on lip balm.

I lifted my head a few inches off the ground and glanced at Gentry before it thumped back down onto the floor. I winced.

"Give me something alcoholic on the rocks," I quipped and struggled to sit up. "Ow. Damn. Ow. What, nothing? Oooh, shit, that hurt. Not even a chuckle, Gentry? Ow. C'mon you bastard, that was fun—oh hell with it. Oooooh damn damn damn."

It took a few tries, but I finally managed to get back on my feet. I was woozy, ached all over and was pretty sure I looked like someone who had gotten their ass beat. Well, no surprise there, given my day. Still, though, I was alive and Gentry…wasn't?

I looked at Gentry's frozen form. He was nothing more than a statue now. I had no idea if his newfound abilities would allow him to recover if he ever thawed out. The liquid nitrogen had done the trick, even if it had almost suffocated me during the process. I made a mental note to mention the idiocy of using it as a coolant for the exterior balancing of the station's panels to whoever designed the damn place, assuming I made it out of this hell alive. While it was a good idea as a whole, the shit had allowed for me to do something that no person should be able to do. I had literally frozen a vampire on a space station and lived to tell the tale.

My life had sailed past strange, skipped crazy and was now threatening to reach Lewis Carroll territory. Ah well. *C'est la vie.*

I pulled my handgun from its holster and took careful aim at Gentry's frozen form. I wasn't certain what would happen, but I had a feeling that it was going to be final. I could almost hear him pleading for his life even if his lips did not move. He wasn't even breathing. There was no way he would survive being frozen.

Fuck it. I wanted to make certain.

"Seen this one, Gentry?" I said as I cocked the hammer. "I loved that movie."

The round hammered into his frozen chest and embedded itself deep into the frozen mass. I was a bit surprised. I'd expected the frozen man to shatter when the round hit him, or the slim possibility of a ricochet. I hadn't expected the round to actually penetrate.

Still, a large crack had formed in his chest. I looked behind him. The steel floor of the corridor was awfully tempting. I gave a little mental shrug and pushed Gentry.

The upper half of his chest cracked fully and fell backwards, taking his arms and head with but leaving his lower torso and legs standing upright. I jumped back a little as the chest shattered into large chunks of frozen man. I could identify what looked like red ice cubes lying across the floor. *Blood. That's frozen blood. And that little piece over there looks like frozen brain. Huh. Is that his tongue?*

"Jesus Christ," I muttered. I'd done some nasty things in my life, but this...this was something far worse. This was absolutely heinous, ranking up there with psychotic mass killer shit. A massive wave of nausea crashed over me. I turned my head and suddenly spewed the last remnants of the Chef's Special all over the place.

It had tasted far better going down than it did coming up, in case you were wondering. Throwing up with bruised ribs is no picnic, either. It took me a few minutes to regain control of the dry heaving and pushing through the pain which racked my body before I could even think about anything else. I spit the last remnants of corn and bile from my mouth and activated my comm.

"Lockhart, you there?"

"That you, John," a reply came back almost instantly. "You sound like hell."

"I feel worse," I admitted, "but we're good. Hangar is secured."

"That's great news! We're heading up to the Observation Desk in five," Lockhart reported back. "Patching you in to the civilian's channel. See you in a bit."

I acknowledged and killed the connection. I tried not to let relief overwhelm my cautious state, but it was difficult. Things were finally looking up. I exited the hangar and headed for the stairs. The only thing we needed to do now was to get the civilians onto the shuttle and get off the planet, then get the Navy to drop a rod or ten on this place and call it a day.

Easy peasy.

CHAPTER TWELVE

*No man is an island, entire of itself; every man is a piece of the
continent, a part of the main; if a clod be washed away by the sea,
Europe is the less, as well as if a promontory were, as well as if a
manner of thy friend's or of thine own were; any man's death
diminishes me, because I am involved in mankind; And therefore
never send to know for whom the bell tolls; It tolls for thee…*
–John Donne

"All right, civvies, coast is clear," I said into the comm. "Let's do
it just like in grade school." No reply. I started down the corridor
to the Observation Deck. "Poole? Lockhart? Hello?" Still no
answer as the hairs rose on the back of my neck. There was only
one way in or out, but I hadn't been paying attention when I blew
up the hangar and I'd kind of lost track of everything during the
fight with Gentry. "Guys, we haven't got all day…"

I stopped at the foot of the stairs. Blood. Blood everywhere.
Great pools of it running together on the floor, growing larger as
what was on the wall slowly flowed into them. Here and there,
solid pieces of flesh and gristle stood like islands in a crimson sea,
broken only where it was smeared across the floor. The smell hung
in the air, thick and metallic, invading my nose and forcing its way
into the back of my throat. I averted my eyes before I could see too
much. My reflexive reaction, though, brought my eyes onto a pile
of what looked like ears. I gasped in horror and gagged, unable to
get the taste of the putrid air out of my mouth.

*Jesus. If it's this bad down here, I don't want to see what's up
there.* Unfortunately, the part of my brain that demanded
thoroughness insisted that I check. I climbed the stairs, expecting
the worst, hoping for the best.

My fears were not unfounded.

The observation deck was covered in blood, splashed on the
walls and windows. What was left of the gathered scientists was
scattered around the room, seemingly strewn at random by a rogue

wood chipper. Careful searching would've been a waste of time—the room left no place to hide for any survivors. A smear of blood, starting in the center of the room, continued down the stairs. I followed it, back the way I came.

The trail led down the hall, long streaks of red apparently made by clawing hands. Whoever had been drug away was still alive. At last check, only two inmates were left unaccounted for: Holomisa and Baptiste, and this definitely didn't seem like the work of the mild-mannered and heroic Holomisa.

I checked weapons, not able to shake the feeling that I was walking towards a death trap. Someone able to rip through a room full of people in only a matter of minutes wasn't going to be stopped by a few bullets.

The trail led to the elevator. The supposedly non-working elevator.

Oh hell no. No way am I getting in there. Not only would it give away my position and allow whoever to know exactly when and where I'd be when I arrived, it was a great place to set an ambush. *I've seen this movie. The hero gets in, complains about the music, and then gets attacked by the monster on top of the car. All that's missing is the scary music and glowing footprints. Stairs it is. Although...*

I was at the top level of the station, the elevator had stopped at Research. Chances were good that the bad guy was there, and that it was a trap. Why, though? As bruising to my ego as it was, I had to be honest with myself: that thing would likely shred me, pick its teeth with my leg bones, and wear the body armor as a trophy. Why not hit me up here, close to the shuttles?

I racked my brain, trying to remember something Jou had said. "The boss wants you alive." Holomisa had still been in his cell, and Baptiste had been loose.

Pretty much eliminates Holomisa as 'the Boss.' So why would Baptiste want me alive?

I punched the call button, watching the numbers above the doors. Agonizingly slow seconds passed before the car arrived, the doors opening to my raised rifle. Empty.

I worked fast, pulling the stop button to make sure I had time to set up. One charge went on the ceiling, roughly a foot from the door; the other, on the panel. I pushed the button for research, deactivated the stop, exiting as the doors slid closed.

Again, time crawled as the numbers reversed themselves, finally stopping at research level.

"Three, two, one…" I triggered the charges.

The muffled thump of the explosion brought a smile to my face. Hey, I was still a Marine, and boomy things make me happy. I could only hope that Baptiste had been waiting close by in ambush. I started down the stairs, rifle at the ready, keeping my movements as quiet as possible.

The stairs were empty. I was thrilled about this, but I had to admit that I was completely *done* with stairs. If I survived this I was installing a fucking elevator or three in my house whenever I got around to buying one. Hell, screw that. I could just build a house with no stairs at all, with everything on the same level. Yeah, that sounded much better.

Kansas. Kansas was flat. Yeah, I was going to buy a single-story house in Kansas.

As I made my way down the stairs, I began to grow dizzy and breathing grew a little more difficult. My ribs were aching, though not the flaring, stabbing pain I typically associated with broken bones. That was the good news. The bad was that my body was extremely beat up and my mind was starting to wander because of it. I knew it would happen eventually. I probably had a concussion from the continued beatings.

My comm chirped. I ignored it. I knew who it was and had no desire to deal with him. It chirped again, this time seemingly a little more insistently. I scowled and answered it as I arrived at the proper level.

"What do you want, psycho?"

"Tell me, Johnny," Baptiste said over the comm as I exited the stairwell and hobbled down towards Research as fast as I could manage. "Did you think you could save everyone?"

"I could try, you sanctimonious prick," I grunted. I knew I shouldn't engage him. It's what he wanted, but I had to say something. He was so far inside my head that he should have been paying rent. Plus, I was running out of good insults. I needed something to get me back in the game.

"I love your enthusiasm and dedication," he said. I came to a stop and looked around. *Where was I?* This sure as hell wasn't Control. I rubbed my sweaty face and grimaced. I'd gotten my ass kicked so hard and so often that I'd forgotten about getting my nose busted. It was swollen but I could still breathe, thank God. I reminded myself for the third time not to mess with it. Baptiste continued to taunt me as I tried to gather my bearings. "Oh, this isn't Research, is it? Dear me. You must have gotten turned around somehow. Perhaps you should have...taken a left at Albuquerque?"

That asshole. It was a good line, which made me hate him all the more.

"Well, since you're on a mission to save people, Johnny, perhaps you can start with these lost, deluded souls," Baptiste said. I blinked and watched as the lights came up around me. I recognized the layout of the room from base schematics and swore vehemently. I wasn't anywhere near Control. Baptiste had mind-fucked me somehow and I was in Maintenance, which was near the absolute bottom of the station. Perfect.

Maintenance was a strange section of the station, designed in a honeycomb pattern to diffuse and displace the massive heat signature of the station's generators. Sure, a lot of the station's energy was created by converting the ultraviolet light and solar winds created by the massive gas giant Saturn, but it still needed the generators to keep up with some demands of the station. These were fueled by the liquid methane on the moon. Not a huge surprise, really.

Even though the generators were up and running, they were more of a backup system than anything else. Still though, even generators idling created some sort of heat. The heat had to go somewhere or else it would turn the station into the universe's most expensive oven. Hence, polycarbonate-constructed honeycombs filled Maintenance, directing the heat out and into the tubing system, which would then send all the heat throughout the station to keep it warm as it sat within the unbelievably cold methane lake.

It was also the only area of the station that featured rough flooring. I wasn't sure why it was there other than it made the footing more secure and prohibited anyone from slipping. Then again, if moisture buildup happened, it could create a safety hazard for anyone working down here. And everyone knows just how important being safe is.

Safety third, as my great-grandpa used to say while showing off his missing middle finger.

Not all of the lights seemed to be on I noticed as I carefully stepped deeper into the area. I could hear some sort of sharp, steady beat somewhere within the room's shadows. The lack of proper lighting created long shadows in the room itself, dividing it into area of bright light and pure blackness. My eyes adjusted as well as they could and I could faintly make out human forms standing in the shadows.

They were here, waiting. I swallowed nervously and waited. I hated dealing with mind-wipes, and now I was in a room full of them. For some sick and demented reason, Baptiste had guided me down here. I was about to find out what that was.

The maintenance workers came out of the shadows, their faces devoid of any emotion, each one of them snapping their fingers in a rhythmic pattern. Each one was dressed in their usual white partial jumpsuit, which covered the necessary parts but left everything below their mid-thighs bare. It was warm enough in the lower half of the station to merit such a strange looking outfit. None of them were wearing shoes, which I found odd. The floor was not something I would have wanted to walk on without some sort of protection. They moved in unison together, though it was slightly stilted. It took me a second to realize just what, precisely, was going on. It made me sick.

Baptiste was playing puppet master, and each maintenance worker was his own personal marionette.

"Oh, swing it Johnny, you fat cat you," Baptiste sang out, his voice reverberating through my skull and across the room. The maintenance workers all stopped moving suddenly, though they continued to snap their fingers. "Boop de bop, wham bam a diddly doo wop."

The first maintenance worker slid across the floor on his knees, his bare legs leaving a bloody streak behind him as the skin was peeled off by the grated flooring. If the mind-wiped maintenance person noticed, he didn't seem to care. He popped back to his feet and spun in place, an improvised dance move that would have worked had he not been trying to do it on a surface that inhibited sliding movements and had bare feet. I heard his ankle crap and he faltered slightly. His face showed no signs of even feeling the pain, however. He continued to dance, though it was a mockery of a number. Blood began to drip onto the floor, trailing behind him with every step he took. I could see the tip of his ankle bone jutting grotesquely out the side.

"They feel it all, Johnny," Baptiste taunted me, reading my thoughts, "but they can't complain. They have no minds left, no sense of self. I own them, and they will dance for me for as long as I desire them to."

Another snap. The guy's other ankle snapped. He continued to dance on the broken bones. I watched, horrified. I had to stop this. But how?

"Only one way to save them from this, Johnny. Only one way to free these poor souls, and you know what it is."

A second maintenance worker began to dance, a series of macabre movements that looked like a cross between a hipster and a drunken zombie stripper. It was horrifying to watch, especially since there was no sign of life behind those eyes. There was nothing but flat emptiness, and there was a decided lack of rhythm to his movements. If it hadn't been such a disturbing sight, I would have probably mocked Baptiste about his obvious lack of dance aptitude. The mind-wipe continued to dance, his bare feet leaving behind bloodied footprints with each step. I growled. Baptiste was an animal.

I understood that mind-wipes are controversial, but they served a purpose for mentally handicapped convicted felons. It enabled them to be a productive member of society while it regrew their neurons and tried to work around the handicap. At the end of five years, the convict was supposed to be able to be a free person once more, though with no memory of his or her past life and a skill set so they could find work. At least, that was how it was supposed to work.

Something slammed into my shoulder and knocked me to the side. I managed to stay upright only because whoever had hit me had not managed to build up enough speed. I snap-kicked towards my attacker and recognized the first maintenance worker. I realized why he hadn't been able to push me much harder: bone was sticking out of both ankles, which made walking hard even if Baptiste was making him ignore the pain. I let my bag slide from my shoulder and onto the floor as I turned to face my attacker. I tossed the rifle down on top of it as well. There was no sense in killing these poor bastards, not while they were under Baptiste's control at least.

"Meet Ghordahn," Baptiste crowed in my ear as the maintenance worker began to weave towards me. "He's thirty, loves Thai food and had a wife and four kids. He was also what I would call 'retarded.' Funny, that. They let him breed and marry in spite of his being handicapped. I personally would have drowned him at birth or, barring that, neutered him so that his stock could not pollute the Earth. But what do I know? I'm just a crazed, psychotic asshole, am I right?"

Wasn't going to argue with him there. I blocked another weak punch from Ghordahn and shoved him away. He stumbled and fell on his ass, his feet flopping hideously around on his broken ankles. I didn't pursue the attack, though. I didn't want to fight him. This seemed to piss Baptiste off a bit.

"Johnny, I'll make them all abuse themselves until they are nothing more than standing, ragged piled of flesh and meat," Baptiste growled in a dangerous tone. "I will hurt them worse than I have hurt anyone before in my life. You know what I'm capable of. You know what I can do. Do not test me, Johnny."

"What do you want me to do, you bastard?" I fairly screamed into the comm.

"I want you to reach down into that dark pit you call a soul, Johnny," Baptiste whispered seductively, "and I want you to bring the monster to the surface and play with my toys. Or better still, let that dead bitch of yours come out and you can be her white knight once more by removing these poor, captured men from their earthly bonds. Be the hero if you insist, though we both know that you have a desire to be the villain."

I don't think he realized just how badly he screwed up just then. Whatever illusion or spell he had pulled over my psyche snapped apart with that comment.

Ghordahn managed to crawl back to his feet, a pool of blood forming beneath them. The poor guy was trying to do what Baptiste wanted, but the body could only take so much abuse before it stopped working. Compound fractures were murder on the body and were usually a good indicator that a person was seriously hurt and should stop what they were doing.

Only Baptiste wasn't going to let him stop, or let any of them stop. It was up to me to do something about it, even if it was something that I would probably hate myself for afterwards. I decided to take the initiative instead.

I delivered a brutal kick to the inside of Ghordahn's knee, the sickening *crunch!* audible to everyone in the room. I probably broke his leg as well, but whatever I had ruined, he was out of the fight. He lost his balance and fell to the ground. He tried to push himself up off the ground, but without ankles and a knee, there was no way he could fight me any longer.

"I'm impressed, Johnny," Baptiste said. "That was a surprising bit of viciousness I hadn't expected out of you. Can you do it again? For me?"

Two more maintenance workers joined the routine, bringing the number of mind-wiped dancers to three. The others continued to snap their fingers in a timed beat and dance a small two-step number, hands twirling in the air.

This was starting to go way past absurd. What was Baptiste's end game?

The three men charged me at once, moving as a single unit to take me down. While hand-to-hand combat during recon training had covered being outnumbered, as a sniper it wasn't something I really focused on. If I was in a fistfight and not on base or in a bar, it meant that somewhere along the line I had seriously screwed up.

However, just because it was something I hadn't focused on didn't mean I was hopeless at it.

I charged towards the lead mind-wiped and kicked him as hard as I could in the chest. He fell back onto the floor, hard, his head smacking the steel grate beneath. I landed on top of him and slammed the back of his head down into the grate a few more times to make sure. I could feel his chest rising and falling beneath me, so I knew he was still alive.

The other two grabbed me and hauled me off of him, each taking turns punching my ribs. The blows hurt but weren't debilitating. Not yet, at least. I think Baptiste was causing them to pull their punches, though I didn't know why. Or maybe something else was going on that I wasn't aware of. It's entirely possible, since I was simply focused on staying alive and not killing anyone else—except Baptiste. I was going to take great pleasure in murdering him.

"Come on, Johnny. Stop trying to hit them and hit them."

That bastard was stealing all of my classic movie lines. I was going to kick his ass whenever I got ahold of him.

I ducked slightly, weaved and managed to avoid another elbow to the ribs, instead letting it bounce off the top of my head as I slammed an open palm into the solar plexus of the mind-wiped man holding me on my left. He stumbled back far enough to allow me room to maneuver and I used my momentary advantage. I grabbed the closest mind-wipe around the waist, twisted slightly and tossed him over my hip. He slammed down hard onto the floor and I used my own momentum to put a knee on top of his chest. I punched him a few times in the face to disorientate him before the other one came roaring back into the fight.

I rolled away from him, using the body of the man I had just taken down to cushion the move. It must have caught Baptiste off guard because the mind-wipe stumbled over the other and fell flat on his face. I kicked him in the temple with the heel of my boot and hoped like hell I didn't kill him.

"Daisy, Daisy, give me your answer, do," Baptiste sang over the comm as I scrambled back up to my feet. Three more of the finger-snapping maintenance workers came rushing in, trying to all use their weight advantage to pin me down. Meanwhile, as I fought to maintain control, Baptiste continued to torment me with his horrid singing. "I'm half crazy, all for the love of you. It won't be a stylish marriage, I can't afford a carriage. But you'll look sweet upon the seat of this bicycle built for two."

I tried to block out what Baptiste considered music as I redirected two swift punches with my hands. It's difficult to time just right but if done properly all you have are stinging hands. It also opened them up to a counterstrike. Thank you Senior Drill Instructor Jonathan LaForce.

Blows were coming in from all directions at such a rapid pace that I felt my control of the situation slipping. I still refused to kill the men, even if they were trying to kill me. They had no control over their actions, and I'll be damned if I let Baptiste beat me here as well. But I had to do something, and do it quick. The solution came to me after I stepped over the downed mind-wipe with the busted ankles.

Broken legs are painful and debilitating. The mind-wipes may not feel pain, but I'd already proven that they couldn't stay upright with broken bones. I felt like shit for doing it, but it was the only way I could keep them alive while making certain they couldn't keep attacking me.

Brutal? Definitely. Necessary? Of course.

The tibia and fibula don't require as much effort to break as the femur does, which is why they are the most broken bone in the human leg. They also have the least amount of muscle go through to hurt them as well. It's why banging your shins on the coffee tables hurts so much. There's just not much there to protect them.

It's also fairly easy to break someone's leg when they're already on the ground.

I grabbed the nearest ankle of a felled foe and twisted as hard as I could while I delivered a stomp directly onto the upper part of the tibia. Combined with the pressure I'd put on it with the ankle grab, it splintered like a cheap piece of balsa wood. If he hadn't been unconscious and under the mind control of a psychotic killer, I'm sure that he would have screamed and passed out. So I guess he was fortunate to have skipped a step.

"You're avoiding the issue, Johnny," Baptiste's voice cut through the sound of flesh being pummeled. I wasn't fighting fair at this point. You don't fight fair if you were trying to stay alive. Legs were choice targets and Baptiste the Puppetmaster did not know quite how to counter the attacks. The guy knew how to play mind games, but physical confrontation without a huge advantage?

I could tell that he was stretched to the limits of his abilities while trying to control the remaining two mind-wipes who had yet to enter the fray.

His hesitancy allowed me to wreck the two poor bastards who had already attacked me. They went down hard and fast, both legs ruined. I felt a little guilty but I also knew that modern medicine could heal those broken bones inside of four days. It was painful for now, but it was far better than killing them. Even if they weren't precisely innocent.

Me? My body ached, my nose was bleeding again, I had a numb spot on my elbow and the top of my head was throbbing. To the victor, the spoils.

"Fine. Time to change the rules a bit."

"Wait...what are you doing?" I asked, confused as I watched the two men who had remained behind turn and look at the other. Baptiste clucked his tongue.

"You disappoint me, Johnny. I expected a little more out of you."

The two men grabbed each other by the throat and began to squeeze simultaneously. Both men were large and strong, and I could see the veins on their arms pop out from exertion as they tried to strangle one another. Neither fought back against the other, and both refused to let go. I realized what now what was going on.

Baptiste was making a point.

"Stop it," I told him. He chuckled.

"Stop what? This is what you wanted, since you refused to put them out of their misery for me," Baptiste said. He sounded convincing, but I knew he was full of it. He was toying with me.

The duo continued to strangle one another, their lips taking on a blue tint as their bodies began to suffer from oxygen deprivation. Still they hung on, controlled completely by Baptiste. I had to stop him before he made them kill each other.

"Catch-22, Johnny," Baptiste continued to mock me over the comm. "You do nothing and they kill each other, or you can kill them. Either way, I have determined that these two die. You get to choose how."

Damn it. I was out of options. Even with broken legs they could still strangle each other. Especially with Baptiste controlling them.

"Fine!" I shouted and threw my hands into the air. "I'll surrender if you stop them from killing each other."

The strangling paused. The two men remained motionless but they had loosened their grasps on one another.

"Surrender? What in the world makes you think that I want you to surrender?" Baptiste asked, his tone incredulous. "I have you precisely where I want you."

"Then why'd you stop them from strangling each other?"

"Well played, Johnny. Well played." Baptiste paused for a moment, the comm falling eerily silent. I thought that the connection had failed and was just about to turn the comm off when he spoke again. "But while you are quite a catch—you really are, you know—I already have a chew toy in your little pal Doctor Isaac. I don't need a little chewy Marine. No, Johnny, I want the real prize. The *grand* prize, so to speak. I want the traitor."

"Traitor?" I asked, confused. "What traitor?"

"That bastard Holomisa was given a gift unlike any the universe had ever seen and he *spat in my eye!*" Baptiste roared. "He betrayed his brothers for the sake of his precious honor!"

It may not have been evident before the prison break had begun, but it seemed pretty obvious now that Baptiste was the sort to hold a grudge.

"I have no idea where he is," I said. "Last I saw him, he was still in his cell." This was true, I hadn't seen him since things went south. The computer in Central said he was still in the cell, though I had never actually checked inside his cell to confirm what the computer told me. Still, the way things were going, I doubted that he would have escaped and made problems for us. Well, added to our growing list of problems, in any case. I could have checked my PDA but I wasn't sure if it was working properly. Things had gotten decidedly strange over the past few hours.

"*I know this!*" Baptiste fairly screamed at me. It took him a few moments to regain control of his composure, which told me quite a bit about his mental stability. In a nutshell? He was crazy, plain and simple. If it hadn't been obvious before, he was making certain everyone knew it now. After he had managed to rein in his heavy panting he continued. "I want you to track him down and eliminate him."

I laughed out loud. Probably wasn't the smartest thing I could have done, but I couldn't help it.

"You want me to kill the man who has broken out of more prisons and escaped more search parties than all of us combined on this station? The one guy who could kill me without me ever even knowing he was there until after the knife enters my spine?" I laughed some more. "Yeah, that's not going to happen."

"Then they die," Baptiste said and without a moment of hesitation the mind-wiped maintenance workers renewed their efforts to kill each other. I raised my hands in a defeated gesture.

"Fine! Just stop! I'll do it," I grudgingly agreed. I was still playing the role of the good guy, damn it. I needed to get that problem checked.

"As added motivation, I think I'll bring these two up to my playroom," Baptiste said in a silky voice. It was a tone which raised the pucker factor exponentially. "Now go and find the traitor. Kill him, and we'll talk about saving these two—as well as your precious little doctor."

"What guarantees do I have that you won't simply kill them when I'm done?" I asked.

"None," Baptiste replied, "but if you accomplish this, we can discuss your evacuation from the station. I can promise you that you will be in one piece and breathing, as long as you do as you're told."

He was lying. I knew that he was lying. He knew that I knew that he was lying. The problem, though? I did not want to be responsible for the deaths of the mind-wipes, or Doctor Isaac for that matter. Baptiste, the bastard, had factored all this into his plan. So he knew that even if I figured out that he was full of it, I would still struggle on in hopes of saving a few more lives. He knew me well enough by now and I him.

"Is he still in his cell?" I asked, stalling for time.

"I have no idea," Baptiste said. "You should go find out."

His cell was upstairs. Three levels. I glanced back at the ruined elevator, once more wondering if its destruction had been such a good idea after all. After a few more contemplative moments I decided that no, it wasn't.

Damn it. I hated those stairs like a Bostonian hated a New Yorker.

Kansas, by God. Flat, boring Kansas.

ᛘ

I managed the stairs without too much difficulty, all things considered. Yeah, I was wheezing like a spent race horse afterwards, and my ankles and knees had begun to throb painfully, but I made it up in one piece. That had to count for something.

Control was deserted, as expected. I tried to ignore the bodies of my fellow guards as best as I could but each one left a small hole in my soul. It was rough, but I couldn't afford to do anything for them at the moment. I limped painfully over to the control desk and looked over the screens. The display showed the Holomisa was still in his cell, thank God. I didn't have the energy to try and chase him down for Baptiste. I had a little niggling of doubt in the back of my mind that this was all an exercise in futility but damn it, I had to try. Wipes weren't exactly innocent but they were still human, and not whatever Baptiste had turned them into.

Even if that meant working with the villain.

I slid my index finger up on the desk and activated the door for Holomisa's cell. I walked over quickly, hand drifting down to my rifle I had managed to snag before I had run. I frowned at that. *Wait a second*, I thought as I watched the cell open up, *where did my big bag of boomies go?*

I thought back. I vaguely recalled having the bag when I was in the hangar, but after that it was a little murky. I tried to remember if I had had it when I stumbled into the Maintenance section by mistake but wasn't certain. Maybe I had dropped it?

Still, I had my Fullminster-Kurkai 25 high-velocity rifle and a few flash grenades, so I wasn't completely hosed. I had two magazines plus the one I had in the rifle, and that would normally be more than enough to ruin anyone's day. The aptly named FUKU-25's standard magazine replaced every fourth round with a high-explosive shell, which was very useful when you wanted to spread the hate amongst a group of targets. It was a tracer that would leave a smoking crater in its wake.

It was a fine weapon, though it didn't hold a candle to my beloved .50 caliber sniper rifle I'd used back on my own personal Hell, Soma.

I shook off the idle thought. Tired, beaten, and exhausted were a few words that could start to explain my wandering mind. I felt muzzy and heavy, like a shroud was over my head. I grunted as I recognized the sensation. I had a concussion. Provided I survived this, it would make my fourth documented one. Hooray for the marvels of modern medicine.

I brought the rifle up and peeked into the cell. I didn't want to kill him like this but it was the only way where I stood even a remote chance. In a straight head-to-head fight I was certain that Captain Holomisa would wreck me.

The achy feeling in the front and side of my head, remnants of the concussion, made my eyes water. I blinked and tried to shake off the sleepy feeling. It was starting to mess with me pretty bad. It took a few more tries before I could see clearly into the captain's cell. My eyes widened in shock.

The cell was empty.

"No," I whispered as I looked frantically around Control but there was no sign of Holomisa. The captain was gone, and there was nothing I could do. "Wait—the trackers..."

I looked at the screen, then Holomisa's cell, shook my head, and looked back at the screen. The tracker showed Holomisa in his clearly empty cell. I checked the other inmate's locations. All were where I had either left them dead, or, in Baptiste's case, where I knew he was camping. Hell, the damned thing even showed that the door to the captain's cell was closed. I slammed my fist down on the release in frustration, unable to hold back the barking laugh as nothing happened.

There was no way I was going to be able to save anyone now.

Holomisa had somehow pulled out his tracker and hid it within his cell, undoubtedly. The device normally would have alerted Control if someone had done such a thing but with the Things wrangling up the remaining civilians and everyone else dead, the alarm had probably gone unnoticed. Chaos like the prison break was a great cover to do one's dirty work.

I didn't see any blood, but that didn't mean anything at this point. Holomisa had gone through the same procedures that the eleven others had, so there was no reason to think that whatever change had occurred to them hadn't happened to him as well. After seeing Jou make himself twice as big and Gentry... I shivered at the memory of the convict. Hindsight seemed to make him scarier. I was glad that I had managed to put him down for good. That was one scary bastard.

Had Holomisa gone the rogue path? That was a terrifying thought.

A sudden wave of nausea overwhelmed me. I dropped to my knees and vomited bile, the bitter acid burning my throat and leaving a nasty aftertaste in my mouth. I let the rifle go and used my hands to keep from falling flat on my face. Once the heaving stopped, I tried to spit the last remnants of the bile from my mouth. The heavy sensation in my head had lessened a bit, but I was still feeling less than optimum. The concussion was starting to kick my ass in a major way.

I grabbed the FUKU and crawled back up to my feet shakily. I needed a new plan and I needed it quickly. I glanced back at the open cell door and cursed under my breath. I nearly gagged when the smell of dried blood and bile hit me. I'd almost forgotten about the bodies nearby.

What's this universe coming to?

I pressed my head against the cool plasteel and closed my eyes. I needed to think, to formulate, to try and get rid of the godforsaken headache that was ripping my skull apart. I focused on my breathing for long moments and tried to relax as best as I could. Tension aggravated my headaches in the past, and I figured that the reason doctors always told me to take it easy after suffering from a concussion was due to this. So I tried to erase every thought from my mind. I tried to envision nothing but darkness overwhelming everything. Not shadows, but something far deeper. Not covering, but eliminating. I tried to see nothing but darkness in my thoughts.

Most people don't realize this, but it's almost impossible to think about nothing. There has to be *something* in the mind, whether it's insignificant or not. The mind is always working.

Always projecting, and there is literally no way to turn it off. So a trick I learned a long time ago when I had trouble relaxing or even sleeping was to imagine empty space. No heat, no cold, just a conscienceless floating midst the vastness of a dark void.

It was here that the dreams usually came. This time, though, there was nothing. No ideas, no sense of direction. Nothing. Not even my subconscious was going to be able to bail me out of this mess. Not this time.

"Screw it," I muttered under my breath and opened my eyes. I pushed the familiar darkness away. If I was going out, I would at least make an effort to save Isaac and the two mind-wipes. If I was lucky, I would even find out where the Things disappeared to. I hadn't seen them up on the Observation Deck, so I was holding out hope that they had squirreled themselves away somewhere safe and were simply waiting for me to show up so we can get the hell out of here.

The light in Control was bright, but I needed my eyes open if I was going to have any shot at taking down Baptiste and saving everyone on the station. That included the mind-wipes, Thing One and Two, Doctor Isaac and even Captain Holomisa. I double-checked my rifle and made certain that my flash grenades were secure and in place.

Did I have a plan? No, not really. I had something that was almost as good.

I needed to go down to Research, confront Baptiste and kill him. Barring that, severely injured would work. Surviving would be an added bonus. I had a goal now, a mission, though not necessarily a plan. Whatever. This was going to have to do for now. I moved out of Control and down the hall. I paused as I realized something I had overlooked.

That meant taking the stairs again. I looked at the ruined elevator shaft and then the stairs. I shook my head. I was a complete moron. Yes, the boom had been immensely satisfying, at the time. Now? Not so much. I sighed and shoved open the door to the stairwell.

"Christ on a crutch…"

♃

I listened carefully at the door to Research, almost—but not quite—thankful that I had to descend the staircase. Had I been required to go up, I'm not sure I'd have heard anything over the pounding in my chest or the ragged breaths caused by my bruised and battered ribs. I turned the handle carefully, easing the door open just far enough to see the hall.

Clear.

This is playing hell with my nerves.

Checking what was left of the elevator, I saw the charges had performed as expected. The emergency brakes had kicked in fast enough to stop it just above the floor level, with only enough space to see the sparks coming from the blown-out panel through the smoke. It wouldn't be going anywhere, ever again. While I wasn't looking forward to humping any survivors up several flights of stairs to the shuttles, I couldn't repress a self-satisfied grin.

Excellent. Now all I have to do is stop the bad guy, rescue anyone still alive, and figure out how to call in the rescue team. Piece of cake.

The hall leading to the main research area was short and gave me a fairly open line of sight across the Well to the back wall. So far, so good. I kept the rifle level as I approached. I didn't know how many civilians had been taken, but based on the amount of gore upstairs, I wasn't expecting many. The smell, similar but weaker than in the staircase leading to observation, hit me after only a few steps. I stopped at the corner, mentally psyching myself up for what I'd find. A few deep breaths, a few seconds of pep talk, and I was ready. I stepped into the room.

I thought I was prepared for the worst. I was way off.

"Hello, John," Baptiste said, smiling. "I was hoping you'd drop by and spend some quality time with me." He stood, gently placing the arm in his hand on the counter next to him. "I do apologize about the mess, you caught me right in the middle of putting this little puzzle back together."

At his feet lay a collection of what seemed to be random body parts. Arms, legs, hands—two sets of each, by my count.

"You know, it is just so difficult at times to tell what goes where." Baptiste turned slightly, reaching behind him. "Especially when it comes to these two."

He faced me again, holding Poole's head in one hand, Lockhart's in the other, faces frozen in identical expressions of horror.

"Give up now, Baptiste, and I won't kill you," I said, my finger stroking the trigger. "I will put you down."

"Oh, John," Baptiste said, "That you think you can, I just— well, I find it adorable."

The rifle barked, three 10 mm slugs impacting the wall behind Baptiste.

"What the…" I missed. From less than ten meters away, *I missed.* The edge of my vision felt blurry, as though I had just woken up with a killer hangover. Blinking didn't help. The rifle muzzle swung left to center again on Baptiste's chest, the recoil of the next three shots causing it to rise slightly. A monitor died with a shower of sparks. *I missed again?*

"You see, John," Baptiste said, now meters closer and strolling towards me, "You can't hit what you can't perceive. And I can make you see what I want you to see." I blinked, and he was on my left again, against the far wall of the room. "Am I here?" My vision blurred, and he was closer, on my right side. "Or is it over here?"

I leveled the rifle, forcing myself to keep my eyes open. Baptiste shimmered, appearing to shift suddenly around the room.

"As much fun as this is, let's step it up a notch." His smile grew. "Are you even sure you're trying to kill the right person?" Another shimmer, and my rifle was pointed at Gerry. I hesitated, the muzzle wavering slightly.

"Why are you waiting, John, I thought you were a stone killer?" The voice was Gerry's, but the tone underneath was all Baptiste.

I pulled the trigger, another computer dying as Gerry disappeared.

"Oho! So not quite as fond of your old boss as you thought, eh?" I whipped around, just in time to see Gerry's image shift, April Voecks taking his place. "Maybe someone a little closer to your rung on the corporate ladder?" Her face took on a pleading look. "Please, John, I thought we were friends? I saved your life!"

"April died in my arms," I said. "I know it's you, Baptiste." Three more missed shots, and Baptiste's position changed again. I tracked him, squeezing the trigger as I moved, trying to focus on the blurry image before me.

It solidified, rocking slightly as the bullets struck. My heart caught in my throat.

Concy. I had just shot my dead wife.

Her features were filled with pain, blood streaming from the wounds in her chest. I dropped the rifle on its sling, anguish coursing through my body. I knew, deep in my mind, that it was just Baptiste playing another trick, but I couldn't stop the rush of emotion. I took a hesitant step in her direction.

"And, that, my dear John," Baptiste's voice came from directly behind me, "is why you will fail."

I felt myself heaved off of my feet, Concy fading out as I was slammed to the floor. The breath left my lungs as the rifle slammed into my kidneys, pain causing me to gag soundlessly for air. Baptiste's kick caught me square in the chest, the ceramic armor plate cracking at the impact. I slid backwards, unable to do anything but try and breathe, watching helplessly as he closed, flexing his fingers.

"Poor little Johnny," another plate cracked at his next kick. The impact felt like a .45 slug at close range. "You couldn't save them. Any of them. No matter how hard you fought and tried, it was beyond your level of skill."

Baptiste squatted down next to me, his face above mine. "Why do you think you were cashiered so quickly after Soma? You want to believe it was skill that saved you, but deep down, where you don't want to look, you know the truth. It was sheer luck. The Marines knew it. They could see you for what you really are—the boy playing war while all the grownups die around him. Too many old action movies and adventure books gave you a false sense of manhood."

I couldn't help myself, flinching as his hand stretched out to tousle my hair, hating myself for giving him some satisfaction. "See? The scared child never strays too far from the surface."

I drew in a ragged breath, finally able to get my wind back.

"Fuck you, Baptiste."

"Profanity is the first resource of the immature, my dear boy. You should really work on your vocabulary." A sharp slap across my cheek, faster than I could follow, bounced my skull of the floor. "Normally, I'd wash your mouth out with soap, but that will have to do for now."

"You realize you're not getting off this station, right?" I coughed, body complaining with every motion. "The U.N. knows about the breakout, and will only allow those shuttles to leave with the correct codes." I jerked my chin at the remains of Thing One and Two. "And you killed the only two guys that had them."

"Oh, Johnny." Stars exploded in my eyes with the next slap. "That's for lying. I know those codes are firmly nestled in your little jar head. Getting them out is going to be sooo much fun."

He lifted me up again, handling my body weight and assorted gear like it was nothing, the straps of the body armor biting into my armpits as he raised me with one hand. I went for a pistol, only to have Baptiste lock my wrist in an iron grip.

"Johnny, Johnny, Johnny… When will you learn? You're beaten. I'm faster, stronger and smarter." To prove his point, he forced my hand, pistol and all up and out, the muzzle aiming at a point somewhere over his shoulder. Before I could stop him, the butt of the gun cracked into my temple. "Now, stop this foolishness before I'm forced to really hurt you."

He squeezed, the tendons and bones in my wrist creaking at the sudden pressure. The pistol fell from nerveless fingers, clattering to the floor before Baptiste kicked it away. Still holding me aloft, the former prisoner stripped me of every weapon I had, tossing hardware around the room as he found it.

"Now that you're sufficiently harmless, let's have a chat." With a sudden move, Baptiste hit me with a rabbit punch, his fist angling up under the body armor to catch my side. I felt a rib go, the sharp pain causing me to gasp. "I pulled that one, Johnny. Can't have you dying on me just yet."

I struggled to breathe as he dropped me into a chair, pulling up another and reversing it to sit with his arms crossed over the back. He didn't even bother tying me up. There was no need. I was a beaten man. It hurt to breathe, much less try to make a break for it. I knew it, and Baptiste knew it. He smiled sardonically.

"I grew up in a small, rural town in Indiana," Baptiste said as he gently touched the side of my cheek. The touch, light as a feather, opened the skin. He looked at his sharpened claw and frowned.

"Oops. I am so very sorry about that. Anyway, in this tiny, redneck town there was absolutely nothing for a kid to do."

"Great," I growled, blood trickling slowly down my face, collecting in a drop at my jawline. My entire body let me know how it felt about the beating I had taken. I told myself I still had some fight in there, somewhere, because Marine, dammit. Granted, that could have been the blood loss and traumatic head injury talking. "You're just another psychopath who blames all his problems and everything he's done on his fucked up childhood."

"I'm surprised that you would think that, John—I can call you John, right? I mean, we're practically blood brothers now, considering how much of yours is all over me." Baptiste shook his head. "Sadly, I have no one to blame for the way I am but myself. I decided my actions, and this is the result. I have to be frank with you, though. I used to think that maybe I'd done wrong, that perhaps this prison was my punishment for all the crimes I've committed. Now? Well, now I'm rethinking that assessment. Perhaps this isn't so much of a punishment as it is a reward."

"Lunatic."

"What was I talking about again... Oh, that's right." Baptiste nodded and leaned away. His eyes, molten puddles of red filled with insanity, were lost in memories past; his voice a hushed, almost reverent whisper. "This town, there was nothing to do at all for the teens as we got older. Sure, there was little league and soccer for the young kids, but once you hit high school, unless you made one of the few sports teams, there was little else to do. So the kids had three option: get drunk, get high, or get laid. Oddly enough, my hometown had a high teenage pregnancy and high school dropout rate. Strange, right? Nobody could figure it out why fourteen and fifteen year olds kept getting knocked up. The strangest damn thing.

"Then one day a new business opened up. It was amazing, this new place. It was a place where the teens could hang out and not get chased off by cops. It wasn't anything special, really. Just a pool hall with some retro videogames in it. But it was *something*, and naturally kids flocked to it. For a time, the parents in town were happy. No longer were their kids out doing stupid things.

"This 'peace,' for lack of a better word, lasted for about a year. Then the drug dealers noticed that their clientele had moved, and followed suit. Soon enough, drugs were being sold out of the pool hall and police began to patrol. Parents were angry—not at their kids, though. Oh no. That would have made sense. No, they were angry at the pool hall. They wanted it shut down, so they tried to revoke the business license. That failed because the business brought in money for the town, money that was much needed, since there was little else there for the small town to tax.

"One night, an angry father of a girl who had gotten pregnant and eventually dropped out of high school torched the place. Burned it right to the ground, no muss, no fuss. Police investigated and, even though everyone knew who did it, there wasn't enough evidence to bring him up on charges. Other parents covered for him, saying that he had been nowhere near the fire. So the owners of the pool hall collected their fat insurance check and were given two options: build elsewhere, or risk more accidents.

"They took the risk and rebuilt. Now the pool hall had even swankier games and had enough money to hire an off-duty police officer to guard the place to chase away the drug dealers. Unsurprisingly, this worked, and the pool hall was safe again. Well, safe from the criminals. Safe from concerned parents who thought that this blight on their precious community should leave permanently? Safe from concerned citizens who blamed their own poor parenting skills on something else? Well, that was a different matter altogether.

"It was little things at first. Tires on a car being slashed or having the air let out of them, threatening messages on their voicemail, graffiti on the walls of the hall. But the owners were convinced that they were doing a good thing and pressed on, trying to keep their business open. Petitions were started, online hate campaigns pressed forward, and for the owners it was as if they were running a pornography den out of the basement of a church.

They were hated by the parents, no matter how much the kids like them.

"Then the place was burned for a second time. Completely scorched, nothing saved. The volunteer fire department, for reasons unknown, were a bit slow in responding to the fire. The subtle message was obvious to any and all. This time the owners packed up and left. There was no insurance check this time, since the insurer had figured out by now that it was going to continue to happen. Poor, destitute and hated by all, the owners never looked back. And the proper people in the town rejoiced, because now things can get back to the way they were before. The teens slid back into old habits, and once more the parents were left blaming society for their own misdeeds. The circle of human life. So sad, so cruel, so absolutely pathetic."

"What…has that to do with this?" I jerked my chin at the bodies around us. "You think that's some sort of good reason to murder innocents?"

"Them? Your so-called innocents? No, John. They're the little things. Ah. I see confusion on your face. Well then, let me explain it to you in easier terms then. After all, you're just a simple Marine," Baptiste hissed through his pointed teeth, his hot breath on my forehead as he leaned in closer. "This planet? A small, boring redneck town for your beloved kraken. This station? This…*prison*? This is the pool hall. The kraken that seem to follow your every move and move freely about? Those are the fourteen and fifteen year olds of their species. All that we're missing is the angry parents, no?"

The entire station tremored slightly, causing my blood to run cold. A distant thunder reverberated throughout the supposed indestructible structure.

"Ah, it seems I've struck a nerve," Baptiste said, grinning. "Someone's getting a little worked up."

My heart raced as adrenaline poured into my system, realization dawning on me.

Psyops. An almost forgotten detail of his bio came to the front of my mind. As an officer, he'd run psyops in one of the wars. Whatever it was had apparently been bad enough to cost him his commission. The lack of details in his court martial, combined with the catch all 'conduct unbecoming' made me think it was something the military didn't want to make public.

Baptiste wasn't done with me yet. He wanted to drive the fear into the mind of a man who had already survived Hell once. He wanted to break me, and in doing so, break the Kraken. That's why he needed me alive. The empathic link was stronger than it was with anyone else, and the resulting backlash would cripple their morale.

Why, though? Why did he have a need to harm an alien species that, for all intents and purposes, was harmless? What made him want to kill the very species which had helped the scientists make him into... whatever he was? The many questions and complete lack of answers made my head spin.

Baptiste's mocking, evil smile was wide upon his elongated face. He grabbed my chin, forcing me to look him in the eye. That's when I felt it. Pressure at the front of my skull, rapidly increasing to a throbbing pain. It felt like my head was trapped in vice, and Baptiste was slowly turning the screw. Those red eyes bored into mine, the brightness fading as my vision grew dark. Through the ringing in my ears, I could just make out his voice, harsh as steel wool on sheet metal. Another tremor seemed to shake the entire station.

"Daddy's here...and he's ready to burn this fucking place to the ground."

Baptiste was crazy, that much was obvious. What his little monologue meant was lost on me. I wasn't, however, in any position to critique his style, so I kept my mouth shut. Besides, had I said anything, he may have decided to write a dissertation.

On my chest. With a rusty spoon

Darkness consumed me, penetrating my brain, extinguishing any thoughts of resistance. I couldn't beat him, there was no point in trying. Everything I had gone through—Hell week, mission after mission against difficult odds, Soma—everything in my life leading up to this moment meant nothing. I wasn't strong enough to fight Baptiste. There was no hope, I wasn't getting out of this. I needed to just let go, give in, and give up.

A bright flash of pain, a small white light in the overwhelming black cloud, flared behind my eyes, growing steadily brighter and larger as it became a familiar figure.

"You're not done yet, John," Concy said, a fierce smile dominating her features. "I didn't fall in love with a man that would just quit."

A sudden wave of hope washed over me, flowing from the fiery form of my dead wife, growing stronger as her light grew brighter. Her voice echoed in my head, joined by every drill sergeant and NCO I'd ever met.

"Get up, Marine!"

The other voice, formerly seductive and quiet, transformed into a grating parody of itself.

"There's no point, give in, don't listen!"

My vision slowly came back, the desperation fading as it was replaced with grim determination and something else. Anger. I felt my jaw clench as I looked Baptiste in the eye, spitting my words through gritted teeth.

"Get. Out. Of. My. Head!"

The fire in my mind grew blinding, burning out the darkness surrounding it. Baptiste rocked back, as though hit by a lead truncheon, releasing his grip on my chin.

I followed through with a sharp head-butt, the heavy bone of my forehead smashing into his nose with as much force as I could throw behind it. Adrenaline and fear forced away the various pains in my body, giving me the strength to surge forward and land a vicious uppercut. Both feet slamming into his chair sent him toppling over, the sound of his skull striking the floor giving me a grim satisfaction. I jumped up, using the momentum to deliver a snap kick to his temple on my way past.

He wouldn't stay down for long, if Jou and Gentry were any indication. I needed to get clear and regroup. I took a very quick assessment of my gear. The pistols were, for all intents and purposes, gone, thrown who knew where. Seconds mattered, and I didn't have time to crawling around looking for them. My pack was close though, and—Thank you God—the rifle was on my way out. I grabbed the pack and bolted for the door, scooping the carbine up on the run.

"Ohhh, Johhhhhnnny…" Baptiste's moan reminded me of the disappointed tone my mom gave me, "That was not a very nice thing to do."

He spasmed as the two rounds hit him high in the chest, the elation I felt only momentary as the wounds began closing almost immediately. I turned and ran towards the stairs, pulling the pin on a flashbang and tossing it over my shoulder as a parting gift.

I needed to play to my strengths, not his. A straight up fight was out, I couldn't take the chance on his mind mojo screwing with me again. Whatever I had done in retaliation…well, I didn't know how I'd done it, much less how to do it again.

I took the stairs down two and three at a time, trying to get as much distance between Baptiste and myself.

"Johnny…" Baptiste's voice floated down the stairwell followed by his laugh, the chilling sound fading into echoes in my head. "Run, Johnny, like the scared little boy you are."

Ignoring him as best I could, I kept running, my abused ribs starting to complain. Not to be outdone, everything else decided to chime in as well. I ground my teeth together and kept going. Control might not be ideal as an ambush location, but it did give me a few more options. A few more flights and I'd be there.

"What do think you can accomplish, Johnny? You know you can't save yourself." Baptiste's voice came directly into my head, the scrape of dead tree branches on a window. "You've failed everyone, Johnny, it's what you're good at." He fell silent, the sound of my steps and pained gasps filling the void. "I sometimes wonder what that's like. The feeling that no matter what, everything you do is futile. Tell me, Johnny, do get so used to it, that you just become numb? Or is it more comforting? Do you embrace it?" Another pause. "Do you lie awake at night, going over every poor life decision you've made, looking for the one place that you can say 'Aha! That's where I really fucked up!' or is it more of a continuous loop of abject failure after abject failure? Serious question, really. I've never failed consistently, so I'm genuinely curious."

I didn't know if my thoughts would pinpoint my location, so I kept a tight rein on them. It was tempting to engage, spit back insults and bravado, but I knew that would only give him more to work with. Didn't mean his taunts weren't effective or distracting, though. It took everything I had to keep focused.

But dear lord, he knew exactly where to hit me hardest. My sense of duty. My feelings of inadequacy. My survivor's guilt. Each snarky comment felt like a jab to the gut. I needed a distraction.

It occurred to me that he could read my mind, or at least pick bits here and there if they were fairly fresh. It explained why he could pull up April, Gerry, and especially Concy's images and make them seem so damn life like. Hm. Vivid scenes...distracting... A slow grin spread across my mug.

Oh, motherfucker, just wait to see what I have in mind.

In space, even the short trips take days to weeks. What a company of Marines can find on the net with that much time on their hands and no one to kill? It sticks with you. Especially the really disturbing stuff.

I started with the pictures someone had found involving two dudes, a basket of exotic fruit, and a gallon of motor oil. After that, I moved on to the video of the German ladies and the model train set. The fully functional model train set. Some things just can't be unseen.

You know that feeling you get when someone is staring at you, but you can't see them? That's what Baptiste's reaction felt like, but instead of the hair on my neck standing up, a subtle wave of queasiness worked its way through my gut. I grinned and sent another image his way.

"Jesus, John. And I thought I had issues."

The mental slideshow wasn't just to tweak his tail, it had another purpose. I could let my mind focus on the images while letting my hands work without thought. I wrapped the paracord twice around one flashbang, tying the spoon loosely to the body, repeating the process with the other end of the cord. A little duct tape on the door jamb in a few places, and I had what I hoped was a decent booby trap. I pulled the pins and moved to the hallway across the room.

With any luck, Baptiste would hit the tripwire, the paracord would release, and both grenades would go off right at eye level.

Bonus points if they did enough damage to put him down. I'd settle for disorientation and terrible disfigurement, though.

The hard part would be not thinking about the trap or what I hoped to do when he showed. I thought hard about one of the tamer things I'd seen, a XXX recreation of Snow White, from a German film company. I mean, really, where the hell do you find not just one, but seven midget pornstars? An ad in *Der Spiegel*?

I checked the magazine on the carbine, making sure the armor piercing rounds were in place. I didn't want to take the chance he'd hardened up after the last go round. I drew a bead on the doorway and waited, ears straining for any sound that would give him away. Fortunately, the onslaught of images I had in my head seemed to have shut him up for a while, if not shut him out.

The scuff of a shoe on the hallway floor brought my heartrate up. I took several slow, deep breaths to get it back under control, fighting the adrenaline shot that rushed through my veins. Baptiste's voice floated towards me, almost more terrifying in my ears than it had been in my head.

"Johnny, I know you are a stubborn bastard, but this is getting…well, silly is a good word. You can't beat me in a fight. What is that saying the snipers are all so fond of?" More footsteps, closer this time. He still wasn't visible, but I figured he was about five to ten meters from the door. "Oh, now I remember. 'Go ahead and run, you'll just die tired.' Aren't you tired, Johnny? You've been very busy today."

A wave of exhaustion rolled over me, accompanied by blurriness at the corner of my sight. It was difficult to determine if it was Baptiste playing Jedi mind tricks again, actual fatigue and damage, or some horrible combination of both. I shook my head, ramping up the porno images. As I recalled, in exquisite detail, the American-made live action tentacle Hentai one of the Corpsmen had shown us, my vision cleared. The bone deep physical weariness stayed, but that was something I'd fought through my whole career. It was surmountable, and oddly comforting. A familiar obstacle that I'd overcome before, as opposed to all the weird new shit I'd been dealing with the last few weeks.

"Come on, Johnny, you're just delaying the inevitable here. The old cliché of the lone badass, surviving against all odds is just that—a cliché." A shadow, cast from one of the flickering emergency lights, stretched into view. Even taking into consideration the distortion of the light, what was coming was only vaguely human shaped. His voice had changed, as well, becoming more sibilant, as though he were trying to speak through a mouthful of teeth. I suppressed a shudder as he continued, "I get it though, really I do. You jarheads love to see yourselves as the ultimate warriors, the one flare of light blazing defiantly into the overwhelming tide of darkness. It's admirable. Stupid, but admirable." He stepped into my line of sight.

"Semper Fi, Motherfucker." I pulled the trigger.

Bullets tore through his chest, a three round burst that made him stagger slightly. He recovered quickly, snarling as he sprinted forward, hands elongating into talons as he moved. I put another burst into him to keep him focused on me, and not the path in front of him. I threw my arm over my eyes as he hit the tripwire.

The concussion caused me to lose my balance briefly, precious seconds wasted as I stumbled and caught myself. I regained my balance, opening my eyes to get a fix on Baptiste.

While not the best-case scenario, the grenades had done some damage. Baptiste clawed at his face, tearing strips of flaming skin from his skull as he lurched towards my position. I took advantage of his disorientation, firing as quickly as possible, putting round after round into his torso as he closed. The sound of a thousand nails scratching across blackboards erupted from his throat, giving voice to his pain and frustration.

Damn, but even as damaged as he was, Baptiste could still move.

"For Christ's sake," I couldn't keep the exasperation from my voice, "Would you just die already?" I pulled the trigger frantically as his enraged form got within arm's reach.

Nothing. Magazine empty.

Baptiste's laugh of defiance filled the room as his claws slid around my throat.

"It's time to end this, Johnny," he said, grip tightening. The now familiar black veil appeared at the edge my vision. "I have grown tired of your games. You have two options: tell me the codes, and I'll make this quick. Or you can try to continue to play the hero and I'll drag them out of you inch by agonizingly slow inch." He moved his other hand to my ribs, applying gentle pressure to the tender spot, grinning as I winced involuntarily. "Ever peeled an onion, Johnny?"

It took everything I had to keep the scream inside as his talon slid through my shirt and into the top layer of skin, the sharp claw paring away a strip of flesh and cloth. He held the piece of bloody meat in front of my eyes before slowly bringing it to his mouth.

"Mmm…tastes like pork rinds." As he chewed, the seared portion of his face began to heal, charred and blackened pieces sloughing away to reveal raw pink tissue. "A quick history lesson for you, Johnny. Did you know that flaying has long been a tradition in human culture? Extremely versatile, and useful." Another sharp pain, followed by a tearing sensation. "Oh my, I seemed to have been clumsy with that one." Another piece of me went between his jaws. "As a warning, there's nothing like leaving the face of a thief or a political enemy on the door to deter others. As a method of torture? I'd say it's in the top three." Another slice, another strip of my skin dangling in front of my face.

"Did you want a nibble? No? More for me, then." Around his latest morsel, Baptiste kept talking. "The average human could stay alive for anything from hours to days while being flayed. It all depends on shock and blood loss, really." His face grew thoughtful. "I say you would probably make it at least twenty-four hours."

Through the white fire of pain in my side, I could feel Baptiste trying to force his way in again. I tried fighting back, grinding my teeth while focusing on building a mental barrier, to no avail. It was too hard to concentrate while his fingers and mind violated me.

It would be so easy to just let go, I thought, give him what he wants and make the pain stop. I could be with Concy again, for all time. All I'd have to do is tell him what he wants.

"That's it, John," Baptiste's voice became a seductive purr. "Just let go of your pride, your stubbornness. It's only making this last longer."

Something caught my eye through the haze of pain. Kraken lined the windows, as many as I'd ever seen in one place, with still more joining them. I glanced quickly at the large methane filled tubes, surprised to see them packed with the ray-like creatures. Hope washed over me, a gentle blanket of calm with a thread of defiance running through it.

It hit me. The kraken were using their empathic abilities to bolster my resolve, sending me wave upon wave of positive reinforcement to counteract Baptiste's assault on my mind.

Baptiste picked up on it as well, his wrecked face registering mild surprise at the passive resistance.

"Oh? So this is where your defense is coming from, is it?" He turned his head, slowly regarding the aliens. "Interesting. I wasn't aware the smaller ones were that strong." Grip remaining firm, he closed his eyes. I could feel the pressure on my mind shifting, still present, but focused on something else. "I've wondered, you know, if I could…"

Muted pain knifed through my brain, the psychic wake of a mental torpedo as it surged toward another target. Several kraken fell away from their position on the window, plummeting into the depths.

"That was…strangely satisfying." A grin spread across his face. "Let's do it again." Another ripple of psychic force, and another kraken plummeted. I swear, if he could clap his hands together, he would. With sniper-like precision, Baptiste sent Kraken after Kraken into the abyss before turning back to me.

"Do I have your attention now, big guy?" He called out. Yeah, he was crazy. Pretty sure that's been established. "Well, that was fun, but I really should finish what I started. Okay, maybe just one more." Another Kraken writhed in agony as it fell away. He guffawed. "Now, where were we?"

"You were about to let me go, and commit seppuku?" It was worth a shot.

"Ah, right—the access codes." The pressure on my mind came back, a wrecking ball slamming into my head, breaking through what little resistance I had. The Kraken's defensive shield crumbled under the assault, leaving me open to Baptiste's will.

"And there we are." The self-satisfied smirk on Baptiste's face didn't give much insight into how much time I had left. Could be minutes, could be days. Either way, there was no doubt that I was in for a boatload of excruciating pain.

"Since we have some time left together, Johnny, let's experiment a little." The mental fingers poked inside my head some more. "… No, not there…maybe over… Hm. Ah!" Like he had flipped a switch, the pain in my body disappeared. Not that it did me much good, I was still firmly in his grasp. "Now, what if I do…"

I went numb. Not just the absence of pain type of numb, but 'My foot's asleep and I can't feel it or walk' kind of numb. Baptiste released his hold on my neck. I remained upright for about half a second before slumping to the floor in a heap.

"This power is truly amazing, Johnny. Frankly, I'm giddy with excitement. All this potential." The prisoner hunkered down next to me, resting his chin on a palm. "Just think—in a few weeks, I'll be anywhere I want to be, getting anything I ever wanted or dreamed about. Now there's a thought—what do you think about a few hundred kids, some mini-me's running around in about ten years? Introduce this little genetic quirk of mine into the gene pool. A few generations from now, and I'll have a loyal army of supreme beings, all willing to do whatever they want. Homo Sapiens Sapiens would be supplanted as the dominant species. Homo Sapiens Baptiste, the new masters of destiny." He paused, a twisted grin dominating his features. "The name may need some work, but you get the idea."

The ghost fingers brushed across my mind again, and I felt the numbness recede. Not that it did me much good. You know that recovery period between your foot falling asleep and the ability to walk on it? Now imagine that, but all over. Warmth spread up from my toes to my knees as the feeling came back, intensifying as the seconds passed.

"How about those codes, Johnny?" Baptiste raised an eyebrow as pain erupted in my lower extremities. "I can do this all day, and night, and the next day…" Another twitch in my skull, and I could use my vocal cords again.

"Eat…shit…asshole…" It felt like my feet had been held in boiling oil, and the sensation was spreading.

"Hmm…." Baptiste said, tapping a finger on his chin. "Pain isn't much of a motivator, it seems. Must be that hero worship we discussed earlier. I was hoping I wouldn't have to do this again, but, well, you leave me no choice."

The two remaining maintenance men marched into the room, stopping at crisp attention directly in front of me, each holding a pistol. The pain in my legs disappeared as suddenly as it had come.

"So here we are again, John, someone's life in your hands. You remember what I can do, right?" At his words, the two men began to dance again, each placing his hands on his shoulders, forearms crossed at the chest before moving them behind their head. The prisoners dropped their hands to the opposite hip, again crossing their forearms, grabbed their ass and jumped. Behind them Kraken performed an intricate sequence of perfectly synchronized maneuvers, rings of the manta-like creatures weaving in and out of each other in time to Baptiste's hand motions. "Just tell me the launch codes for the shuttles, and they stay alive a bit longer."

The two mind-wiped prisoners raised their guns to their temples.

"Oh," Baptiste continued, "I found your pet scientist as well. He's currently holding a scalpel to his throat, just waiting for me to give him the word."

I could wiggle my toes, but that was about it. Nothing else on my body was responding to my will. Granted, Baptiste had me dead to rights, even if I could move. The rifle was technically within reach, but for all intents and purposes, might have well been on a different planet. To make things worse, I had no way of knowing if the lunatic was bluffing about Isaac. I could probably justify letting the mind wipes die, for the short amount of time I had left, but knowing that I sacrificed the scientist?

Shit.

"You win, Baptiste." The bitter words practically gagged me as they left my mouth. "You win. I'll give you the codes."

"I'm listening…"

God help me, I gave him the codes. I hated doing it, but the thought of being responsible for the deaths of the mind-wipes was too much. I had to, and I hated myself for it.

"That wasn't so bad, now, was it?" Baptiste said, smiling.

Twin gunshots rang out in the room, each mind controlled man's brains painting the other's skull with pink gore.

"Goddammit, Baptiste! We had a deal!"

"True, we did. You were to locate Holomisa for me. You failed to do so." False pity morphed his features into a parody of a sad puppy look. "This is all your fault, I'm afraid."

Deep down, I knew he wasn't going to let those men live, but there had been a glimmer of hope. That glimmer disappeared in a wave of guilt and fear. I looked over Baptiste's shoulder to the window. The kraken had mostly disappeared, either driven away by Baptiste's command, or scared off by his demonstration of cruelty and mental powers. *Can't say I blame them.*

"That's enough, Baptiste."

The voice came from behind me, in the vicinity of the open cells. Apparently, it had shocked Baptiste enough to release his hold on me partially— the pain lessened slightly, allowing me to roll my neck around, and get a better look. I blinked, hard, trying to clear the blurriness at the edge of my vision, not trusting my eyes.

Captain Emery Holomisa faded into view, seemingly coalescing from thin air as I stared at what had been a previously-empty spot in the cell.

"You want me," he said, "You got me."

CHAPTER THIRTEEN

The more I know about people, the better I like my dog
-Mark Twain

The former captain strode forward, stretching and rolling his shoulders. A panther uncoiling from a nap, he exuded casual grace as he moved, weight naturally on the balls of his feet, each step measured and careful. In comparison to his clean-shaven and groomed appearance, Baptiste looked like twenty miles of bad country road; I looked like something that had wandered in front of the car.

"Now's your chance, Baptiste." Holomisa brought his hands in front of him, one curled into a fist, the other, palm open and perpendicular to the floor. "You talk a big game. Can you back it up?"

Baptiste's grin, frightening before, took the number one slot for my nightmares as it stretched across his face. Moving like a heavyweight champ, he reached in between his shoulder blades with one hand, then the other, before bringing both hands into a chin-level guard position. He bounced slightly, shifting from one foot to the other in rapid succession.

Holomisa's breathing slowed—long deep breaths making his chest swell twice its size. He began an intricately paced series of hand motions.

The two men closed, measuring each other. Baptiste feinted, a pulled left jab that came nowhere near Holomisa, before a quick uppercut sought the other man's chin. Holomisa didn't look surprised, watching as the fist occupied the space his head had been only moments before, the motion becoming part of an open-handed strike to Baptiste's Adam's apple.

Baptiste rocked back, gagging, shaking off a blow that would have crippled a normal man. He recovered quickly, anger flashing in his eyes as Holomisa began weaving his hands in front of him, still breathing slow and deep. Baptiste advanced, more carefully this time, keeping his elbows together, fists in front of his nose.

Holomisa's hands stopped for a split second, seemingly leaving him wide open. Baptiste took the opportunity, throwing a jab towards the other man's chin, following it with a hard right hook to the torso. Holomisa's hands were flickers as he deflected both punches, redirecting the energy with graceful ease before lashing out with his foot. Baptiste staggered, breath leaving at the force of the kick to his stomach, doubling over slightly as he fought to regain his balance. Holomisa followed through with a heel to the temple.

The shot broke Baptiste's concentration, causing him to lose his hold on my brain. The agonizing pain left me, as though a switch had been flipped. I slumped, drained.

Holomisa pressed his attack, two quick steps leading to a flurry of punches. Starting at the other man's solar plexus, Holomisa worked his way up, finishing at the chin with a spinning elbow. He continued the movement while setting his feet, before grabbing Baptiste by the arm and heaving with a grunt of exertion. The look of shock on the monstrous prisoner's face as he found himself airborne was almost worth the pain I felt.

Almost. I still hurt. A lot. Moving was the last thing I wanted to do, but the thought of being close enough to catch a badly aimed punch or kick gave me a good incentive to try.

The agony of trying gave me all the incentive I needed to stop.

Holomisa closed again, trying not to give Baptiste time to recover. Unfortunately, he was a fraction of a second too slow, the next strike whistling as it passed Baptiste's ear.

Baptiste rolled, gaining his feet and deflecting Holomisa's kicks with crossed forearms, before stepping in and throwing his weight into a head butt. The muffled crack of bone as his forehead connected with Holomisa's was loud in the relative silence of the room.

The captain, slightly stunned at the sudden move, but still functional, turned his stagger into a sidestep, narrowly avoiding Baptiste's wide haymaker that would have taken his head off if it had connected. He sidestepped again, allowing Baptiste's momentum to carry him out of reach and giving him room to breathe. Holomisa shook his head before returning to his relaxed ready position.

"You lack discipline, Baptiste, counting on brute strength and dumb luck to carry you through." Holomisa watched the other prisoner as he slowly circled, his steps bringing his back into my line of sight. "That and what you think is unpredictable behavior."

From my angle, it was difficult to see exactly what Baptiste tried—all I saw was Holomisa's lightning fast blocks and redirects. He didn't press, though, allowing the other man to exert himself with no reward. Holomisa was on the defensive, trying to keep himself between me and Baptiste.

I needed to move, soon, or risk becoming a weakness in the captain's strategy. That, and I couldn't expect Holomisa to finish this on his own. I'm all for a fair fight when needed, but there was no need for one today. I just had to wait until Baptiste was completely focused on his adversary.

Holomisa turned his head slightly and gave a small nod.

"I'm not even breathing hard, Lieutenant," he said. "I knew you Navy spooks were soft, I just never thought you were *that* soft."

I don't think the sound Baptiste made could be replicated by any other living animal. At least not something native to Earth. He launched himself towards Holomisa, arms wide, fingers extended into claws. His face, still in its nightmare form, morphed and distended as his emotions played themselves out on the canvas of his skull.

Holomisa moved, flowing under and to the side of the leaping prisoner, hardly exerting himself as he grabbed an arm. The motion turned into a spin, launching the other man to the far side of the room.

Baptiste seemed ready for it this time, or at least able to adapt faster, turning in midair to land on his feet, facing away from me.

I took the opportunity to test the limits of my mobility, making it about six inches before I had to stop. Any effort to support myself was met with violent shakes and a massive spike in pain. Whatever Baptiste had done in my head was still lingering. I needed more time.

"You're weak, Baptiste," Holomisa said, walking forward as the other man spun around. "Always have been. You give in to the darkness because it's easy." He dodged a swipe, easily dancing to the side and landing a jab on Baptiste's chin. "You see power as a way to produce fear." Another jab. "Men like you always want the control, but not the responsibility that comes with it. That takes work," he punctuated the word with a right cross, "strength," -left hook- "and hardship." He finished with a quick right-left combo, knocking Baptiste back a step. "You don't have what it takes."

Holomisa sounded like a fucking Jedi. I would have loudly approved except, well, the pain. I did manage to gurgle out something that may have sounded like 'Woo hoo,' if you listened closely.

Baptiste grunted as he took two solid body shots, one to each kidney. Holomisa may be the more honorable man, but it didn't mean he fought by the Marquis de Queensbury rules, it seemed. Baptiste swung, a haymaker that could have taken Holomisa's head off had it connected, leaving him open for another punch to the torso. I heard bones crack, audible even over the sounds of the fight. Baptiste recovered quickly though, catching the captain unaware, and scoring a nasty gash to Holomisa's side. It was only the captain's reflexes that saved him—a split second slower, and he'd have been gutted. Baptiste smiled, long tongue flicking over his fingers.

"You taste good, Captain." He continued to lick the blood from his hand, appearing to savor each drop. "You have a lot of heart." Baptiste brought his hand down sharply, the remaining blood splattering on the floor. "I can't wait to eat it."

Holomisa's face became hard as the wound closed.

"Do your worst, Lieutenant." He stepped forward, features set in grim determination. "I doubt it will be good enough."

I became enraptured in the conflict. Granted, there wasn't much else I could do—any attempt at movement sent spasms through my legs, and my arms were damn near unresponsive. I took several breaths, as deep as I could make them, mentally and physically preparing myself for one last ditch effort.

Baptiste, even after all the punishment I had dished out, and on top of everything he was getting from Holomisa, was still fast, strong, and extremely deadly.

However, if Baptiste was fast, Holomisa moved like Mercury. Quicksilver strikes flowed into each other, making it difficult to determine where one ended, and the next began. I had only seen a fighter move like that in old Kung Fu movies. It was mesmerizing.

A feral howl of frustration and pain erupted from Baptiste as another of his punches failed to connect. Holomisa's kick cut the sound short as it slammed into Baptiste's lower jaw, knocking the lunatic backwards. He held the pose, one foot extended at eye level, both fists even with his hips, for about three seconds before lowering his leg slowly.

"Control should be exercised by a leader on himself before it will be accepted by his subordinates." Holomisa was barely breathing hard. "Trying to control those around you, but not yourself, is the sign of someone who fears losing it. This is why you will fail, Baptiste."

He watched with Zen-like calm as Baptiste caught his balance, shifted slightly, and rushed. Talons hissed through the air, narrowly missing the captain's face and ribs as Holomisa danced out of reach. He was slowing down, though. A minor hesitation allowed Baptiste to counter a strike, opening up an opportunity to land a solid shot to the wounded side. Holomisa's face paled briefly, before launching into a furious attack, hands and feet blurring into a kaleidoscope of motion. For every strike Baptiste blocked, two more made their way past his defenses. In desperation, Baptiste grabbed the other man, pulling him forward as he brought his forehead down. The impact bought him some space and time, allowing him to take a step back.

The ferocity of the assault had taken its toll—both men were gasping for air as they broke contact.

"I don't understand you, Holomisa," Baptiste's words were labored, separated by short wheezing sounds. "What has anyone done for you in this life that demands your loyalty?"

"It's a concept you can't grasp. Honor." He moved, watching the other man carefully. "You lack honor, Baptiste. You only see people as a means to an end, a tool to get what you want. It's why your men hated you, your superiors hated you, and no one trusted you."

"You've got a point, old man. I do have issues with 'honor.' It's what allows me to do whatever it takes to win." That nightmare grin reappeared. "Like this!"

Holomisa had misjudged his opponent slightly, allowing Baptiste enough room to maneuver. With a large step, he moved towards the closest desk, grabbing it under one end and heaving in one smooth motion. It flew in the captain's direction, spinning on both the horizontal and vertical axis, giving Holomisa only one way out.

Holomisa dodged, a quick step to his right which placed him behind the projectile and a half second behind Baptiste. I could only watch in horror as Baptiste's next two steps brought him within arm's reach of me. My desperate lunge for the rifle fell short by a good foot.

Joy filled Baptiste's eyes, echoing the laughing yell of triumph erupting from his throat as he reached for me.

Time seemed to slow, the murderous prisoner's hand closing the distance between us in agonizing seconds, seemingly to prolong the dread of approaching doom. My traitorous legs wouldn't find purchase on the floor, skittering across the smooth surface as I tried to get any amount of space I could. Baptiste's talons locked on my foot.

Holomisa's angle of attack was wrong, but the only one he could take. He leapt, extending one foot in front of him, the other curled under. It was the opening Baptiste had been waiting for. The trap was laid, Holomisa had no choice but to walk into it.

A quick step forward and the kick missed. No matter how good Holomisa was, he still couldn't fight the physics of a flying kick. You just can't change directions in mid-air. Baptiste's other hand locked on Holomisa's ankle, becoming a fulcrum for the other prisoner, using the forward motion of the flying kick to slam him to the floor. Holomisa tucked, taking the impact on his shoulder and rolling to his feet

Directly into Baptiste's combo.

The uppercut snapped Holomisa's head backwards, stunning him and putting him in perfect position to take the overhand punch square in the teeth. Holomisa dropped like a sack of potatoes, stunned by the ferocity of the attack. Another scream of triumphant joy from Baptiste heralded his final assault.

Kick after kick pummeled Holomisa's body, a nonstop barrage of violence that left the downed man broken and bloody.

"Where is your self-righteous indignation now?" Bloody froth dripped from Baptiste's jaws as his teeth tore into his lips and tongue. He didn't seem to notice, focused as he was on his raving. "You could have ruled with me, *Captain*! But you had to cling to your precious *morals!*"

He reached down, taking the other man by the throat. I watched in horror as his free arm reformed, skin peeling back, the bones of his hand and wrist fusing together. In seconds, what used to be a hand became a wide, flat blade.

It was now or never. I lunged again, screaming as the pain tore through my body. Every nerve ending erupted in fire as I closed my hand around the rifle's grip and brought it around.

Baptiste dropped the limp form of Captain Holomisa and turned to me. "Give up, Johnny," he hissed. "It's inevitable."

"The only thing that's inevitable is death and taxes," I shot back angrily. I risked a quick glance down at the charge handle and reaffirmed that I had pulled it already. The carbine was primed and ready for any move that Baptiste might make.

"If you put it that way…" Baptiste's voice trailed off. He cocked his head and it twisted unnaturally. Whatever the scientists had done to the prisoners on the station was something that never needed to happen again. Ever. He continued. "I have conquered death, and taxes can be avoided if you have a good enough accountant. Tell me, were you an accountant before all this?"

"Uh…no," I said. I'm pretty sure that I sounded very stupid, but it was only the fourth strangest question I'd been asked that day. I was off my game.

"Pity. It would have made one hell of a story, the accountant who does battle against monsters like me."

He moved almost faster than I could track. He weaved back and forth, his form almost a blur as he closed in. I whispered a silent prayer as I pulled the trigger, firing off four shots in rapid succession. Each round impacted solidly into flesh, distracting him enough to give me an opening as he staggered closer. Ignoring the lessening, but still present pain, I lashed out with a steel toed boot. While the shattered knee didn't stop him, it did slow him down just enough.

I flipped the firing selection on the rifle from semi to full automatic and jerked back the charging handle one more time. A quick check confirmed that the proper round from the bulky magazine was chambered. While normally the high explosive was pretty worthless in a pitched battle, in close quarters it was almost as good as a bayonet on a rifle.

The FUKU had a forty-round magazine, and every fourth round a high explosive cartridge. It wouldn't go through standard battle armor, but it could wreck holy havoc on unprotected areas and even cause concussive damage upon impact, better even than standard ammunition.

I shoved the smoking barrel into his chest and felt it break through the thin skin, my earlier suspicions confirmed. Baptiste was extremely strong and fast, but, like Isaac had said, they could not make their mass disappear or to create it from nothing. To add the extra strength to his bones and muscles, his body had to pull it from somewhere else.

And one of the most overlooked, yet largest organ of the human body, was the skin.

Baptiste looked at me in wonder as I shoved the barrel of the carbine deeper inside his chest. I looked him in the eye and saw a complete and utter lack of humanity within. If the eyes are a window to the soul, then that place had been burned to the ground a long time ago, ashes scattered by a million storms and all traces of it blown away. There was nothing left of his soul in those pitiless eyes.

"Ouch," Baptiste hissed, his elongated tongue flicking out to wet his lips. "That actually hurt."

"You ain't seen nothing yet," I whispered and pulled the trigger.

The explosive round went off inside Baptiste like a grenade, showering white-hot fragments throughout his chest cavity and damaging his heart, lungs, and stomach. The damage from one single round like that had the potential to be devastating. He jerked spasmodically from the impact and explosion. He howled in pain and fury, an inhuman sound that scarred the soul. Most people would flinch and run at the sound. It was very unnatural to the ears.

So of course I went ahead and unloaded the entire magazine into him. One bullet for every goddamn stair. Yes, I counted.

Shrapnel peppered my hands and arms, with a few managing to make it to my body armor. The fragments of the five-five-six millimeter, high-explosive rounds were stopped by the standard armor, preventing me from taking the same type of damage that had ruined Baptiste's body as every fourth round exploded inside him.

Little rivulets of blood practically exploded outward as the HE rounds expanded on the damage that the standard rounds were causing. I was yelling loudly and incoherently as the sustained rifle fire nearly ruined what was left of my hearing. I kept the trigger pressed, however, even after it was obvious that I wasn't firing any longer.

He fell to the ground, quivering. His eyes were wide open in shock, and I could see something other than pitiless rage in them for the first time. Now I could see pain and, more comforting, fear. Baptiste was afraid, and he had good reason to be: he could feel my emotions, and the only thing coursing through my soul at that moment was wrath.

I looked down at Baptiste's twitching body, my ears ringing from the gunfire. He was still alive, but just barely. The high-explosive ammunition of the carbine had done one hell of a number on him, rendering his entire midsection to pulp. He was bleeding from dozens of small holes in his skin, and I could only guess as to just how bad he was internally. The largest hole from where the barrel of the gun had been jammed into him was oozing with guts and blood.

"You're one tough bastard, I'll give you that," I muttered. At least, I think I muttered. It might have been a shout, I'm not entirely certain. My hearing was absolutely shot to hell, and there was a dull ringing in the background.

I grabbed the last flash grenade I had and looked at it before letting my gaze drift down to Baptiste's ruined form. A particularly vile idea came to mind, one that almost made me shiver. I grinned viciously as I stood above him.

"I'm not the hero of this piece," I growled as I clenched the stun grenade tightly in my hand. "I'm nowhere near it. But I'm not the villain. No, that's you. Just because I'm fighting on the side of light doesn't make me the hero."

I pulled the pin and slammed it into Baptiste's mouth. I shattered his teeth with the steel edge as it went past his lips. Baptiste's eyes widened as he realized what was going on, but he couldn't move his arms. I'd done too much damage to him. One of the HE rounds must have done something to his spine, and while I was certain that he could heal himself eventually, there was no way I could let him. He was an evil that had to be eradicated, even if it meant damning my soul. I backed away and turned. I closed my eyes and covered my ears.

The *bang!* from the flash grenade was surprisingly muted. It could have been due to my damaged hearing, but I was pretty sure that his brain matter, bone, and flesh absorbing most of the blast had more to do with it. The light from the magnesium flash was bright enough that I could see it through my eyelids, but it didn't really hurt. Though it was muted, it was still loud and wet sounding.

I opened my eyes and looked at Baptiste. Though I was fairly certain I knew what I was going to see, I had to make certain that the monster was well and truly dead. What I saw confirmed my suspicion of what a flash grenade would do when shoved inside someone's face. While the flash grenade was designed to disorientate and stun, it was still an explosive device. And when the force of an explosion is compressed, it tended to be far messier than if it had exploded in an open space. Such as what happened to Baptiste's head.

Bits of bone, blood and brain matter had splattered all over the floor, the force of the explosion angled down and away from me. He must have tried to turn his head to spit out the flash grenade, to little avail. More blood dripped from his neck and pooled on the floor around where his head should have been.

It was nasty. It was necessary.

There are some evils one can live within this universe. Taxes, in-laws, and redheaded younger siblings come immediately to mind. Even if we don't want to admit it, these are simply minor annoyances in the grand scheme of things.

Baptiste was evil, plain and simple. The sort of evil that should not be allowed to survive or loosed upon the universe. He had been a convicted murderer before they'd pumped him full of alien shit to make him a powered-up killing machine. With the abilities he had before I had killed him, the damage he could have done to humanity as a whole was terrifying. Especially if he had made it off the station with Isaac in hand.

I had been trying to save Isaac. In the end, I may have saved myself.

"Is he dead?" a voice asked from behind one of the heavy cabinets in the corner.

Baptiste was dead, that much was clear. Not just mostly-dead, either, but the type of dead where all one can do was rifle through his pockets and search for loose change. Doctor Isaac came crawling out of his corner, surprisingly healthy and unharmed for someone who had been in Baptiste's not-so-gentle hands. He stood up and brushed his hands off on his pants. His hair was mused and his face covered in sweat and grime, but otherwise he looked fine to my trained eye.

It's amazing how Murphy seems to love some people while making others Her absolute bitch.

"What was he rambling? He was yelling about a grand kraken or something?" I asked as my hearing slowly began to come back. Isaac flinched. Okay, I may have asked louder than I wanted to. "Sorry. Hearing is shot to hell."

"The grand kraken is something he was going on about for long periods of time when he wasn't babbling about how he couldn't wait to get his hands on patient H-6– I mean, Captain Holomisa," Isaac explained, his voice tinny and small in my ears. "He kept talking about how he was going to summon the grand kraken to destroy the station."

"Uh, okay?" That was weird. I knew that Baptiste had been a sick and twisted individual, but this pretty much cemented my opinion that he was batshit crazy as well. I chalked it up to my lack of experience in civilian matters and moved on. "That sounds...strange?"

That's me, Mister Eloquent.

"It's theoretically possible that there's some larger version of the kraken in the depths of the lake that we haven't reached yet," Isaac said as he wiped his face off on his laboratory coat sleeve. He shook his head and removed the coat and tried to clean himself as best as he could with it as he continued, "I'm not going to say it's definitely there, but it's a plausibility we can't dismiss."

"Okay," I nodded. My hearing was coming back at a surprisingly good rate, "but not likely?"

"I didn't say that."

"Shit."

"A 'grand kraken,' as that deranged lunatic espoused, would have a mass that would probably be unsustainable in the lake's high-pressure environment," Isaac put on his metaphorical doctoral cap and began to lecture me, "but that still leaves a small chance of it occurring. Of course, feeding a creature that is large enough to damage the station in a lake this small is highly unlikely and improbable. There just isn't enough food to keep them alive."

"What if they eat each other?" I pressed. "What if they are like the Aztecs and sacrifice each other to appease a god?"

"That's actually a valid idea," Isaac nodded, a grave look on his face. It was a bit unnerving to see a guy I had considered one of the friendlier people on this hell to be so dour, but then again we did just blow the head off of a shape-shifting maniac.

"That's not comforting me, Doc."

"Sorry."

"What if," I began, my mind wandering as I thought about how the kraken had reacted to me since I had arrived on the station, "we try something out of the ordinary? What if—and this is going to sound a little weird—we ask the kraken?"

I swear Isaac's jaw almost dropped to the floor.

"That's insane!"

"So is the idea of a telepathic shape-shifter."

"Point," he conceded. He looked at me, slightly confused. "So how would you do it?"

I jerked a thumb up at the tubes running throughout the station. There were a few dead kraken inside them, but most of the aliens had cleared out sometime during the battle after keeping me alive and relatively sane. There were one or two, however, that had remained behind and were watching us now. I could feel their alien gaze on me, though it no longer freaked me out. Isaac followed my movement and his eyes widened.

"They always follow me," I explained, "remember?"

"You think they can understand you?" he asked.

"I think that they can sense my intent," I allowed. "Pretty sure that my mangled English is beyond them though."

"That's a clever idea," Isaac nodded. "Projecting your own intentions onto the aliens empathically. How you going to do that, though?"

"Interpretative dance? Hell, I don't know," I admitted. "You're the scientist, figure it out."

"This sounds like pseudoscience to me," he replied, his voice full of doubt. "You think that some random alien is going to understand what you want to tell you where to go?"

...down The Well...

"What the actual fuck?" I exclaimed and looked around. Had I heard it, or had I imagined something telling me about The Well? I shook my head as I remembered when this had happened to me before. "Oh, damn it..."

"What?" Isaac was confused.

"I know what to do," I said as I rubbed my nose. I grimaced as a new wave of pain washed over me. *Right*, I thought. *My broken nose. Well done, idiot.*

"What are we going to do?" Isaac asked, his youth and nervousness obvious in his voice.

"We have two options," I said in a low tone, trying as best as I could to remain calm. "One option is that we can go down The Well and into the deeps to placate the grand kraken—at least, I think it's the grand kraken. He can't crush the station—dropped this place from orbit, remember?—but tipping it over would work just as well, if the kraken's as big as I think it is."

"I don't like that option," Isaac whined. "What's the second one?"

"We stand around in here and wait to die," I stated.

Isaac was silent for a moment before responding. "You know what? I've given it some more thought. I like the first option better."

"I don't like either option," I admitted with a shrug. The voice, whatever it was, did not offer me any more insight. Even in the classics, spooky voices inside people's heads were always cryptic at best. I had to make do with what I knew, even if it was admittedly little. "But I hate sitting around and waiting to die. I'm very proactive. Ask anyone."

CHAPTER FOURTEEN

No sooner does man discover intelligence than he tries to involve it in his own stupidity.
–Jacques Yves Cousteau

"The DSRV was added to the station almost as an afterthought," Isaac said as we descended down The Well, the liquid methane flowing past us outside the plasteel windows someone had thoughtfully provided. "We thought it would be neat to explore the lake further. Unfortunately, once we discovered that the kraken weren't migratory and lived here, it was decided that we shouldn't traipse around in their yard."

"You already dropped one ugly lawn ornament into it *from orbit*," I emphasized, jerking a thumb over my shoulder. "What's a little tromping around in the yard and letting your dog shit all over the place after that?"

"That was Doctor Marillac's call, not mine," Isaac replied hotly. I could see the veins in his temple popping out a little and his face was beginning to grow flushed. I must have been getting on his nerves a little. "I wanted to explore the depths, to see if the kraken made any sort of rudimentary housing down there. My proposal was politely but firmly declined."

"What, you thought they were tool users from the start?" I asked as I toned back my sarcasm a bit. I was a bit surprised by this revelation, though. As far as I could tell, Isaac had been the most junior person on the team. At best he was the guy who ran for coffee. Well, that's what I always assumed the low man on the totem pole did. Coffee and answer calls for the big boss. "You're telling me that you're not the coffee guy?"

"Oh, you're hilarious," he huffed, his hands glued to the steering controls. "I'm a grad student doing research on my dissertation for my doctorate in xenobiological sciences. My doctoral thesis was noticed by Doctor Marillac and I was chosen, from thousands of applicants, to further my studies under her tutelage."

"Aw, shit. You *are* the guy who gets the coffee for the real scientists."

"I'm also the only person still alive who's certified to drive this thing."

"Great. Lattes to go. Oooh! Maybe I have a gift card..."

"Shut up."

I'll be the first to admit that I'm kind of a dick when I'm nervous. Being in a miniature submersible vessel deep under a lake made of liquid methane and petroleum on a strange moon with an alien who could probably swallow me whole would definitely make anyone just a little twitchy.

The DSRV exited the open bottom of The Well and into Kraken Mare. I almost didn't notice at first, as the light from The Well kept the immediate vicinity well lit. The currents of the lake, though, pushed the DSRV around and reminded me quickly enough. Isaac did a good job keeping us both on course and level, which was impressive given that I don't think he had actually driven the thing before.

We stared out of the DSRV in silence as continued down into the depths of the lake. At over five hundred meters deep at some points, Kraken Mare was largely unexplored beneath the surface. A cursory survey had determined that the station could be landed safely in the lake without harming too much of the environment— though how they determined that a massive space station being dropped into the middle of a lake wouldn't disturb things was beyond me—but beyond that, there hadn't been too much exploration. I heard that scientific teams had journeyed across some of the land parts, but the atmosphere and weather of the moon was brutal enough to render almost all of the current environmental containment suits worthless.

I joked once that an army could be dropped right on Mayda Insula, the island which the station was named for, and all die before making it across. Gallows humor for certain, but it was valid as well. There was simply no way of safely trekking across the surface of the planet. Hell, even the shuttles which came down from orbit had to be strenuously cleaned and maintained before lifting off again.

The surface makes traveling beneath the waves of Kraken Mare a breeze by comparison, which is why I was so shocked to discover that nobody had taken the DSRV out for a spin to look at things. Granted, there were some nasty currents in the lake which could drive the DSRV way off course, but the majority of those were near Seldon Fretum, the so-called "Throat of the Kraken." We were far enough away from that narrow channel that the currents shouldn't have affected any sort of basic exploration.

Still, not my monkey, not my circus.

The deeper we went, the stranger the color the lake became. The lights from the DSRV created a rainbow effect throughout the methane, and as we went into the deeper, darkest part of the lake the colors began to change in hue and intensity. I swallowed nervously as the DSRV began to creak and groan as we descended further.

"Uh…" I glanced nervously at Isaac, who was sweating slightly.

"It's okay," he said in a tone that did not have much confidence in it, "it's settling."

"Settling?" I asked, the nervousness doubling my heart rate with his simple statement. "Houses settle. Lawsuits settle. Deep Sea Reconnaissance Vessels *do not settle!*"

"Ssshh," he whispered at me, "concentrating."

I left him alone and instead focused on my aching body. I had taken one hell of a beating from Jou, Gentry, and Baptiste. The sealant spray that Isaac had applied to the gashes Baptiste had created was holding for the time being, and while I was going to have some wicked scars from where the psycho cut me, they weren't bleeding any longer. Isaac had done good work and had been thoughtfully prepared when we had made it to the DSRV by insisting on using the first-aid pack on me before we began our descent. I was also fortunate that whatever Baptiste had done with my brain, the effects were temporary, and faded after he died. I was sore, sure, but I wasn't writhing on the floor in absolute agony. That was something, at least. I lifted my shirt and inspected the damage.

Aside from the flayed area, I had purple and red bruising on my ribs and stomach, a few scratches that weren't very deep but burned like crazy, and a strange circular mark near my right hip that almost looked like a bike handle. I pulled my shirt back down and began to carefully inspect my skull with my fingertips. I winced at the egg-sized knot on the back of my head and wondered how I got it. Stairs? Probably. Or maybe when Jou slammed me into the wall. Or had that been Gentry?

Memories of the fights were fuzzy and blurred together. The main thing I remembered was getting hit a lot and running up and down those damned stairs. Oh, and Baptiste eating me, but I would give my left arm to forget that little incident.

"John," Isaac's tone and well-placed elbow shook off much of the fuzzy sensation in my head. He motioned out the window of the DSRV. I looked out but saw nothing important. Okay, maybe it was getting a little easier to see, but—

I stopped. *Why is it getting easier to see?*

"It's getting lighter out," Isaac stated, "but we're not going up to the surface. Some sort of artificial light is creating this."

"Saturn's light doesn't reach down this far?" I asked. Stupidly, as it turned out.

"Saturn barely breaks through the cloud cover," Isaac pointed out. "There's no way it could be bright enough to reach down to this depth. On Earth, light can reach about six hundred feet down, but that's rare. Considering that we're at eight hundred feet, there's absolutely no way."

We crested a large rise on the lake bottom and the source of the light suddenly became apparent.

In the deep crevice lay a city larger than anything I could have imagined ever existing on this godforsaken rock. They were obviously buildings melded into the side of the cliff, but unlike any design that I had ever seen before. The light was coming from each building face, which were somehow glowing in the dark and murky liquid of the methane lake. The colors created by the combination made for varying hues to dance in the currents and swirl around. It reminded me of the old psychedelic paintings and movies, only better. Much, much better.

The sight before us made my soul weep. There was a pure, unadulterated beauty in the flowing designs. Each building seamlessly blended into the surroundings while still standing out and being original. The material looked to be a cross of white coral and opal, twisted and blended together to make them appear to dance within the hazy liquid methane of Kraken Mare.

The kraken had designed and built all of this, and we humans had not had a single clue that it even existed. I chalked it up to scientific arrogance. We should never cease to ignore anything from which we could learn, even if it's something we cannot easily explain.

Look, I'm not that guy who appreciates beauty in art. I'm the guy who looks at the canvas with red paint and ask just how much they paid for it and then, afterwards, mock them mercilessly for paying anything at all. I don't see the subtleness in a brush stroke or the layering that goes into it.

This, though…this was so utterly *alien* that I had little choice but to feel something.

"I thought you said that they ran an ultrasound scan on the lake floor," I whispered as I drank in the view, my hand on Isaac's chair as I leaned over his shoulder to peer outside. "How did they miss all of this?"

"It's beautiful," Isaac said in a hushed tone. I silently agreed and continued to stare at the city. The longer I looked at it, the more I became enraptured.

How did they build all this? I wondered. *Not like they have opposable thumbs or anything.*

I couldn't answer the unspoken question, not in a million years. The structures were magnificent, well beyond even the most architecturally stunning designs of Earth. There was a beauty in the designs which seemed to swim in the lake, the same way that the kraken seem to move.

It was simply a stunning sight, and it completely distracted me for the surprise attack on my mind.

I felt a strange consciousness reach out to envelope me, much like when I had seen Concy on the station. Isaac looked at me with a curious expression on his face. I grimaced as it continued to prod into my psyche and delve into the innermost reaches of my mind.

- 187 -

The overwhelming *presence* in my head was almost too much. I jerked my head to the side and a strong sense of being drowned pushed aside most of my reasoning. I was about to lose myself to the presence and there was absolutely nothing I could do about it.

Everything went gray as the alien entered my mind. The foreboding sense of doom and despair was greater now. My heart felt as though it would burst from my chest. My head felt like it was trapped in a vice grip. My hands were cold, clammy. It was too great, too powerful for me to even begin to fully comprehend. Oil running down a canvas and creating images filled my mind. The alien was taking memories from me and trying to talk.

It hurt like hell. I began to scream.

Greetings, came the soft emotion into my soul.

I wept, tears unwelcome upon my cheek. It was too pure, too familiar. The alien had tapped into a part of my mind that I had not wanted to have brought forth from memory. It had been a long time since I had seen her face in anything but a memory, yet there she was, regal, beautiful. Not a ghost, like before. She was not ethereal. She was here. Her dark skin was flawless, exactly as I remembered it. Her smile was wide and welcoming, the corners of her eyes slightly crinkled in amusement. Laugh lines at such a young age. Perfection like that would never be matched, plain and simple.

She was beautiful. She was long dead. She would always be my wife. She would forever remain my first and only.

Too many feelings, a rush of emotions that no human being should ever try to cope with alone, sentiments which were both alien and mine own, crashed over me. I tried to focus on her face, her cheeks, something which would let me push through the crushing weight of it all. I reached for her but, just like in the dreams that I refuse to admit that I still have, she remained just out of my grasp. I cried out for her, but she just smiled sadly at me.

No, I cried out to her. *Don't leave me again.*

I couldn't handle the emotional onslaught. I was psychologically, emotionally and physically beaten. I was nothing more than a shell of who I once was. I was a broken man. I was ripe for the taking. Whatever that had forced its way into my head made certain of this. I was nothing more than a helpless child, finally ready to listen, to learn.

I clung to her memory. It was all I had left.

Please?

I blacked out.

CHAPTER FIFTEEN

Calon lân yn llawn daioni,
Tecach yw na'r lili dlos:
Dim ond calon lân all ganu
Canu'r dydd a chanu'r nos.
(A pure heart full of goodness
Is fairer than the pretty lily,
None but a pure heart can sing,
Sing in the day and sing in the night.)
–Daniel James, *Calon Lân*

The grey matter was pushing against my subconscious, prodding me to wake up, so I pushed back. I was warm, comfortable and in desperate need of rest. The horrors of the nightmare had receded into the dark corners of the mind. Men were simply men once more, not horrible monstrosities which had been created from condemned men. The kraken would tear apart the station and everything would be okay. The mutated bodies of the dead prisoners would be hidden, their corpses eventually being devoured by the plankton in the liquid methane, lost to time and space. All I had to do was stay asleep.

No.

The force of the protest surprised me. It shocked me even more when I realized that the thought had come from my own mind. I was the one protesting, not…whatever else was there. The grey matter was trying to wake me up, but was going about it in a way that was not human.

I refused to stay calm. I let loose all the inner turmoil and anguish into the grey, the years of self-doubt and loathing, the hatred, the anger. The raw emotions became mental barriers to protect me from the grey. I'd been beaten, abused, manhandled and damn near killed, but I was not about to give up yet.

Concy would not have approved if I did.

I could feel the grey pressing back. Its anger and rage was palpable, pushing against the mental barriers I had erected. Beneath those emotions, however, I felt something else. Something far different. The gray was closing in around me, blocking out all thought and reason. Whatever was attacking me psychologically was too strong, too powerful. There was no way I could last much longer.

I reached.

Fear.

A bright flash exploded from within the gray. Reality shifted sideways. I wanted to puke but couldn't. There was something shrouding my mind, like a blanket had been thrown over it. The images of my mind, the grey, everything disappeared for a moment.

It was terrifying. I was convinced that I was dead. No, I was definitely alive. I was less than before, but at the same time I was far, far more. I was human and I was…not. Darkness was everywhere and the grey was gone. I screamed helplessly into nothing, my throat making not a sound. My lungs would not move. I was paralyzed, alone, and in the dark. I was dead. I had to be dead.

Just as quickly as the darkness descended, light filled my eyes. I was blinded for a moment as my pupils tried to adjust to the rapidly changing spectrum. I winced and tried to shield my eyes as best as I could manage, but the pain remained. Tears blurred my vision as my body sought to protect itself. After many minutes, I was finally able to make out my surroundings.

I found myself standing on the lake's edge, my toes inches from the liquid methane. The haze overhead prevented me from seeing the massive gas giant, but I knew that somewhere above sat Saturn. I could feel the gravitational pull, which was really weird. I'd never felt it before. I inhaled sharply but the gas had no effect on me. I blinked, surprised.

"I'm not dead?" It was supposed to be a statement. My mouth decided otherwise. Traitor.

I knelt down and touched the ground. My hands were bare and the strange sand clung to my skin. I felt it squish between my toes. I could feel the liquid methane on my feet as a tiny wave lapped against them. It was cool but not overly so. I wasn't wearing any shoes. A breeze cut across the lake and sent chills up and down my body. There was no protective gear on my person. In fact, I wasn't wearing anything at all. I was standing nude in a poisonous environment which would kill anybody.

"What the hell?"

"I'm sorry about that," a sincere voice said from behind me. I turned.

Standing nearby was a normal looking man dressed in digicamo and wearing a strange-looking beret. It took me a moment to recognize the UN logo, though as I stared at it more and remembered how they looked when I had last seen them, the image began to sharpen, as did the details of the uniform.

I was in my mind. Or rather, someone was in my mind with me.

Probably.

"I can only dredge up images from your subconscious with a lot of effort," the man explained, his voice annoyingly calm. "The more you think about things, the better that image I can use."

"What?"

"You are confused," the man said. "That is entirely understandable. Let me explain. No, there is too much. Let me sum up."

Great. Now even my subconscious was stealing my best lines that I had stolen from movies.

I was suddenly bombarded with alien images and feelings, emotions and thoughts that were unlike anything humanity could even dream of. I could see it all. The seemingly endless war between the kraken and the invaders. The carnage it has wrought upon their home. The sliding of the scales as the great kraken began to slowly die off while the invading species continued to be born anew. It shattered my soul to watch such a beautiful and elegant alien race be wiped out as an invasive creature outbred and outfought them. I'd seen it before throughout human history and knew precisely what the being meant.

The figure before me nodded. "We've fought them for so very long, but we're dying. We cannot control the magma any longer. They will feast on our home and, when they are done, they will move out into the stars for more planets to devour."

"You thought we were with them," I began to understand. My mind was still reeling from the images. "That's why you attacked the station."

"You placed your 'station' right in the middle of our dinner table," the being replied in a brusque manner. "But yes, we only attacked when it became clear that some of you had become influenced by the magma."

"Influenced by…what?" I was confused again.

"The magma."

"How did it influence us?" I was confused. Lava? No, that couldn't be it. I was missing something vital. My mind wasn't translating something correctly. Magma meant something entirely different between our species, it seemed.

"Not you." The figure smiled. It was disconcerting. "If it had been you, we would have eliminated you already."

"Huh?"

"I am unfamiliar with that term."

"Can you tell me how they influenced the…others?" I said, trying to wrap my head around everything. It was still very confusing, but the longer the being was in my head—and I'm pretty sure that's where we were—the easier it became to understand some of it. It was as though the kraken was influencing my thoughts and opening venues I could never have dreamed of finding on my own.

"The magma pollutes our younglings," the being said as it began to pace around. The scenery changed as the lake began to ripple and lights appeared. The clouds of Saturn began to swirl madly, racing across at a maddening speed. I could see the entire length of eternity and the deepest pits of nothing. Metaphorically, I guess you could say that it was a journey through the soul. I would have said it was more akin to the universe's worst acid trip. If everything hadn't been in my head, I probably would have puked. The man continued to talk, ignoring my plight. "We have existed for eons as peaceful denizens of this part of the galaxy, and we believed we could handle everything the magma could possibly do to us—until it began to infect our children. This immediately heightened the state of war between our kinds. The one who traveled with you? He called the magma plankton."

"Holy shit," I breathed. "The plankton is the magma?"

"A byproduct of their habitation of our home. You would call it…their bio waste."

Oh, wow. The scientists on the station had been pumping psychotic lunatics with shit of an invasive alien species on a planet inhabited by one of the oldest sentient species in this part of the Milky Way. Talk about strange days.

"How do I know all this?"

"You share your thoughts with me, and I share in return." The being shrugged. "Once we too walked the stars, sailing the pathways of the elders upon great ships. Many eons before we explored every known pathway between worlds, charted the many stars, and delved deep in to the sciences."

"What happened?" I asked. Images flashed before my eyes. Darkness. Light. Conflict. I saw stars exploding and black holes forming. I saw peril, danger, and war. There was no peace, only…death? I couldn't tell, precisely. It was a dizzying and confusing vision.

"The End happened."

There was such a finality in his tone that I didn't want to press any further. Whatever had happened had been powerful enough to cause him a tremendous amount of pain. It must have been hell, though. I've only seen reactions like that from Marines who had seen some bad shit in their day.

Considering the mental fortitude it takes to become a Marine, bad shit would break a regular person.

"Is Isaac okay?" I asked, changing the subject.

"The young scientist is doing well for the time being," the man answered. "We are probing his mind to see what he has done and what harm he has led in his pursuit of knowledge, but so far it appears that he was not using his knowledge to harm life. We approve of his curiosity."

I sighed with relief. The little guy was my responsibility, since it had been my idea to go out of the safety of the station to meet the kraken. If anything had happened to him, assuming I made it out of this alive, I'd feel pretty horrible about losing him as well. He might not be some innocent kid, but he was a decent-enough guy.

"How do we stop the magma from spreading?" I asked. "How can we stop it from reaching Earth?"

"If not for your discover of space flight, the magma would have easily remained contained on this moon for time immemorial," the man replied. "Since you have begun exploring the pathways of the elders, however, the magma can…'hitch a ride,' I believe the expression is. They will find your planet eventually, and devour it over time. It is their nature."

So much for human progress.

"How can we stop it?" I wondered. "The magma…how do we stop it?"

"You must destroy it all," the man said.

"Okay, so how do we do that?"

"You must destroy us."

I hadn't expected that.

"I'm sorry," I blurted out before I could stop myself. "What did you just say?"

The man heaved a great and weary sigh. I could see the exhaustion on his face and in his body language. He had been around for a very long time, though he didn't look a day over thirty. I realized that whatever I was seeing was a mental projection of something greater, something far older than I. The man before me was what the kraken wanted me to see, a way so that I could perceive his kind better than I would if I had been looking at his true form. Or hers. One could never be absolutely certain when dealing with aliens.

"Your species is so very war-like, so aggressive," he began, his eyes staring off into the distance. "You have proven time and time again to be something that we do not strive to become. You frighten us, and make us believe that there is no room for a species like us in the coming millennia. And yet…your species may be the only chance for the continued survival the galaxy. Humans are the ones who are needed to protect the galaxy against what is to come."

"We've created art, music, and made breakthroughs in science to better mankind!" I retorted hotly.

"Yet for all the times we have reached out to humanity, shared our voice with them, the only ones to ever hear our song and reply have been the warriors," the man answered back, as calm as I was agitated. He saw how frustrated I was becoming and began shaking his head. "It's not a judgement of you, more of the state of mind your warriors must attain. It is something we cannot fathom, but your minds are by far more flexible than any other human we have managed to reach. It is strange that warriors would be the easiest to communicate with."

"How long?" I asked. "How long have you been trying to talk to us?"

"Hundreds of years."

That didn't surprise me much. We could barely talk to one another, and as a species we tended to be pretty insular looking.

"But to prevent the magma from becoming a symbiotic parasite with your species, you must destroy it here, now," the man continued, waving away my protests as he continued on, directing the conversation back on course. "This threat must be contained."

"But...to destroy you..." My thoughts drifted back to all the kraken that I had seen swimming around the station. I recalled something that Baptiste had said during his rantings. My stomach dropped as realization hit me hard. "That means I'd be killing kids!"

The man nodded. "Our youth, yes. It is necessary."

"No," I said forcefully.

"Why do you resist to acknowledge what you must do?" the man asked. He motioned around at the beach, the waves of the lake, and frowned. "I know what you are feeling, what you are thinking. This is inside your head. I already see that you have analyzed everything and agree with what I have said. So why do you continue to deny what must be done?"

"Because..." my voice trailed off. He was right. Damn it all to Hell, he was absolutely correct. I *had* accepted the fact that it needed to be done. I was lying to myself about everything else. I hung my head. Jou hadn't beaten me, and Gentry had been unable to make me quit. Even Baptiste, may he rot in Hell for eternity, hadn't managed to force me to throw in the towel.

Now, though? With an alien intellect in my mind, begging for me to kill it and all of its children in order to save humans?

I dropped down to my knees and hung my head. I closed my eyes and listened to the gentle sounds of waves crashing on the shore. I could feel the man staring at me. I chuckled darkly at the idea. I should feel everything he was doing. After all, this was my mind and not his we were having the discussion in.

I sighed and gave my answer.

♂

As it turned out, Isaac was able to do far more than just fetch the coffee.

The shuttle ride was mostly a blur, with Isaac handling the controls of the craft as we managed to break orbit and exit the volatile atmosphere. The approach to the waiting warships was long and dull after the excitement of navigating through the atmosphere. This gave me some free time, alone to my thoughts. I had much to think about.

I couldn't even begin to explain why I had agreed to do it. Who the hell was I to think that I could dictate the death of two species? I mean, I'm not squeamish about killing people. Not usually at least. But there's killing a man, and then there's eradication, which is what the kraken were asking.

It's what I agreed to do. God help me, why did I agree?

I never thought I would be a person who destroyed something beautiful and pure in order to save the universe. War is war, and fighting an enemy to save a population from collapsing is one thing. But systematic eradication of an entire species in order to save the universe? That would be cruel, heartless, and beyond the scope of what I thought I could bring myself to do. It would be inhumane even if they willingly sacrificed themselves for it. It was aliens doing alien things. I hated them for this, and yet I understood their reasoning as well.

It didn't matter what I had reluctantly agreed to do while I was on Titan. The kraken had been in my head, messing with my mind. How did I even know that the emotions and feelings which had compelled me to accept their offer in the first place were my own? There was a fine line between compelling someone and convincing them.

I exited the shuttle and found two very confused Marines waiting to escort me to the captain. They guided Isaac and myself through the maze of the ship. I was so lost in my thoughts I barely noticed any of it. It was still recycled air, still an artificial environment. Nothing had changed, not really.

I found myself on the command bridge of the dreadnaught, the captain asking me for orders. Strange, considering that I was just a lowly guard. Then I remembered the Emergency Protocols, which meant that the order to destroy the station had to come from the senior supervising security officer on the station. That would normally have meant Gerry, but he was dead. As were all the others. It would be my call, my decision. It had to be done.

No, I thought to myself. *I'm not going to kill an entire species.* I couldn't do it. I couldn't give the order. It didn't matter how evil the magma were, I could not destroy the kraken in such a ruthless manner. That was something no man or woman should ever be asked to do. It was not *right.*

We understand, a voice whispered from far away.

I stood there, frozen, unable to move. My mind no longer had control over my body. I felt a presence within me once more. The grand kraken had returned. An image of the most beautiful woman in my world appeared before me, blocking my view of Titan. Concy looked back at me with warm brown eyes. I tried to shake my head but I was still unable to move. Her lips quirked into a small smile. She forgave me for my weakness, even as I cursed the kraken.

"Drop everything on the planet," the command which came from my lips were not words I ever wanted to say, but they came anyway. I screamed silently, trapped within my own mind as the words poured forth. I could do nothing to stop them. I had no control. "Destroy the station and irradiate the moon thoroughly. We have to destroy all evidence of everything there. Tell the entire task force to drop everything they have. Drop every rod we have on it. Destroy it all."

A great sense of melancholy came over me after the last words passed through my lips. I wasn't sure if it was the kraken's emotions or my own. I don't think it mattered anymore. The command had been given, and followed. I was still unable to speak and my feet remained rooted in place. The image of Concy faded and the massive hole in my heart began its slow journey to healing itself at long last. Like a salve to an infected wound, the pain which had been constricting my soul began to ease for the first time in memory.

If you are what humanity represents, we hold great hope for it. We thank you for helping us save the galaxy.

I stared at Titan with tears in my eyes as I eradicated two species to save my own.

"Sir," one of the men on duty called out. "Launch detected."

"Scan and report," the captain snapped.

"It's gone now, sir," he said, turning towards me. The operator's face changed slightly. No one else seemed to notice, but after dealing with the mind wipes, and my own experiences, I was acutely aware of the difference in expression. *Had he been... what the fuck?* "Ghosted. Must've been a glitch."

He turned back to the screen, face resuming its normal appearance, as though all were right in the world.

END

CHECK OUT OTHER GREAT SCIENCE FICTION BOOKS

FURNACE
by Joseph Williams

On a routine escort mission to a human colony, Lieutenant Michael Chalmers is pulled out of hyper-sleep a month early. The RSA Rockne Hummel is well off course and—as the ship's navigator—it's up to him to figure out why. It's supposed to be a simple fix, but when he attempts to identify their position in the known universe, nothing registers on his scans. The vessel has catapulted beyond the reach of starlight by at least a hundred trillion light-years. Then a planetary-mass object materializes behind them. It's burning brightly even without a star to heat it. Hundreds of damaged ships are locked in its orbit. The crew discovers there are no life-signs aboard any of them. As system failures sweep through the Hummel, neither Chalmers nor the pilot can prevent the vessel from crashing into the surface near a mysterious ancient city. And that's where the real nightmare begins.

LUNA
by Rick Chesler

On the threshold of opening the moon to tourist excursions, a private space firm owned by a visionary billionaire takes a team of non-astronauts to the lunar surface. To address concerns that the moon's barren rock may not hold long-term allure for an uber-wealthy clientele, the company's charismatic owner reveals to the group the ultimate discovery: life on the moon.

But what is initially a triumphant and world-changing moment soon gives way to unrelenting terror as the team experiences firsthand that despite their technological prowess, the moon still holds many secrets.

CHECK OUT OTHER GREAT SCIENCE FICTION BOOKS

IN PERPETUITY
by Jake Bible

For two thousand years, Earth and her many colonies across the galaxy have fought against the Estelian menace. Having faced overwhelming losses, the CSC has instituted the largest military draft ever, conscripting millions into the battle against the aliens. Major Bartram North has been tasked with the unenviable task of coordinating the military education of hundreds of thousands of recruits and turning them into troops ready to fight and die for the cause.

As Major North struggles to maintain a training pace that the CSC insists upon, he realizes something isn't right on the Perpetuity. But before he can investigate, the station dissolves into madness brought on by the physical booster known as pharma. Unfortunately for Major North, that is not the only nightmare he faces- an armada of Estelian warships is on the edge of the solar system and headed right for Earth!

BATTLEFIELD MARS
by David Robbins

Several centuries into the future, Earth has established three colonies on Mars. No indigenous life has been discovered, and humankind looks forward to making the Red Planet their own.

Then 'something' emerges out of a long-extinct volcano and doesn't like what the humans are doing.

Captain Archard Rahn, United Nations Interplanetary Corps, tries to stem the rising tide of slaughter. But the Martians are more than they seem, and it isn't long before Mars erupts in all-out war.

CHECK OUT OTHER GREAT SCIENCE FICTION BOOKS

MAUSOLEUM 2069
by **Rick Jones**

Political dignitaries including the President of the Federation gather for a ceremony onboard Mausoleum 2069. But when a cloud of interstellar dust passes through the galaxy and eclipses Earth, the tenants within the walls of Mausoleum 2069 are reborn and the undead begin to rise. As the struggle between life and death onboard the mausoleum develops, Eriq Wyman, a one-time member of a Special ops team called the Force Elite, is given the task to lead the President to the safety of Earth. But is Earth like Mausoleum 2069? A landscape of the living dead? Has the war of the Apocalypse finally begun? With so many questions there is only one certainty: in space there is nowhere to run and nowhere to hide.

RED CARBON
by **D.J. Goodman**

Diamonds have been discovered on Mars.

After years of neglect to space programs around the world, a ruthless corporation has made it to the Red Planet first, establishing their own mining operation with its own rules and laws, its own class system, and little oversight from Earth. Conditions are harsh, but its people have learned how to make the Martian colony home.

But something has gone catastrophically wrong on Earth. As the colony leaders try to cover it up, hacker Leah Hartnup is getting suspicious. Her boundless curiosity will lead her to a horrifying truth: they are cut off, possibly forever. There are no more supplies coming. There will be no more support. There is no more mission to accomplish. All that's left is one goal: survival.

CHECK OUT OTHER GREAT SCIENCE FICTION BOOKS

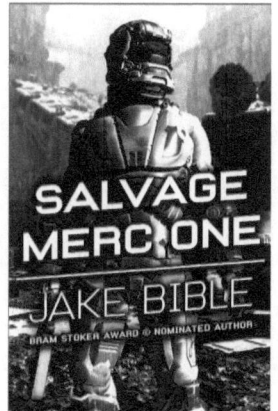

SALVAGE MERC ONE
by Jake Bible

Joseph Laribeau was born to be a Marine in the Galactic Fleet. He was born to fight the alien enemies known as the Skrang Alliance and travel the galaxy doing his duty as a Marine Sergeant. But when the War ended and Joe found himself medically discharged, the best job ever was over and he never thought he'd find his way again.

Then a beautiful alien walked into his life and offered him a chance at something even greater than the Fleet, a chance to serve with the Salvage Merc Corp.

Now known as Salvage Merc One Eighty-Four, Joe Laribeau is given the ultimate assignment by the SMC bosses. To his surprise it is neither a military nor a corporate salvage. Rather, Joe has to risk his life for one of his own. He has to find and bring back the legend that started the Corp.

SERENGETI
by J.B. Rockwell

It was supposed to be an easy job: find the Dark Star Revolution Starships, destroy them, and go home. But a booby-trapped vessel decimates the Meridian Alliance fleet, leaving Serengeti—a Valkyrie class warship with a sentient AI brain—on her own; wrecked and abandoned in an empty expanse of space. On the edge of total failure, Serengeti thinks only of her crew. She herds the survivors into a lifeboat, intending to sling them into space. But the escape pod sticks in her belly, locking the cryogenically frozen crew inside.

Then a scavenger ship arrives to pick Serengeti's bones clean. Her engines dead, her guns long silenced, Serengeti and her last two robots must find a way to fight the scavengers off and save the crew trapped inside her.